On Tripoli Circle

Pat Cunningham Devoto

This is a work of fiction. Names, characters, places, and incidents are the product of the author's imagination or are used fictitiously. Any resemblance to actual events, locales, or persons, living or dead, is coincidental.

ISBN: 1466201193
ISBN-13: 9781466201194
Library of Congress Control Number: 2011914030
CreateSpace, North Charleston, SC

Warm praise for Pat Cunningham Devoto's work:

My Last Days as Roy Rogers

"The literary lovechild of Harper Lee and Mark Twain..."
—*Booklist* (starred review)

"Engaging...Graceful...[with] characters finely drawn... Devoto has an ear and eye for the vagaries of family and loyalty."
—*Denver Post*

"Fascinating...a captivating trip back in time."
—*Dallas Morning Star*

"Devoto is a talented new voice from the South with keen insight reminiscent of Eudora Welty or Harper Lee...a poignant and memorable debut."
—*Library Booknotes*

Out of the Night That Covers Me

"Stunning...This lyrical, moving novel should establish Devoto as a great Southern novelist."
—*Library Journal*

"Written with grace and sympathy."
—*New York Times Book Review*

"A real pleasure...elegant...The whole story rests on [John] and never falters."
—*Washington Post Book World*

The Summer We Got Saved
"A wonderfully poignant, funny, and intelligent book about the coming of age and wisdom...completely delightful."
—*Booklist* (starred review)

"The work of a gifted story teller."
—Robert Inman, author of *Captain Saturday*

"Nicely woven: Devoto captures the internal ambivalence of a society teetering on the uneasy verge of change."
—*Kirkus Reviews*

"Delivers a powerful testimony on the struggle that rocked our nation, leading us to ponder our own responses to difficult choices."
—Southern Living

"Devoto's episodic, nonchronological structure creates potent narrative pull, but her evenhanded, affectionate treatment of her complex characters, each struggling to make sense of their changing world, is the novel's greatest asset."
—Publishers Weekly

Dedication

To the great American neighborhood, wherein lies our real strength.

And to my sons, Mike, and Andy, and their families - great neighbors all!

Also by Pat Cunningham Devoto

My Last Days as Roy Rogers
Out of the Night That Covers Me
The Summer We got Saved

On Tripoli Circle

Pat Cunningham Devoto

England, Jan. 4, 1943
1st Lieutenant J. M. Brownlee,
329 B. Sq. 93 B G,

Dear Mom,

A quick note before chow because rumor has it we are having real eggs for supper and I wouldn't want to miss out on that—but of course we are getting plenty to eat so don't worry about me.

You will be happy to know that Daniel arrived over here right after my group came—couldn't believe my eyes. Two days later the navigator on his plane got sick, appendicitis, I think, so Daniel asked for me and now I'm part of his crew. Carl Tyree was already onboard as his bombardier. Now it's Carl, Daniel, and me, our Tripoli Circle boys—like old home week.

Please thank Miss Delaney for sending the divinity and the Pruitt sisters for the box of pecan fudge. All were delicious. Yesterday I got ten letters plus the package from the Pruitts. Now I probably won't get any mail for another month, but all this will keep me going until I hear from you all again.

Of course we won't know when, or if, we'll leave until the day before, but if hope can get me back home, it won't be too long.

Love to a sweet mama,

Jonnie

Chapter 1

402 South Tripoli Circle
Summer 1950

"He's here ...driving up in her driveway. You better come look."

No answer from the kitchen.

"Chief Kelly—he's turned off the engine, but the light's still going round on the top."

We could see him as we peered out the living room window, through the front porch screen, and across the street into the shade of the huge oak that cooled Mrs. Brownlee's front yard.

Every summer, all those years ago, we would use it as a climbing tree, the ones of us bold enough to reach its highest branches swaying precariously, momentarily, to get one all-encompassing look at our world—up and down the full length of Tripoli Circle. As God must do—as our father had told us God must do, before handing down some decree from on high. This day He was getting ready to send down a real zinger.

I called back to her, "Now he's opening the door."

Hercule said, "He's getting out of da car." Herc was just tall enough, on tiptoes, to see over the windowsill. Jane and I were stair steps behind him—me in the middle. It was, I had discovered early on, the best place to be in the scheme of things. The one in front was forever having to blaze a trail, the one behind was there to be bossed around by the one in the middle.

Still no answer from the kitchen, and the importance of any happening must first be measured through her eyes. We glanced backward toward the dining room into the kitchen to see if this last bit of news might be noteworthy. Smoke was wafting up out of the ashtray on the kitchen table. She was turning a page—probably to the solving. She did not like to be disturbed during the solving part. We turned back to watch out the front window.

"He's pushing the boxes to one side and knocking on the door," I said.

Suddenly Hercule shouted, "A *rat*," so excited that he was jumping up and down on one foot. "It's running . . ." He pointed. "Dare."

"Where?" we shouted back, so she would hear us.

Still the smoke in the kitchen wound a lazy silent path upward.

Hercule pointed again. "See? Right dare."

The neighbors on Tripoli Circle were constantly calling the police on Mrs. Brownlee. She had a house so grimy, so full to overflowing with litter, that rats collected in it and had recently begun to spill out into the surrounding houses. We felt lucky to live on the other side of the street. The rats had not seen fit to cross over, yet.

Most every house on Tripoli Circle was kept trimmed up and neat except for Mrs. Brownlee's, and that summer her house, and her behavior, had been getting more and more bizarre—out on the porch the week before in her slip. It had looked to Jane and me, playing on the swing in our side yard, as if she had decided it was time to sweep, so she came on out to the sidewalk when she had finished the porch, without bothering to dress before she did it—just walked right out with the broom and started swishing, barefooted and in a loose-hanging slip, her shrunken little breasts for all the world to see, wispy gray hair half done up in pin curls—another job she must have started and forgotten to finish. Jane had sent me into the house to tell.

Mother had gone over and told Mrs. Brownlee there was a new town ordinance and that she, Mother, was now in charge of the sweeping of the sidewalk. Mrs. Brownlee's bony little shoulders had sagged in relief as she'd handed over the broom and the responsibility, as if she might have had to sweep all the way to town had someone not come along to help out. Mother put an arm around her and walked her back in the house. She had insisted on giving Mama a warm Coca-Cola for her trouble.

"He's trying the door and it's locked," Jane called, turning around, facing in Mother's direction. *"He's banging on the door."*

Mama brushed a strand of fine brown hair out of her eyes and turned the page with long, delicate fingers. She had, at one time, been a model, she said. She didn't look up but did offer, "He should leave the poor old soul alone. Everybody knows she's crazy as a betsy bug . . ." She caught herself and glanced up at us. "Or a lunatic ...or one possessed as in, a loon. Remember that," and went back to her reading. It was a technique she said she had invented while teaching school out in California—learning three words for one. Of course we didn't quite believe that, about teaching in California, because if she had been teaching in California, before she had been a model and lived in New York City and before she had all of us, then she would have been somewhere around thirteen years of age. By the time Jane took up long division in school and figured it all out and asked, Mother had said they were short on teachers ...that year ...in California ...and she gave Jane a look that meant, *You are spoiling the story*.

That summer, Jane had been receiving a great many of those looks. I, on the other hand, had not been getting any dubious glances because I wanted to believe everything our mother said, and back then I was of the age when wanting to believe and believing were the same thing. It was the last summer I would have that luxury.

Chapter 2

"But Mama, da rats—day is running all over da place. Give me da creeps—yuck."

Mother had read somewhere that the "th" sound took longer to develop than all the others. We were fervently hoping it was so.

"Everybody knows it was the war that did it. Before she lost her boys, she was perfectly sane." Mother picked up the half-burned cigarette out of the ashtray, took a drag, and went back to her reading. She said then, still talking to the page, "It's part of our patriotic duty to accommodate Mrs. Brownlee. She sacrificed two sons for our country."

"What's dat one Mama?"

"*Murder in Mesopotamia*, sweetheart. I'll tell you all about it when I finish ...and we have a meeting ...under the parachute," she mumbled, and took another drag off her Camel.

We turned our attention back to Mrs. Brownlee's house. I was hoping something would happen before Roger woke up. It was my turn to babysit him.

"Chief Kelly's walking over to that window—the one he used to get in last time. He's raising it up and trying to get his chubbo tummy inside," Jane said, then grimaced and glanced in the direction of the kitchen. “I mean ...his rather hefty, somewhat considerable, stomach ...within.”

Mother said, “Adequate, but you could do better,” and kept reading.

We waited a while longer and so did Jarvis, the chief’s assistant, standing alongside the police car out in the drive, looking up at the front of the old house that had been in the Brownlee family for generations. It was baked and faded from years of afternoon suns. One of the shutters on the second floor was hanging lopsided on a single hinge.

“Chief’s trying to open the front door from the inside, but he can’t. I can see the whole door rattling. Must be something holding it closed,” Jane said.

I said, “I see the Pruitt sisters behind their curtains looking out at the goings-on. I’ll bet *they* think this is important.”

“Now he’s opening the front door and kicking a pile of old newspapers out on the front porch, and now he’s coming fast down the steps to the car.... Mama! He’s talking to Jarvis and now Jarvis is calling on the car radio.” Jane was chewing on her lower lip. Hercule was watching intently, sucking away on two fingers. He had been told he was too old to suck his thumb anymore.

“We think this is serious, Mama,” I called back to her.

“Aggie, sweetheart, Jarvis just likes using the new two-way radio in the patrol car. We all know that ...don’t we?”

After another minute, we could hear the siren of another police car and then another—all we had in our cozy Alabama river town. And then we heard the high-pitched sound

of the ambulance from the hospital, off in the distance, getting closer.

"Mama, we think this is serious!"

Mother closed her book, stubbed out her cigarette, got up, and walked into the living room. And then we knew: it was serious.

Chapter 3

We watched as Mother pushed open the screened door and walked across the street to the chief's car. The three of us, openmouthed, had edged onto our porch when they carried out a stretcher covered with a lumpy white sheet. I was juggling Roger, up from his nap, on one hip. No other neighbors had ventured outside, but we could see curtains being pulled back and blinds being bent open. Mother was already deep in conversation with Chief Kelly.

I pulled away just as Jane tried to grab my sleeve, opened the screened door, and crossed over to stand behind her and listen. My excuse would be that I needed to check and see if she wanted me to give Roger some Gerber's.

"Deader than a John Deere with a stole battery," the chief was saying. He took off his hat and ran fingers through a damp flattop; waxed red bristles caught the afternoon sun. I could see the backs of Mama's shoulders wince—it was the "stole battery" rather than the demise of poor old Mrs. Brownlee. "Been dead nigh on to . . . I don't know . . . maybe a week? Been having such a stretch of hot weather and the stench in that house is always so bad anyway . . . and the rats done already commenced on her. It's hard to tell when . . ." He noticed me. "Now, Aggie darlin', I think you oughta take little Roger there and go on home. This ain't fit for kids." Mama turned and shooed me on back across the street, saying she would be there in a minute to feed Roger.

She stayed and talked to the chief for the time it took the ambulance to leave and then for the chief to rummage around in his trunk and find some rope and bring two kitchen chairs out in the yard. Chief and Deputy Jarvis strung it up from one side of the house to the kitchen chairs and then onto the other side of the house, which seemed peculiar to those of us watching. The notice of someone dying would usually be signaled by a black wreath on the front door.

By then the rest of the neighbors—the body having left the premises—felt it was not being indiscreet to come on out and gather around, talking and greeting one another outside the ropes. The crowd got larger as the men came home from work, ties loosened around necks and suit coats slung over shoulders.

As soon as they had had a chance to say how sorry they were about poor old Mrs. Brownlee's passing, the talk turned to other things: How were people going to get along with mail coming only once a day now? And how come Jackie Robinson, being colored, was making as much as he must be making just to play baseball? We sat on the front steps and watched and listened. The Silverbergs, the only family on Tripoli Circle to own a television set, began recounting the latest news, because they had actually seen it, in person, on TV. We were, they informed, headed for a showdown in Korea - no doubt about it.

In truth, it was probably hard for the neighbors to be that heartbroken over Mrs. Brownlee's passing, considering the rats and all—having forgotten her past sacrifices for country. Now a new lot of children were coming of age on Tripoli Circle, on the same sidewalks where her boys had once ridden their bikes, in the same yards where they had once played touch football. Other, newer wars were brewing. The wounds of old conflagrations surely must have scabbed over by now.

Chapter 4

~

After a while, Mother, who was never one to aimlessly chitchat, came back across the street so we could feed Roger and she could tell us all about it. We were waiting. We followed her into the kitchen. I put the baby in his high chair while she got out the Gerber string beans. I was shoveling it in while she talked.

"Mrs. Brownlee—rest her soul, as your father would say—has gone to her reward." She paused. "Happy hunting ground, nirvana, paradise, depending on your particular religious persuasion." She never passed up an opportunity to remind us that there were other possibilities—unlike our father, who was sure there were not. She tied on her apron and got out the hamburger for meat loaf.

"She's . . . *really dead*?" Jane's eyes began brimming. "When we first moved into the neighborhood," she sniffed, "before she went nuts and started running around in her underwear, she used to give me peppermint stick candy. At Christmas she always had fruit in a big bowl"—turning to me—"remember that, Aggie? She would give out to all us kids on Tripoli Circle?" Her voice went scratchy thinking of it. "We . . . we all loved her back then."

"What do you think, Jane? They carried Mrs. Brownlee out on a stretcher with her head covered over by a sheet 'cause she was merely sick?" I was trying for, and not succeeding, a more hard-edged, world-weary persona, in imitation, I thought, of my mother. People said I looked like her, so I felt I must surely be like her. Besides, as far as neighbors went, I was more partial to the Pruitt sisters and their pecan fudge.

I sighed nonchalantly. "What happened, Mama, bludgeoned to death?"

We were all acquainted with the lingo, having listened to Mother's retelling of her mystery stories and all manner of other tales she would read to us or tell us when we would get together under the parachute to hear *The Lion, the Witch and the Wardrobe*, which was not actually *The Lion, the Witch and the Wardrobe* anymore. We had finished that long ago, but this was a title benign enough, and with enough pious provenance, to be accepted by anyone who might ask questions about our meetings, especially our father. What we did under the parachute, she said, was one of the myriad things he did not need to know—to be bothered with, she said.

"Your father is much too busy with the business of the church. Time under the parachute is reserved for people who are developing creative turns of mind . . . for use in the wider world."

We understood this to mean a person like herself, one who lived, or had lived, in larger cities like Nashville or Memphis or even New York City—all places Mother had visited or said she had visited. Details of a story were not that important, she told us. They were just that, details—like little wheels on the larger train that takes you where you want to end up. At my age then, that sounded perfectly logical.

As newlyweds, my parents had gone to New York City on their honeymoon, the summer she met him, shortly before he was to ship out to go fight Hitler. The big city had left an impression. We would all go to New Orleans or Chicago or New York City one of these days, she said, and we would see for ourselves—the museums, the plays, the traffic. In the meantime, when there were gatherings under the parachute—a souvenir our father had brought home from the war—we could say things, do things, and wear things that we would never say, do, or wear in the more conventional world.

"On the outside, we have contractual obligations," she would say before telling us we were going to have to go to five straight nights of revival meetings at the church and sit on the front row the whole time, listening to our father preach. Be still and quiet and pass the baby around to keep him from crying. Ah, but this was good for developing our concentration, she said, and good for developing strong memory skills. She would give us math problems to solve in our heads while we sat there so we wouldn't squirm. It was actually a blessing in disguise, she said. Deep disguise, we figured.

Chapter 5

He was going to be a math professor after the war and she was going to spend her days raising children and writing widely read, wildly popular mystery novels, maybe even become as famous as Agatha Christie. It hadn't worked out that way.

They had met right after her first husband had died in a traffic accident—a very tragic but romantic story she had told us many times. We were enthralled. Jane especially liked this particular tale because he, this Jack fellow, was Jane's real father, and Jane didn't remember a thing about him—how handsome he was, how dashing, how intellectually dazzling. When Mother told it, he seemed to have the brainpower of Albert Einstein and bore a great physical resemblance to Burt Lancaster, but with a personality more down-home, like Jimmy Stewart's.

Our own father was another example of the lofty position of men in the scheme of things. Daniel Wellington Cunningham had been a captain, a bomber pilot in the war, guiding his plane and his crew to victory over the Nazis. Even now, I don't remember calling him Daddy or Pop. It would have been disrespectful, rude even. It was always Father. When I was very young, I had thought he might be *that* Father.

It seemed only logical. He was a preacher. Everyone told us he was perfect. At times I would narrow my eyes, studying Hercule—another man in the family—wondering how, in a mere ten or fifteen years, he too could possibly be so transformed.

Jane had been a baby when Mother had married our father. Still, Jane said, she thought she remembered a little something of him back then, before he went off to war—carrying her on his shoulders to the park. She believed she remembered he used to sing a lot. She said she recalled one day in the fall—he and our mother must not have been married many months by then—when the fair came to Nashville. He had taken Jane to ride on the merry-go-round and stood next to her to keep her from falling off the tiger as it moved up and down to the music. She remembered distinctly that they had both laughed and waved to Mother, by then big and pregnant with me. That day, flags were fluttering in the breeze and people were strolling around in uniforms and she got cotton candy all over our father's uniform. He had just laughed and taken a big piece of cotton candy for himself, and later he bought all of them caramel apples. He had bought her a souvenir dolly.

I had told Jane I thought if she remembered it at all, she was remembering it wrong. He sure wouldn't spend money in such a frivolous way as to buy cotton candy and then turn right around and go out and buy caramel apples, too. Jane swore it was true. She remembered that day, she said, "clear as a bell"—the breeze in her face, the sun shining on the merry-go-round tiger.

I scoffed at the notion of the father she described: comfortable, flippant even. I had never met that father. I was never to meet him, not for any length of time. "If it's true, Jane, how come you don't still have that souvenir dolly you say he bought for you on that day?"

I remember that Jane got mad and began to tear up, saying she had lost it when we moved from Nashville to our house on Tripoli Circle.

"Oh, sure," I had said, "likely story."

During the war and for two years after he came home, we had lived in Nashville, waiting for him to finish seminary. Then he got the call to preach at First Redeemer, not four hours away from Nashville and in his hometown. It was divine providence, he said, and we must not question. So we packed up everything in the Plymouth and came to live on Tripoli Circle, three blocks away from where he had grown up. He said it was three blocks from where he had grown up, but he never took us by the house. He never showed us where it was.

Our new neighbors would say, "That daddy of yours was a war hero, you know. Bet Daniel told you all about how he had his B-17 shot out from under him. Had to parachute right down into Germany." He had not. But in that day and time, I had thought it was not that unusual.

War was discussed by our town's returning soldiers only as it pertained to the lighter side, funny little stories that the ladies, and any others who had not had the privilege of combat, would think amusing. If I biked down to take a load of dry cleaning to Darby's Cleaners, likely as not Mr. Darby and some of his pals might be in there shooting the breeze: ". . . and there I was, right in the middle of the whole dang D-Day landing and my Higgins boat flat dab ran out of gas. You shoulda seen me, sitting there like a dang duck bobbing on the river in hunting season, waiting for the Nazis to blow me to smithereens." Or Mr. Crowe, leaning against the counter: ". . . got drunk and went AWOL for three whole days. Snuck back in camp and old Sarg never knew it." Or Mr. Cramwell, sitting in the corner, smoking: ". . . hid out in a brothel in Paris for a week and had me a time. Them girls was on our side, let me tell you." All to great gales of laughter with each retelling.

Their stories were funny or demeaning or both, or it seemed they did not deserve a telling. It meant you had tossed off the whole war like so much dirty laundry, pitched it into the back of an old clothes hamper, donned new attire, and got on with your life.

Chapter 6

"I've promised Chief a glass of tea when he finishes up at Mrs. Brownlee's. It's blistering over there and I want y'all to make yourselves scarce when he comes. If children are around, he won't tell me the particulars." Mother slipped the meat loaf in the oven and closed the door, to which she attached a piece of bungee cord hooked from the oven door handle to the left front burner, since that burner didn't work anyway. This would keep extra heat in, giving the meat loaf more of a gourmet flavor, as in French meat loaf, which she had loved when she was over in Paris on a weekend jaunt. That meant, she told us, raising an eyebrow, "a trip, an excursion, or maybe even . . . a spree," smiled knowingly at me. And I, in turn, smiled back, pretending that I knew what in the world she might be talking about.

When she had finished, we all moved to the front screened porch—our primary living space in the summertime—to keep track of what was going on across the street. Jane was carrying the potatoes and a peeler – me, Roger's bottle. Hercule took his Lincoln Logs to the far end of the porch and dumped them out on the cool concrete floor, preparing to build a rocket ship. The rest of us gathered at the other end under the ceiling fan, intermittently glancing across the street to Mrs. Brownlee's darkening house.

Before this day, her lights had always come on in the early evening. We had seen them without really seeing them: on downstairs, until she had had her supper and listened to the end of the news with Gabriel Heatter, and then off, until she had climbed the stairs and muted lamp lights came on in the second-floor bedroom windows—like the sun rising in the east and setting in the west, until it didn't anymore.

Early evening shadows were beginning to settle in the guilt. We should have done more for her, been there for her, not made fun of her rising rat population. Now there was no way to make it right.

Now only the chief's car was left across the street, the blue and white of its markings fading in the coming dusk. The women on Tripoli Circle had gone back into their houses to get supper ready. Mr. Wilson, sitting out on his porch next door, had the Yankees game on the radio. At one time I had thought Mr. Wilson—being so sophisticated as to be interested in something that far removed from our world—might just be the person to befriend our mother, since nobody else on Tripoli Circle seemed up to the task. Jane had scoffed at the suggestion. "He is a man and she is a woman."

"So?" I had said. Jane had not deigned to explain.

Across the street next to Mrs. Brownlee's we could see Mr. Oliver sitting on his front porch swing, popping open the evening *Birmingham News* to the sports section. He was partial to the Birmingham Barons baseball team, if there was nothing in the paper about football.

On the other side of Mrs. Brownlee, the Pruitt sisters were setting their dining room table. We watched them through their window sheers, coming and going with glasses and plates.

Jane began peeling potatoes, making long continuous delicate strips of skin that fell into the pan in her lap. I handed Mother Roger's bottle, which she tested on her wrist and then began giving to him while she rocked and looked out at Mrs. Brownlee's.

Years ago, in the early 1900s, it had been the only house on forty acres of farmland, but being a man who could change with the times, Mrs. Brownlee's father had gone out one day, pulled down the hog barn with his tractor, scraped out a road, and cleared the land for home sites—intent on turning a scrub farm into a moneymaking proposition.

Since farming had been his lifelong occupation and he was not skilled in the house-building business, he had sat down one night, thumbed through the Sears, Roebuck catalog, chosen three house plans he liked, and ordered one of each, completely self-contained—everything from roofing shingles, to numbered lumber pieces, to red bricks, to windows and doors, ready for assembly. The three house kits had cost him a whopping total of $4,123, but no matter, he would make it all back. When the houses came in on the train, he unloaded them down at the rail station, transported them by mule to his place, and began putting them together piece by numbered piece. After he sold off the first three, he ordered three more, and so on, until he had finished and named the whole thing Tripoli Circle in honor of his service in the marines in World War I.

It wasn't actually a circle, more like one long block of twelve or so houses with a circular turnaround at the end—cul-de-sac would have sounded pretentious. Our house was on the neck of the street directly across from the Brownlee's. In the turnaround, he had carved out a rounded grassy mound and planted a lamppost squarely in the middle. There was a sidewalk that ran up and down the full length of Tripoli Circle. Mrs. Brownlee's father was an honest man who was out to build an honest, sturdy street.

By the time we moved into the neighborhood, Tripoli houses had been there for thirty or more years and were by then anchored into their surroundings with oaks and maples he had planted. A sprinkling of pecan trees had been left over from his orchard. Crepe myrtles and azaleas framed front porches and side yards. Over the years, other streets and houses had sprung up around us so that we had long ago been incorporated into the general population of our town, but Tripoli Circle remained a standout, one the populace would point to as the Sears, Roebuck block. We lived in the Starlight model. The Pruitt sisters lived in model number 3194A, the Sunbeam. The Olivers were settled into the Avalon.

As extra incentive for buyers, he had added a one-car garage to the backyard of each of his houses, complete with an extra room above that. The garage was meant to say that somewhere inside there was bound to be a car, even if you didn't actually own one at the moment.

Mrs. Brownlee's old farmhouse—being an only child, she had inherited it—and the huge old oak that shaded it had been the odd duck among us. I was told that there had been a white picket fence in her front yard at one time, but after her boys had gone off to war, the fence began to fall apart, a picket here or there, and the neighbors on each side, pretending they were working in their yards, had taken it down little by little. Mrs. Brownlee hadn't noticed or had pretended not to notice. Then one winter, when there was an ice storm, the neighborhood children used the remaining front pickets to pretend they were skiing, children in the South not knowing much about what it was like to ski anywhere else other than on water. Come spring, without the fence, Mrs. Brownlee's house seemed in line with the rest of us, albeit out of a different era. It had a stone foundation that rose up to a second floor of wood shingles. As an added architectural bonus, there was a tiny circular turret in the front. This gave it a small parlor inside and a vaguely Victorian look outside. A stone terrace ran the length of its front—the one Mrs. Brownlee had seemed obsessive about sweeping.

Overall we were, except for Mrs. Brownlee's house, obedient in size and manner to our sister houses.

Chapter 7

Presently we saw the chief locking Mrs. Brownlee's door, checking the ropes tied to the kitchen chairs, and then heading our way. Mother, still holding Roger, gestured with her head for us to leave. I held out my hands for Roger to come to me, "but you'll be sure to give us all the skinny when he leaves, won't you?"

I was almost to the door with Rog when she held up an arm. "The *what*?"

"The skinny," I said, and then quickly backtracked. "To enlighten, to illuminate, and uh . . ."

"To apprise," Jane said as she helped Hercule gather up Lincoln Logs.

Mother lowered her draw bridged arm. "If you must pick up this local slang, I shall always expect compensation in alternate knowledge." We nodded and left, because we knew Mama would give us the lowdown. We just weren't too sure how true it might be.

"She told us to go in the house," Jane said. "She didn't say what part." Although I was loath to ever admit it to her, I did admire Jane's conniving ways. We headed to our bedroom, to the window that opened onto the screened porch.

Jane, Hercule, and I shared this room. Roger's baby bed was in our parents' bedroom.

I sat Roger down on the floor, gave him a banana to smear around, and told Hercule to share his Lincoln Logs.

"No, he'll get banana on dem."

"Hercule," I said in my most lofty tone, which somehow he still mistook for adult authority. He grudgingly gave Roger a Lincoln Log to play with.

Jane and I lolled on my bed next to the porch window. I picked up a book, Jane opened a magazine. From time to time the lace curtains, moving in the breeze, touched my face. We were not eavesdropping so much as we were staying in contact with her, in case she might call. That's what we were pretending.

Chief was the first person we had met when we moved to town from Nashville—pulled right up in his patrol car, stopping in to say hello on our first day. The car, more than the chief, had made an impression. Looking back, I suppose he was the quintessential picture of a lawman, although I didn't see that at the time. He was tall and stout, close to fat, but it suited him, people being comforted by someone in authority who is physically imposing. The red hair and Irish lineage topped it off, gave him instant identity and credibility. Voters would automatically pull the lever by his name. He was a veteran, had trained to be a police officer up in Memphis; it would have been almost un-American not to vote for him.

We knew only that there was some vague connection between him and our father, since they had both been in the war together, but then again every man we knew had been in the war in some way.

Mother was in the kitchen getting the iced tea when Chief pulled open the screened door and stuck his head in. "You there, Sara?" He came on the porch, sat on the glider, took off his hat, and began fanning himself with it. We could hear the glider creak as he stood when she came out with the tea.

"Don't know how long the electricity's been out over there," he said, sitting back down when she did. "Told them TVA boys to tell me if they was gonna cut it off again. I sometimes would scotch her till she got another government check. This last time, they musta forgot."

He put his hat aside and held the glass Mother had given him while she poured. Then he drank down half of it in one pass. "Mighty good, mighty good . . . hits the spot on a day like today." Then he finished it off. Drops from the sweating glass dripped on his uniform. "How long is it since y'all seen her out and about?"

Mama leaned forward with the pitcher, pouring again. "I don't think I've seen her in, oh, probably a week or so, but the children may have. Do you think that's what happened, all the hot weather we've been having?"

He was nodding his head as he started in on the next glass. Mother poured herself one. He rested his glass on the side table next to the glider, his hand still holding it, polite enough not to ask for a third, but hoping. "I don't know if it was the weather or not, but probably. Poor old soul. Feel right bad about it. You know me and your Daniel and her two, Sammy and Jonnie, her baby, we was all in it together—midway through and till the end. Felt kinda responsible for her after they didn't come home."

He smiled as Mother poured another glass for him. "By the way, Daniel in town right now? Heard tell he's done gone and got hisself another church over in Limestone County."

Mama set the pitcher back on the side table. "I believe he's up at the north end, visiting one of his smaller congregations, but I'm not sure. It's hard to keep track . . . somewhere in that vicinity. Why do you ask?"

There was a long pause as Chief studied the ice in his glass, jiggling it back and forth. "Oh, no reason." He downed a third. "I'm rung out from the heat over there."

She poured him another.

"Since she didn't have no family left, I was thinking I'd try to make some kinda arrangements. Ya know, her boys was the last of the Brownlees."

"Is that why you wanted Daniel—to preach the funeral?"

"Yeah, later maybe, but no . . . not yet. Have to wait a while on a funeral. Need to do a autopsy, get the boys up from Birmingham, or send her down to Birmingham more'n likely."

We could hear the ice crackle in his glass as he drained it again.

"Is that normal—an autopsy on someone Mrs. Brownlee's age? Isn't that a little disrespectful? What would her sons . . . what would Sammy and Jonnie have thought of that?"

Jane and I had raised eyebrows at each other; autopsies, ropes in the front yard, boys up from Birmingham . . . Like one of Mother's Agatha Christie mysteries. It seemed that frivolous then.

This was before I had read the first page of Jonnie's journal—before I knew it even existed— before I had stolen it.

Chapter 8

The glider squeaked back and forth. We edged closer to the window. "Well, it is a funny thing. Looks like she musta hit something, 'cause there's a lot of blood dried on the floor and a wound on her head, like she fell, but darn if I can see anything she mighta hit against from where she was when I found her."

Mama leaned back in her rocker, smiling. "Foul play, in our little village? Business must be slow, Red."

Chief chuckled. "Naw, don't worry none about it. Probably shouldn't even waste the money on them Birmingham boys, but it's the law. Being the new chief of police hereabouts and it being election time next year, I wanta be sure I do a job can't nobody complain about, me not being a native." The glider squeaked again as he lifted off his big frame.

"There was one other thing . . . The window next to the back door was broke out. Probably been that way for a long time. If you could see the inside of that house, you'd know she never was proud 'bout her housekeeping. Glass and such, still pieces of it round the back door, coulda been there for ages." He handed his empty glass over to her, but not before he took a piece of ice and settled it in one corner of his cheek. "Thanks for the tea, Sara girl. That hit the spot.

I'll see you tomorrow." He took his hat up off the glider cushion. "And listen here, I'd be obliged if you didn't let none of these kids here in the neighborhood go past the rope yonder in the yard."

"I was wondering about that rope."

He gave her a blank stare. "It's so none of them kids can get past it . . . like I just said. Kids can be a mess of trouble."

When he reached the screened door, he paused and turned back to her again. "Here's a thought. I'd count it a favor if you'd send one of your young'uns out on her bike to spread the word amongst the kids round here. Tell 'em I don't want nobody, I mean *nobody,* getting smart and thinking they got to prove how plucky they are by sneaking in that house stealing some gimcrack to prove they was in there. It would be a insult to Mrs. Brownlee, and besides, that place is a downright mess—full of rats, among other things." He held the door. "Would you do that for me?"

She was picking up tea paraphernalia. "I know just the one to do that for you."

Chapter 9

And so, the next morning, I set out on my bike to spread the word up and down Tripoli Circle. The chief would lock you in the cellar of the jail and let the rats get at you if you came near the Brownlee house. That was my story—to Marilyn McClure, Jerry Silverberg, Harriett Tomlinson, and anybody else I could find and interest in the bloody details. I took such pleasure in being the messenger that I had added a few grisly, perhaps extraneous, finer points, but I felt it was for the greater safety of the neighborhood, what with the rabid rats now lurking in the basement.

I had saved the best for last: the Pruitt sisters. Although they were generations older, we had seemed, from the beginning, to hit it off. I, being relatively new to the neighborhood and loving to hear the local gossip, and they, loving to tell it. Most of my anecdotes (the Oliver's cat got run over by Mr. Oliver, and I think he did it on purpose) couldn't compare with their news (Marilyn McClure's mother was pregnant, and even her husband didn't know it yet), but they seemed to like me anyway.

I would come to know, years later, that they were not really sisters at all but had somewhere along the line been assigned that title, as it was easier for them to fit socially into a round hole than admit to being square pegs. Everyone, all the way around, seemed pleased with this arrangement. The Pruitt sisters were revered contributors to the community good, and no one would think of challenging their lifestyle, as they lived it in a socially acceptable way.

For aeons they had taught English and Spanish in the one and only high school in town. Everyone knew them because they had been through at least one of their classes on the way to graduation. Now they were retired, independent, and owned *two* cars—unheard-of wealth on Tripoli Circle.

I rang the bell, listening to it echo down the inside hall. First they would come peeking out the front window curtains. Then they would smile, seeing it was me, and one of them would let me in while the other disappeared into the kitchen to get the tea and the pecan fudge. I would take the visitor's seat, the overstuffed horsehair club chair with the lace antimacassars, my sandals swinging freely off the ground. The sisters sat opposite on the matching sofa, Miss Lena dressed as though she could just as easily have headed out to a cocktail party as sit there with me: beautiful flowing silk dress, high heels, and earrings with matching necklace. I had even seen her out in the yard gardening and dressed like that, plus hat and gloves. Once I squinted and tried to imagine Miss Lena in blue jeans. The image would not come. Miss Louise was the one who would use the shovel and get things done. She served tea from the coffee table, "so strong," she said, "it'll make you stand up and be counted." Miss Lena would pass the pecan fudge, my favorite.

Everyone in the neighborhood knew that the sisters took a trip every summer for several weeks. “Gone off on one of their jaunts, have they,” people would say, and dismiss it with a flip of the hand. I was the one who got to hear the particulars. In retrospect, perhaps they hadn’t liked me that much; rather, I presented a nonjudgmental audience. Others might have read too much into their outings. “Remember, Lena, years ago, our trip to Mexico? That beautiful dancing señorita, the wonderful mariachi band, the margaritas . . . and you spoke Spanish?” They would smile, remembering. I would smile back, thinking how crazy to go that far just to practice your Spanish.

They would pour another round of tea, always hot. Cold tea was so local, they said. Hot tea was okay with me because their house was always cool—musty cool, as if they might not let fresh air in until winter came.

Their voices were quiet and pleasant, as if they were perfectly content living there with each other in that house on Tripoli Circle, with their two cars. No matter what people might say about old maids being unhappy, to me it looked to be a grand lifestyle, one I might consider for myself.

After I finished tea and two pecan fudge pieces, we got down to business. I told them all about what the chief had said. They cringed, appropriately, when I got to the part about how the chief might lock people up if they crossed the rope line without his permission.

All the talk about Mrs. Brownlee began to shake loose their memories of her. They began telling me about back when she was sane and happy, when her boys were young and alive. "What a wonderful person she was," Miss Lena said, "really a perfect mother, raising them up after her husband had passed. Why, each Christmas she would have a big tree-trimming party. The whole neighborhood would be invited."

"Yes," Miss Louise chimed in, "there was a tree in the living room that her boys would string with popcorn, and Jonnie—I think it was Jonnie—he would make miles of paper chains and circle the whole thing."

"Then Sammy, the older one, he would throw icicles all over the place, trying to hit the top of the tree. All the children would join in and make such a wonderful mess. The adults would become quite amused," Miss Lena said. "I would make pecan fudge to take over every Christmas."

"No, Lena, you would take candied orange rinds, I would take the fudge."

"I took candied orange rinds *one* year. It was never popular. After that I started taking the fudge and *you* made the Toll House cookies."

They stared at each other for a second and decided, I supposed, that it wasn't worth arguing about, so they turned and smiled at me. "We sang carols," they said in unison.

"I can see it now," Miss Lena said, "just like a Norman Rockwell painting on the front of *The Saturday Evening Post*, all the children dressed in their Sunday best and running around . . . Such a happy time."

Miss Louise gazed into the dark hollow of their fireplace. "We haven't been inside her house in years now, not since she lost those precious boys." She leaned back, resting her head on the sofa. "I was partial to Sammy. Such a cutup, and straight A's in Spanish."

Miss Lena touched the back of her hand. "I favored Jonnie. So devoted to his mama, writing her practically every day—saying he was keeping a journal for her so he could tell her everything that happened when he got home . . . only he never got home."

Chapter 10

That night after supper, just as the lightning bugs were blinking at us from the kitchen window and Jane had finished washing and I had finished drying, Mother announced that it was time to have a get-together. Jane and I rushed to haul out our parachute, still smelling of raw silk.

Our neighborhood was replete with keepsakes from the battle—German helmets, Japanese flags, bayonets, tattered U.S. Army canteens. Children who didn't have them seemed odd. Our parachute was rare among souvenirs, as most of them had been long ago cut up to make silk dresses and pajamas. We hung it between the wringer washer and the clothesline that was strung across the back porch. Jane and I had decided that somebody—some German somebody—must have fallen miles to his death trying to get it open. Our father had never told us how he came by it, just that he had picked it up along the way. It had not discouraged our imaginings.

When we met under the parachute, we were free to wear whatever we felt like. Mother sat down on the floor with us, wearing a bright chiffon scarf, *The Lion, the Witch and the Wardrobe* in her lap just in case someone asked. I had on my cowgirl boots, and Jane wore ballet slippers, things we had found at the Salvation Army thrift store. Mother would take us there periodically, opening the front door and sweeping her hand out to us: "Just go right in and pick out your heart's desire."

Hercule had found a bow and arrow set with one arrow, the others missing. I had run across my cowgirl boots in a big cardboard box marked "Etc." Jane had found her ballet slippers at the bottom of the same box.

At the time, we were not sure what all this freedom under the parachute entailed, but thinking back, it seemed that she meant it to be a nice respite for us, given the confines of the teachings of the Church of the Redeemer, especially the confines of the children of the head minister of Church of the Redeemer.

Upon first hearing the news of this place of reckless abandon, Hercule had said that if he could do anything he wanted under the parachute, he would eat peanut butter the whole time. She had let him, once. I, being older, had made more appropriate use of my time. Once, under the parachute, I had silently plotted the murder of Polly Ann Rogers. I had felt it was just what she deserved after she had laughed at Jane and me for riding double on the old Schwinn Mother had bought for us at the thrift store. We were trying to get to her birthday party on time, so we had doubled up and probably did look like something out of Ringling Brothers—me carrying our presents, balanced on the front handlebars, Jane jerking me from side to side, maneuvering around parked cars.

This night, I was mentally rubbing my hands together, ready to get down to the gory details of Mrs. Brownlee's demise. Mother smiled at us and blew smoke that rose up and hovered in a cloud just beneath the parachute and just above our heads. We felt it gave us a clandestine, mysterious look, like the fog in London when Hercule Poirot was about.

We could look out past the porch into the backyard and see a light that was flickering through the trees when the breeze stirred the leaves. It usually meant he had come home and was working on his sermon in his garage office before coming inside.

Hercule noticed. "He's home," and he got up out of his cross-legged position. "I wanta go see him."

"No, not right now," she said, turning our thoughts away from the garage. "Pay attention to this. I want to tell you about *our* mystery." Hercule sat back down.

"I believe . . . ," she said, glancing into dark corners. "I believe we have our work cut out for us. I believe, my dears, there is foul work afoot." She said things like "foul work afoot" when she was in her mystery story mode or trying to divert us.

"What's dat mean?"

"Why, Mrs. Brownlee, of course. A mystery, right here in the neighborhood, right here under our very noses. Chief told us himself not to let people inside the rope around Mrs. Brownlee's front yard."

The light went out in the room over the garage. She glanced up and saw it. "I'll tell you what," she whispered for effect. "Let's continue our meeting in the morning, when it's light and we can think more clearly, without the mysterious dark shadows of the evening swirling about."

Jane was not taken in by this faded melodrama. "Really, Mother, are you just thinking up things to entertain us?"

"Moi?" Mother, hand to bosom, pretending great shock.

We heard the door of his garage office open. We knew he must be closing it and locking it and walking down the outside stairs to ground level. We gathered up the white parachute and stuffed it in its storage place behind the wringer washer.

As it turned out, it didn't matter what Mother's intentions were. The whole scene of the mystery at Mrs. Brownlee's was getting ready to be dumped right in our laps.

Chapter 11

The next morning, Chief came to our house. He stood on the front walk, his hand resting on his gun grip, the underarms of his uniform already drenched. He took out a wrinkled handkerchief and wiped down his face. The cicadas in the oak tree over by Mrs. Brownlee's were tuning up for their midmorning whine. It was going to be, it already was, a scorcher. "Got some boys from over to the jail, trying to clean the place out—cut down on the varmint population."

Mother was standing on the front steps in the middle of morning chores. She put aside the broom she was holding and began to tie a scarf over her hair. "Convicts? On our street?" She joined it behind her neck and flipped the corner of the scarf back over her hair to catch the dust.

"They ain't convicts, Sara. Old Z, we pick him up once a month for hanging one on, and Dummy, he wouldn't harm a fly, when he's sober. Just dryin'em out." He stood watching her, head cocked to one side, as if he weren't sure what he thought of her yet. "Now, I come to you 'cause I know you ain't like the rest, them Pruitt sisters, the Olivers, and all them. Nothing scares you, Sara girl."

"Ah, Red, you're such a flatterer . . . and so subtle." She paused and smiled at him, but not for long, because Mother was one to get to the heart of the matter straightaway. "What can I do for you?"

He grinned his big-man grin at her. Chief was not famously handsome like our father, but he didn't have a mean face, which to my mind would have been perfectly respectable on a chief of police. Rather, it was pleasant and ordinary. His hairline was receding slightly, and his flattop—the fashion of the day—was a bit overdone, crushed down each time he put on his hat and then when he took it off again running his fingers through to make sure it stood upright.

If you took away the uniform and the gun and the fact that he was overweight, we might have approved of the chief, except that he did *not* have a way with words. And that, in Mother's eyes and therefore ours, made him a hopeless case.

"Ain't no telling how long ago they cut off the water over there," he was saying, "and no electricity to even plug up a fan. And the windows, they was painted shut years ago. And I can't start up none of that again, else who's gonna pay for it? And the dust, Lord . . . you take a deep breath a time or two and you're liable to end up with tuberculosis. I was just over there a minute ago—poor old Z was coughing his head off. Him being Italian and all, probably ain't used to it being this hot and moist and—"

"I get the picture, Red," she interrupted. "The working conditions for your prisoners are less than admirable. And what is it you think I might possibly do about that?"

He looked down at the ground, pushed a pebble around with the toe of his shoe, clearing his throat. "You know, people hereabouts, they don't rightly take to such straight talk.

Not me, 'course, I don't mind it, but if you was to want to make friends . . ." He trailed off when he saw the look he was getting. "Well, here's the thing," he continued in his original vein. "I'd be much obliged if you was to take some water over to the boys or iced tea, if you're feeling generous, every few hours or so. Hot as the devil's kitchen in there." He winked at her. "And I can tell from that sample I had yesterday, you're one heck of a iced tea maker."

Mother gave him a rather weary look. She wasn't in the mood to be amused. I knew it must have been residue from the night before. Our father had had one of his dreams, the first one in several months. She called it that, a dream, because "nightmare" sounded too lurid and she had to name it something, since when it happened it would stir the entire household. He woke up yelling something indecipherable—"Key pot or Kriegbot," something like that. The words didn't matter, it was the way they sounded in the dark, eerie and completely unattached to anything we had knowledge of. Jane and I raised our heads and waited for it to subside and for Hercule to be disturbed enough to ask, "Is dat him?" When we said it was, he had his routine. He would push back the covers, grab his teddy bear—mine before I had passed it on—feel his way to one of our beds, and climb in. This night it was my bed. Before we dozed off again, the light came on in the kitchen. She was making a pot of coffee. The comfortable smell of it floated in under our door. Our father had gone back to sleep. We were going back to sleep. She was in the kitchen drinking coffee.

Chapter 12

Mother picked up her broom that was leaning against the screen. She was getting ready to use it to knock out a dirt dauber nest that was building under the eaves of the porch, right where the screen door opened. "I'll be happy to help out . . . on one condition." The chief took a quick step back as Mama let fly with the broom and missed the nest completely.

"And what's that, Sara girl?"

"If you will refrain from calling poor old Dummy *Dummy*," she said. "Surely he must have another name. It's outrageous that you, and everyone else around here, refer to him in that way. He's not dumb, he just can't hear and consequently hasn't learned how to speak." She took out after the nest again, jumping up, swatting, missing.

Chief backed up a few more steps. "Well, if you can find out what it is, I wish you'd let me know. Need it for the lockup records. I've asked him a million times and all he writes down under 'Name' is D-u-m-m-y. That's what everybody's called him since he was in grade school, so I'm told." Chief ducked to avoid another swish of the broom, which didn't seem to be bothering the nest at all, sitting up there minding its own business. I decided to come inside on the porch, easing the screen door shut.

"Nobody means nothin' by it, it's just his name," the chief was explaining, "just like everybody calls Z Z. That's not his real name either, we just call him that." He watched her take another swing. "Kinda like nicknames, you might say—like mine, Red. Didn't they ever have nicknames where you come from?"

Mother sighed and stepped up to the dirt dauber nest again. "No."

Chief tried to get on with the subject at hand. "So if you'll do that for me, I'd be much obliged. I'll come by to check on 'em during the day, have lunch sent out, and I'll pick 'em up and drop 'em off till they finish cleaning things out. Then maybe all your neighbors will give my phone a rest. Been complaining nonstop about them rats coming out of that house . . . and the stench, since we opened up them doors." He waited a second to see if she would object. "Knew I could count on you, Sara girl. You wouldn't want nobody to have no heatstroke over there."

He turned to walk back across the street but paused. "One other thing. If I was you, I'd leave well enough alone with that broom."

"I will not have dirt daubers messing up my front porch entrance."

"Uh-huh." Chief exhaled loudly. "Except they ain't dirt dabbers, Sara. Them up there is wasps. Wasps have the brown nest. Dabbers, they got the red dirt nest, if you didn't know it. You gonna end up with a bunch of swoll-up kids if you don't watch out. You sure you wanta go messing with 'em?"

Not being one to back off, Mother handed him the broom. He shrugged, took it, and with one hefty swat knocked the whole thing, wasps and nest, out to the side yard, then threw the broom on the steps and trotted—I don't think he could have run—back across the street. Mama stepped inside the screen door fast while the wasps buzzed around looking for the guilty party.

He called to her from the street: "Told Daniel, the day he brought you back here, 'Daniel, son, you outdid yourself when you hooked up with Sara.' How *did* he get you, anyway—fancy enough for the big city and ending up down here with us?"

Chapter 13

"I wanta go."

"No, me."

"No, me." Hercule, and Mother, had insisted he be included whenever Jane and I got into a competition.

We settled by flipping to see who would be first to carry the tray of glasses and ice while Mother carried the tea pitcher and some cookies across the street. After Jane lost and wandered away from the proceedings, I won out over Hercule. Flipping, I explained to Hercule, was a complicated mathematical formula that would be hard for him to understand. Sometimes it was best out of three or sometimes best out of five or ten, depending. He pretended to see when on the tenth try I called heads and won.

Once he had asked me about his name, having been teased by some of the other children in Sunday school. Rather than explain Mother's devotion to Agatha Christie—and that we were all, in some way, named after Agatha's people—I had told him Hercule was short for the great Greek god Hercules. I was not sure it was so but knew he would be delighted. The thrift store bow and arrow had only firmed up the image.

And what I saw was "mind-boggling, incredible, and amazing," I said to Jane and Herc when Mother and I had come back from delivering tea for the first time.

Mother said, "Colossal, massive debris over there."

We were sitting out on the front screen porch, looking across to the Brownlee house. "In the first place, the whole thing is filled up to overflowing with stuff, stuff, and more stuff. You see that window on the end, on the left side?" Together they nodded. "Well, let me tell you there must be hundreds of empty Coke bottles in that room alone. Every time Mrs. Brownlee finished a Coke, she musta gone and stacked the bottle in that room."

"Well, da water was off." You could see Herc's brain churning away. "Maybe she didn't drink nuttin' but Cokes . . . which ain't a bad ding, if you dink about it."

"Right, Herc." Jane rolled her eyes. "Have you thought a person might need to wash her hair once in a while . . . or take a bubble bath?"

Hercule wrinkled his nose. The idea of taking any kind of bath was depressing to him. I continued, "And not only Cokes, but RCs, Nehis, Grapettes, Orange Crush, Dr Peppers." I had embellished slightly, for effect. "And the library, it's stacked with canned goods, in boxes and on shelves: old cans of beans, fruit cocktail, peaches, Spam, some oozing this brown, liquid looking stuff. Like the whole of Hill's grocery gone bad in there."

"Did you go upstairs and look around?"

"Are you kidding, Jane? We couldn't get up those stairs if we had a ladder. There're things stacked all up and down the steps—catalogs, magazines, books. Mrs. Brownlee must have had to weave her way in and out every time she used them. Chief said it isn't even safe for grown men till they get cleaned out. Besides," I said with what I hoped was great authority, "we'll get to it soon enough"—part of my scheme to take ownership of this project before Jane could butt in.

"Yeah, but did you see da prisoners up close? Did ya touch 'em in dare jailbird outfits?"

"Oh, that. Nobody over there but old Mr. Z. I see him all the time down by the Trailways station when I ride bikes."

"Da Italy man?"

"The Italian man, Hercule. And Dummy, remember him? He's the one painted our garage that time. He's over there." I tried to say it offhandedly, as if I were not at all skittish where Dummy was concerned, hoping Jane didn't recall that I wouldn't come within shouting distance of the backyard while Dummy had been out there painting our garage. I had spent my time peering around the edges of the house, afraid to come within sight of him. Rumor had it that if you had been looked upon by Dummy, you might be in some way changed for the rest of your life—and not for the better. The particulars of this curse were never mentioned, which made it even worse. That had been a few years back, when we had first come to town. By this summer I had grown older and would not be so easily duped.

"Yeah, but I bet day look scary in dem uniforms."

"*Those* uniforms, Hercule," I corrected, thinking of how scared I had been to step close enough to give Dummy his glass of tea, but then how I had softened to him when he'd reached out his big rough hand and given me the sign for thank you. At least Mother had said that was what he had done.

"You are not to call him that name ever again. Is that understood?" She was standing in the front doorway with a sack of beans, getting ready to string them for supper. She came over to take a seat on the glider under the fan.

In the summer, if you didn't have conditioned air—and no one in our town did, except the Majestic Theater—you stayed under fans as much as possible. At night I could look down the block and see half the families on Tripoli Circle out on their porches, under their fans, yellow lights from their lamps spilling out onto the grass. Children, for the most part, remained out of doors until it was time to be called in, like horses let out for the day and called home for the evening feed. Sometimes there was a big game of hide-and-seek, the lamppost in the middle of Tripoli Circle being home base and all of our shadows darting from behind bushes and around corners. That summer, I played and Hercule played. Jane had all but given up on the game.

Mother got up to check on Roger, who was already pulling up to a standing position in his playpen. We were certain he was above average. "Everybody in town calls him Dummy, Mother. People wouldn't know who we were talking about if we called him something else," Jane said.

She sat back down and peeled open the paper sack to begin snapping Kentucky Wonders into the pan she had brought from the kitchen. "Now let me see, what would be a good name for a person like Dum . . . a person like him . . . which is"—she pointed a bean at me—"which is a person who can't hear so no one has taken the time to communicate with him. Also he is an albino and his looks are somewhat off-putting, but that should not deter." She glared at us. "Should it?"

We all nodded that no, it should not deter, even though I didn't know at the time what exactly albino meant, figuring it must have to do with Dummy's strange, piercing eyes.

"Hmmm"—she bit her lip—"how about Vincent, after another painter? How does that sound?" She smiled and nodded, having made up her mind. "From now on, we shall refer to him as Vincent."

"But he doesn't even look like a Vincent."

She stopped snapping beans. *"Vincent,"* she said.

"Vincent," we mumbled.

"And another thing"—she pointed a bean at us again—"as soon as we find out what Mr. Z's real name is, we will begin to address him properly." Before that summer, I had never given a thought to old Mr. Z, although I knew of him. He was someone, some old someone, I had seen shuffling around town—to a child, part of the necessary landscape to be skirted.

Chapter 14

Our father had come home for supper. It was an exception rather than a daily habit. He came to the table looking tired and bleary-eyed from long hours on the road tending to his ever increasing flock. In addition to Redeemer, he had taken on two smaller churches that needed a preacher. "And people know your father won't refuse," Mother had said, weary of it. "He can never refuse—has to carry the weight of the world on his shoulders."

More often than not, he would stop for the night with some parishioner who had an extra bedroom and needed advice. For us too, it was like having an honored guest. Once, I had overheard some of the ladies of the church say, "Doesn't matter if Brother Daniel can preach a lick or not, he's that good to look at." And he was—tall with white blond hair, beautiful blue eyes, and honey-colored skin. I had thought the ladies of Redeemer were not exaggerating one bit.

He came in and kissed each of us on top of the head, seated himself at the end of the table, and took down his napkin. Giving us a tired smile, he began to talk about his new congregation in a little town up near the Tennessee border, good people all, "and I think I will be of use to them." Then he turned to us, asking what one particular thing we had been doing this past week to glorify the Lord's name. It was a question always asked and one we were never prepared to answer correctly or with any eagerness, as we were not quite sure what glorifying the Lord's name entailed. After a pause and eyes darting back and forth to one another, Jane announced that she was cutting the grass all summer so we would not be a worry to our neighbors. I, looking at my plate, mumbled that I was helping her out with that chore. Hercule, ditto. Already, we felt we must be a disappointment.

He slowly brought his hands together over his dinner plate. We could tell it was going to be a long prayer by the way he had kissed us and looked into our eyes, each one as he kissed. We were all born sinners, and long blessings would somehow help. We were happy to listen because we were receiving, on a somewhat regular basis, what everyone else in his various churches seemed to be clamoring for.

After a time I looked up, and Mother was taking Roger out of his high chair and holding him because we were getting so hungry that Roger was beginning to whimper. We sat there in our innocence, listening or half listening, not realizing what was to come.

"And Lord, we know You will always provide even when there seems to be no way." He paused and we thought it was over, but he continued, "I was at a loss about what to do for the Briggs family, that sick little baby and three other children to feed and not a scrap of food in the house, until I remembered the wonderful bounty You had allowed us to save for our family vacation." He paused again. I sneaked a peek at Mother. She had opened her eyes and was looking right at him and then around to the rest of us, eyebrows questioning. She was that surprised. We were all that surprised.

"Lord, I bought only the necessities with that money. I knew they would need . . ." He went on to say other things, but by then Mother was up, putting the baby in his high chair and rushing to the kitchen. I still had my hands clenched together over my plate but was looking at Jane to see if she was the one who had told. She was looking back at me to see if I was the one. We could hear Mother jerking down the flour canister and dumping it on the kneading board to see if he was talking about our secret money we had been saving up under the parachute for two years now, so Mother could take us to Gulf Shores on our first vacation ever, to see the ocean. We heard her fists banging on the kitchen counter, eight, nine, ten times. Then there was silence, and our father was saying, "Amen." He took up a piece of meat loaf and proceeded to serve our plates.

"Besides," he said, smiling wearily at the meat loaf, "I like going to the river and using our old Chris-Craft to ride around, and I like cooking hot dogs over a fire on the shore. That's a vacation, isn't it?"

We all nodded, knowing he never had taken us to the river, with the exception of that one time when we'd first moved back to town, just to look at the old boat. That had been so long ago that Hercule didn't remember ever seeing it. He said he had skied behind it when he was a boy, before the war. Now it just sat at the river marina, slowly sinking into the water, like some old relic from yet another story we hadn't heard.

A few more minutes and Mother stalked back into the dining room, yanked out her chair, and took her place at the table, her jaw clenching and unclenching.

"It was the Lord's way of providing," he said to her calmly. "We are instruments of the Lord, Sara. I had to do it. I couldn't let that family suffer. You should have seen the children—their eyes . . . when they looked at me."

"How did you know about it?" she said, jerking down her napkin.

"Hercule was so proud of his last contribution, the money he made from washing the Pruitt sisters' front walk, he had to show me." He turned to Hercule. "And a fine contribution it was, Hercule. The Lord looks with favor upon those who provide for His people."

Hercule sat there grinning like some crazed Cheshire cat until he looked over and saw Jane and me ready to pounce.

"That was *my money, too*," Jane almost shouted at him. "I put in thirty-five cents last week—all I made from selling scrap iron pieces I found in the garage, to Mr. Mallory down at the junkyard . . . and there aren't any more to sell."

"And me"—I reached over and grabbed Hercule's collar—"I spent two whole days washing old Miss Jim Weakley's windows and listening to her tell me every spot I missed, all for a lousy seventy-five cents, and you . . . you . . . ," I snarled, pulling back to deliver a punch, but thought better of it when I saw our father frowning at me. All I could do was give Hercule a look that I was sure would burn through wood. His little face scrunched up in horror at having wronged his big sisters. Small comfort, but I took it.

At our last meeting under the parachute, we had taken a vote about where we might go when we got enough saved. We were constantly changing our travel plans. Time before last, we had decided on a safari in Africa. Last time, we had changed our minds and I had said Paris, France, after all the stories Mother had told—the Eiffel Tower, the sidewalk cafés, the Seine. Jane wanted Gulf Shores and so had Mother, so we'd settled on a beach vacation and knew it would be another year before we had saved half enough. Truth be known, I probably would have been in high school before we had saved enough, and our destinations would have changed ten times over by then, but that wasn't the point. "Let your minds wander out anywhere on the planet you might like to go," she had said. She would take us to the library to study up on safaris, the Eiffel Tower, the Serengeti. Then we would change our minds and go back again, looking up Iceland, the Nile River, and the Pyramids. Now Hercule had gone and blabbed.

We already knew the Lord came first with our father and we came in second. She had told us there was nothing wrong with that. It was, however, one of the reasons we didn't tell him everything. For his own good, she had told us. If he had known about the money, it wouldn't have lasted five minutes, and sure enough, it hadn't. We were, she had explained, actually doing him a favor, not giving him a temptation. That was her take on it, and therefore that was our take on it, because we were secure in the knowledge that we came first with her.

Chapter 15

Our loss was twice as bad because the secret had lasted so long. We had saved up so much and now nothing. Hercule jumped up out of his seat, ran to Mother, and buried his head in her lap. I was itching to get at him as soon as we got to a meeting under the parachute. He would rue the day.

Our father didn't look at Mother but ate his meat loaf and told us how happy the Briggses were to get the food. And how proud we should be because we had helped them. "Remember the Good Samaritan," he said. "We should all try to emulate the Good Samaritan."

He glanced up at Mother as she took the last cigarette out of the pack and lit it, her jaw still working, fingers trembling as she held the match. She knew he hated for her to smoke, especially at the table, and she usually didn't, to avoid the long, biblically punctuated discussion of it.

"We must all humble ourselves before the Lord," he said. "Your mother has never completely given herself over to Him." And then he smiled. "But we are always hoping, aren't we, Hercule?" When he asked for an opinion, it was always addressed to Hercule, because men were supposed to make all the decisions, according to the Church of the Redeemer, and Hercule was the only other man around to consult with, baby Roger being incommunicado as yet. It was never in a cruel way that he deferred to Hercule, but he always did.

"*Hope* was what I was going for. . . ." Her voice trailed off with the smoke she blew out over the table. "Hope . . . at the bottom of the flour bin."

"The only hope is in the Lord," he said, casually asking Jane to pass the biscuits, as if he had no idea he had taken away our hard-earned twenty dollars and twenty-five cents—a fortune.

Iced tea and Camels for dinner . . . She blew smoke in the air until there was another cloud hanging over the table. "Daniel?" She looked to him as if she might say something else but must have thought better of it.

His face had gone gray. He was gripping his knife and fork so tightly his knuckles had turned white around the edges. "I was the one who had to make the decision," he said.

We were not then aware of the appalling decisions he had already had to make and of the toll taken.

Chapter 16

Supper finished, he had gone back out to his garage office to work on his sermon and left us sitting at the table, stunned and penniless. Mother adjourned us to a meeting under the parachute, and after we had ranted and raved, especially me at Hercule, Jane at Hercule, Hercule at Mother, me at Jane, etc., we calmed down and Mother began to explain that what had happened at supper could really be considered a test of sorts, to see if we could keep things to ourselves. She said we must remember that old motto from the war, "Loose lips sink ships," and that from now on only certain ones of us would be clued in as to where the money was stashed, duly named by her "Assets Assistants." And those who were warriors—and Hercule would be a warrior, thank God—would not have to bother themselves with high finance. Warriors, she explained to Hercule, were charged with protecting us all; she didn't say from what.

Jane and I were much relieved to be the only designated Assets Assistants. Hercule seemed just as pleased to be assigned to something that involved only himself and his bow and arrow.

Mother gave us the money to start over, five cents, and we were told to find a new hiding place. It looked like such a paltry sum lying there in Jane's palm, especially given that only hours before we had been in possession of gigantic wealth. It was hard to even imagine taking a vacation to Tahiti or Africa on five cents.

"Starting over," she said, "is what you have to do a lot of times in life, and you might as well learn that lesson right now."

We were hard-pressed to see the wisdom in that. It did, however, give Jane and me a new project. We spent the rest of the afternoon secreted away, plotting where to hide our money. It must be in the most clandestine place imaginable. "The devil himself," Jane vowed, "would not be able to find this money when we finished hiding it, not if he looked for a thousand years to come." The only problem I saw with that was that it had been the very opposite of the devil himself who had found it in the first place.

Chapter 17

Perhaps he felt some guilt at having taken away all of our vacation money, or perhaps a little of the old self was seeping through. I will never know why our father decided that a vacation day on the river was in order, but the next time he came in off the road he said we should take one, "like we used to do," he said. Jane and I and certainly Hercule had never had an outing on the river with him, except when we first came to town and went to inspect the old Chris-Craft that had been his in his youth and now was left half floating in the backwaters of the river marina. We hadn't thought to wonder about the why of it because we were thrilled to go anyplace with him, especially Mother. He might have intended to take us to the river on so many occasions that the intention and the actual event had become one in his mind. In any event, it was a day we would not forget—for the pleasure and the pain of it.

We would get out the old boat, he said, take it to a beautiful spot on the riverbank, cook hot dogs over a fire we would build, go swimming, sing songs, gaze up from the river bottom, and watch cars cross the bridge high above us—things he had done as a boy.

He kept his word and was home right after lunch on the appointed day. He came into the kitchen with the rest of us, keen to help with the preparations, taking all the ice out of trays in the refrigerator and dumping it in the ice chest, loading in hot dogs and chips and Ball jars of sweet tea Mother had made and anything else he could find in the cabinets. She laughed at his eagerness. "Daniel, sweetheart, we don't need to take everything in the house." He had just pitched a can of baked beans in the cooler.

"What are you talking about?" He came over and grabbed her around the waist, ruffling her hair. "Baked beans, they're one of the four basic food groups. I used to live off of them when I was coming up, baked beans and hot dogs, baked bean sandwiches, baked beans straight out of the can, baked—"

"Wait a minute, *wait* one minute here," she said, smiling and grabbing his shirt collar. "I am not falling for that one. Baked bean sandwiches?" She was laughing as she picked the can of baked beans back out of the overflowing cooler. "Nobody ever ate a baked bean *sandwich*."

"You are looking at the inventor of the baked bean sandwich. When Carl and the Brownlees and I used to camp out at the river, we would live off of baked beans." He took the can out of her hand and put it back in the chest. "Gotta have 'em." His big arms circled her waist again and pulled her close, turning her in my direction. "Isn't that right, Aggie? Ya gotta have hot dogs and baked beans if you wanta call it a real day on the river."

She was grinning, shaking her head at me. "Have you ever heard of such a thing, Aggie?"

I smiled back at them, never before having heard them talk to each other in such a frivolous, playful way.

We were off to the river with swimsuits, towels, quilts, an overflowing ice chest, a large wicker basket for plates, napkins, a tablecloth, baby food, and everything else we could possibly think of needing. Hercule had to take along some of his Lincoln Logs. Jane brought a few back issues of *Seventeen*. Me, I took an old fishing pole I had found in the back of the garage when we moved into the house on Tripoli Circle.

Mother sat next to him in the front seat, holding the baby, the ice chest wedged in between her and the door. Jane, Herc, and I were in the back holding quilts and baskets and a large beach ball with a slow leak that we had patched with a Band-Aid.

He announced that we should sing on the way there. My jaw dropped. Jane mouthed, "I told you so," remembering how I had scoffed at her notion that before the war he would sometimes sing with her. It was an off-key version of "In the Good Old Summer Time." We sang along. Mother laughed uproariously when he would end a line loudly off-key. He took one arm off the wheel and put it around her shoulder. I watched from the backseat, holding a large stack of quilts in my lap, looking over to Jane and Hercule and shrugging. Next we sang "Row, Row, Row Your Boat" in rounds. We were pretty good on that one.

The marina was situated near the highway, which rose up in a steep grade to cross the river bridge. We turned off the main road onto a dirt road and bumped down toward the docks, all of us bouncing and laughing as our old car hit potholes and deep gullies that he was not trying to avoid. He stopped a few yards down the road and turned back to Jane. "Come on up here, Jane girl. You need to start learning how to drive." Jane was astounded. After she had asked two or three times if he was serious, she jumped at the chance.

"Serious as I'll ever be." He smiled. "Come on up here, Janie." He pushed the big bench seat of our old Plymouth back as far as it would go and Jane sat on his lap, steering all over the road and loving it. Even the baby was laughing when we finally zigzagged our way to the marina, stopping in a swirl of dust that wrapped around our car.

"This boat . . . ," he said as he opened the door, let Jane out, then went around to open Mother's side and grab the ice chest that had her pinned. "This boat is the one that Carl and the Brownlees and I used to use in the summer. We'd come out here with enough supplies to camp along the river for a week or two. Caught some giant catfish out in the main channel back then." He slung the immense ice chest onto his broad shoulder as if it weighed nothing, talking all the while. "I would work at the marina by day and then stay in the camp at night. The others would join me when their parents would let them."

For the first time, I imagined him as a child and felt sorry for the other boys, for Carl and Sammy and Jonnie Brownlee, not being able to stay with him in his camp on the river. I could see him wild and free of any responsibility, coming to the water's edge, building his own secret hideout, living the life of Robinson Crusoe—an existence children of my era could only dream about. Now, as I look back, I see a teenager, still a boy, really, cut loose from any binding ties of love and responsibility, his old aunt not caring whether he lived or died and he desperate to build his own version of home and family.

Mother scooted out carrying Roger, smiling—actually grinning—at Daniel. "How did you boys ever afford to buy a boat back then?"

"I worked down here in the summer for Miss Madine, the marina owner, and this boat was sitting half-drowned in one of the slips. She said I could have it as part of my pay if I would move it out of the marina and free up the slip." Jane got out carrying the big wicker basket. Hercule had his box of toys. We would have to come back for the other things in the car. "Worked all summer on that boat. And it was a beauty when we finished." He walked fast ahead of us, searching the riverbank. "You'll see."

Jane and I and Hercule walked behind them, remembering the only other time we had visited the marina. The boat had been half-submerged then and must still be unless some miracle had taken place. "I thought I remembered that that boat wasn't—," Mother began, but stopped herself and walked on behind him.

Chapter 18

We came to the river's edge. There was a bow rope that ran from a willow down into the water. The old boat wasn't half-submerged now, it was fully submerged. Silt that had settled in on the wood ribs was obscuring what had been the top. I was holding my quilts and my fishing rod, looking down at the muddy outline in the water. I could barely make out a cracked windshield.

Hercule said, "I taught you said it was a nice boat when you . . ."

Mother touched Herc on the shoulder. "Your father was just remembering wrong." She shifted the baby to her other side and took our father's arm. "I've done that many times." She watched his face which had suddenly gone dark. "That can happen to anybody . . . remembering wrong."

"I thought . . . I thought I remembered that the boat was still here where . . ." He trailed off, staring down at the dark outline in the water. He had a bewildered, almost frightened look, as if he had suddenly lost track of who he was, of what he was there for. She caught his arm and tried to pull him away.

"Daniel, we'll come back here another time. Why don't you take us to the place on the riverbank where y'all used to camp out. . . . Remember . . . you and the Brownlees and Carl? We can build a fire . . . cook hot dogs. That will be great fun, won't it, children?" Her look to us insisted that we agree, with gusto. Jane caught on immediately.

"Oh, yeah, let's do *that*. That should be great fun."

And I, the less subtle among us: "How am I gonna fish if I don't have a boat?"

And Hercule, my backup: "Yeah, she can't fish if she ain't got no boat."

"You can fish off the shore, stupid." Jane turned me around and marched me back toward the car. Herc followed. We waited by the Plymouth and watched as she talked to him, her arm on his back, rubbing it. When they finally joined us, he seemed in a somewhat better mood than the darkening furrowed brow we had left staring into the water. We all got back in the Plymouth and headed down the marina road another quarter of a mile, past the marina and some distance from the river bridge but with a good view of both of them. Soon enough we came to a long, beautiful stretch of sandy shore where the lapping waters of the Tennessee gave up periwinkles and mussel shells and afforded us a grand view downriver. For children, dark moments don't last long. We jumped out excitedly and began unloading.

"So this is the place of many happy memories," she said to him. He put the ice chest down and walked over to her, looking out at the water. Off in the distance there was a tiny speck of a barge coming toward us. "This would be it." He grinned at her as he rolled up the sleeves of his shirt. "I spent many a day camped out here, cooking over hot coals—fish, quail, you name it."

"And baked beans," she teased.

"Oh, cute," he said. "Your mother is a comedian, kids." And rubbed his hands together, seeming to be back into the spirit of the day. "I'll get the playpen out of the trunk, and then Hercule, let's us men gather some firewood while the ladies set up camp."

And so we did, spreading out a tablecloth on the grass, loading it down with plates and forks and glasses, collecting river rocks to place in a circle as a firebreak. He showed us how to cut off tree branches and skin them for roasting hot dogs. He strung clothesline between two river birches and hung quilts over it to make a changing room. Once, in his enthusiasm, he called to Herc, "Jonnie, catch that line for me, buddy." Then we all went swimming.

The day proceeded at a leisurely pace. Hercule built a fort on the sand using his Lincoln Logs. Jane and I played catch but soon enough lost the beach ball to the current and watched until it floated out of sight. We took turns swinging into the shallows on an old rope someone had left tied to an overhanging oak branch.

Late in the afternoon, Jane and I started the fire. It wasn't close to suppertime yet, but all the swimming had us starving. Our father had taken the quilts and laid them down for us and stretched out on one himself. Immediately he had fallen into a sound sleep.

When the fire was ready, we began madly affixing hot dogs to roasting sticks, poking them into the flames, and burning them to various shades of black. Hercule was so hungry that he was eating his dog right off the stick. Jane and I, being more sophisticated, burned ours on the outside, then slid the dogs, the insides still cold, into a bun and drowned them in catsup and mustard, trying to assuage a mighty hunger stirred up by a day on the river. Herc, his mouth stuffed, "We should wake him up so he can say da prayer before we eat, like always."

Mother nixed it. "He needs the rest more than the food. He hasn't been sleeping well lately." She whispered, "Look how contented he seems."

We glanced over to see him sprawled on the blanket, breathing slowly and deeply, late afternoon shadows dancing across his face. She was sitting close by and brushed a ladybug from his forehead.

It was dusk when it happened. The day had cooled slightly, just enough to give our crackling fire another reason for being. Swirling eddies in the river current had gone black, and a tugboat with barges—as big as they came on the river, two across and eight long—moved toward us, its front navigation lights positioned on the leading barge, warning oncoming traffic: red right, green left, and an ominous blinking yellow in the middle. The tugboat, bringing up the rear, had just turned on its massive searchlight. The captain was swinging it from side to side, lighting up the riverbanks, making sure his cargo was centered in the channel. At this point, the barge began crossing the river in front of us, headed for the dam lock. The captain gave two earsplitting blasts on his air horn, signaling his cargo's arrival to the lock master. Being children of a river town and knowing it would happen, we had automatically put our hands to our ears, waiting for the deafening noise to subside so we could get on with our cooking.

But he had been sound asleep on the quilt. The sudden blast of the air horn along with the roving searchlight, that intermittently swept over us, woke our father into a different world. He sat up abruptly as the beam of light hit him full in the face and then whipped on down the bank. He jumped to his feet, his eyes narrowed and terrified. "Get down . . . *get down*!" he shouted to us—or probably not to us—and grabbed Hercule, the closest one to the fire, lifted him up, and threw him through the air, away from the firelight, searching all the while into the woods and then back out to the darkening river for what, we had no idea. He shoved me and Jane hard to the side away from the flames, sending us sprawling in the dirt, then kept up his assault on the fire. "Get it out, Sammy . . . *now*," he yelled, furiously smothering any sign of our fire, desperate to have it gone.

Jane and I were bewildered and terrified, watching this stranger obliterate the burning tree branches that he and Hercule had earlier gathered. Hercule was sitting on the ground where he had landed, tears running down his cheeks, still holding his stick, the hot dog on it half-eaten. I had been in the process of making s'mores. My scorched marshmallow was dripping on the ground. The baby had begun crying from his playpen as the tugboat captain let loose with another blast from his air horn.

At first Mother sat there transfixed, watching him scatter us about like so many rocks he was heaving out of his way. And then, as he stood in the middle of the fire, stomping at its remnants, sparks rising up around him like some born-again Satan, she jumped to her feet and leapt into the fray, grabbing him around the waist, clinging to his back, shouting to him over and over to stop: "What in heaven's name are you doing? . . . Daniel? . . . *Daniel?*" There in the fire with the beam of the barge searchlight swinging past and sparks still flying, they looked to be staging some strange tribal dance, struggling one and then the other for control.

By the time Mother's words finally sank in, they had wound down to a standoff in the smoldering ashes. He stood still, blinking at his surroundings and then slowly pulling her arms from around his waist and turning her to face him, then abruptly pushing her away. He began to back off, his eyes darting from one of us to the other, until he had moved back into the shadows and then into the trees. She watched him go, not trying to follow but dealing now with the casualties he had left behind.

Mother gathered up Hercule, wiped his tears, and checked him over. He was going to be fine, she said. Jane and I were inspected and found whole. She went over to crying Roger and picked him up out of the playpen to comfort him. By that time, she must have thought of just how she would explain this whole episode to us.

"Your father . . . was trying to protect us," she said, holding Roger on her hip and stomping her feet to get rid of the excess ash and soot left from the fire.

Jane was over being scared and tipping into being mad. “Protect us from *what*—in the world?”

“Sometimes . . . sometimes, down here near the riverbank, there are wild boars . . . wild pigs.” Mother put the baby back in his playpen, brushed off her skirt, and, having decided on her main theme, began gathering up quilts, creating an explanation as she went along. “Remember that story Mr. Mitchell at the bank told us, Hercule—the one about shooting a wild pig as a boy, when he went hunting . . . remember?” Hercule nodded his tear-streaked face, remembering and immediately accepting. And in truth, we had heard tales of wild pigs near the river. We had been told they could be dangerous.

“Sometimes . . . ,” she said. “Sometimes they are attracted to light, and your father probably thought the wild pigs might see the firelight . . . and charge us . . . and so he was trying to protect us.” She thought about it for a moment. “Yes, that could happen,” she said mostly to herself, satisfied now. She grabbed another quilt off the ground and began folding it.

“Are you serious, Mother?” Jane was standing there with hands on hips. “You think he was trying to protect us from a wild boar or pig or . . . something? Really!”

“*Yes*, I do,” she said, and nodded toward Hercule. “And we will leave it there. Do you think your father would do anything to hurt you if he didn’t have to?”

Jane stared at Mother, her resolve melting. Her arms dropped to her sides and she began to shake her head. “No . . . ’course not.”

“Aggie?”

Slowly shaking mine, too: "No, ma'am."

"Well then."

We had been given a plausible explanation—to Hercule, anyway—and she expected us to go along. "Jane, you and Aggie gather up the hot dogs and"—she flung her arm out in the air—"all the other stuff. We need to be heading home. It's past Roger's bedtime."

We had almost finished loading the car when he came out of the woods, walking up to our camp, mumbling his apologies. He must have had a bad dream, he said. He was sorry for what happened . . . for whatever happened. He didn't seem to know. Mother left the playpen she was breaking down, stood up, and started toward him. He stepped away—the distant countenance was back. She stopped where she was and took up the slack. "I was telling the children, you probably thought you heard a wild boar in the distance. They are in this area sometimes . . . aren't they?"

He stared at her for a long moment and then nodded slowly. "Yes . . . they are." He walked cautiously over to the ice chest and picked it up. It seemed almost too heavy for him to lift.

"Dem wild pigs . . ." Hercule was throwing Lincoln Logs in his cardboard box. "Day is scary. I am not coming back to dis river place ever again."

We packed what was left of our picnic, stumbled to the Plymouth, and headed for the safety of home.

Chapter 19

The day after the picnic on the river, he left for another preaching trip up in the hill country of north Alabama—left early in the morning before any of us were up. We wouldn't see him for days after that. Our world settled back into the security of Tripoli Circle. This was fine by us, safe for us. For a child, an unpredictable parent is terrifying. Mother tried to turn our attention to the Brownlee house and what was going on there. And we were happy to have our attention turned. Soon the dark side of that day on the river began to fade, because whenever it was mentioned, Mother would immediately begin talking about what fun we had had—the taste of the hot dogs, singing "In the Good Old Summer Time," swimming in the river. We did not discuss the other, even under the parachute.

It was decided that no one would be allowed to go in Mrs. Brownlee's except the prisoners and Mother, with her assistants, of course, who were now me or Jane—Hercule being too young, as had been noted by his tattling ways with our vacation money.

The upshot of the whole thing was that Jane and I would become the stars of the neighborhood, the only persons mature enough, according to Mother, to accompany her across the street to deliver drinks and look inside Mrs. Brownlee's house to see exactly where the body had been. Hercule was too small to carry glasses anyway. He had done it once and had dropped them off the tray, breaking two of them.

Of course, my first leak of important Brownlee news was always to the Pruitt sisters, who would be out watering their caladiums or some such when I rode by on my bike. They would just happen to look up and I would just happen to stop to adjust my chain and sigh, noticeably, while looking over to Mrs. Brownlee's, where Z and Dummy were beginning to amass great mounds of trash out on the curb. I would shake my head knowingly and say, "Abominable, monstrous, vile," or something to that effect, and the sisters would say, "What, dear?" And then would begin my telling of the food stacked up the walls and the dust a foot thick on the sofa, that was covered over with stacks of old newspapers—perhaps embellishing a tad, just to give flavor. Mother had said that flavor or zest or literary license didn't hurt, it merely made for a better story, just held the interest of your audience. As a result of my creative retelling, there were all sorts of rumors flying, especially on Tripoli Circle, about what had gone on in that house. I did not, however, start the one about the dead body in the basement. I had merely said that the cellar was dark and dank enough to hide a dead body—and it was, what I could see of it from the top of the stairs.

The Pruitt sisters had been the ones to tell me, inadvertently—or maybe not—things I hadn't known about my father's childhood, had not been told.

From time to time, they would pay me to bike to Hill's grocery for an ingredient they had forgotten and hadn't realized until they were in the middle of baking. Thinking back, I was never sure whether my errand was for the ingredient or a way to give me extra spending money. In any event, I was just back from Hill's grocery one day, delivering a bottle of vanilla extract, when they mentioned that my father, as a youngster, had clerked at Hill's. When he finished with football practice, he would restock the shelves after hours because it was the only time he had to earn money. "And that aunt of his, the one who raised him when his good-for-nothing mother ran off and left him high and dry—that aunt was not worth killing." Miss Lena was sitting at the kitchen table cracking pecans for whatever it was they were making, filling up a teacup.

"I remember . . . ," Miss Louise began while sifting flour. It was after she had given me a nickel and a Coke for my trouble. I had taken a chair at the table in the kitchen to finish my Coke. "I remember, walking by her house, when he was still a baby. Why, in the summer, she would leave him out on the porch all day long in his playpen. Sit him down out there in the morning and go about her business, leaving a stack of clean diapers in case anybody wanted to change him. Neighbors walking along the sidewalk would come up into the yard when they heard him."

Miss Lena said, "Miss Jo Bell Hosey, remember her, Louise? She lived next door. She would come over and take him up and sit on the porch and rock him for hours at a time because she couldn't stand to hear him crying, because that aunt of his was too cheap to get a sitter when she would go off and leave him almost all day. He was practically raised by the town, not that aunt of his."

"All of us in the teachers lounge, remember that time, Lena? We were sitting around one day when he was a senior and had just won that big football game. We all chipped in and bought his senior ring for him, remember?"

"Your daddy was a big favorite with all of us, Aggie." Miss Louise cracked two pecans together in her bare hand.

"And that aunt of his, she was the biggest miser you ever saw. Why, if it hadn't been for Carolyn Brownlee when he was in high school, he wouldn't have had a nourishing meal half the time. A lot of days he would finish football practice and head to the Brownlee house with Sammy and Jonnie to get something to eat."

"People thought he lived with the Brownlees, he was over there that much." Miss Lena was measuring out vanilla extract.

"Well, you would have thought so, but no, he lived with his aunt over on Dorsett, that house that's for rent now—not the one on Maple, where his real mama lived before she dropped him off one day at her sister's and never came back. It was the talk of the—" Miss Louise stopped abruptly, as I supposed she thought better of getting into the more unflattering details of my father's past. They could probably tell from my expression that this was all news to me. I had been told only that his parents were dead and that his aunt had raised him.

After that conversation, I had on numerous occasions passed slowly by the house on Dorsett Street, pausing on my bike to imagine him there in his little playpen, crying and diaper soaked. It was a little square cracker box of a house with a sagging roof, vacant with a FOR RENT sign out front. I had walked up to the front porch, looking for the scratches the playpen might have made on the floor or the marks the rocker might have etched out as Miss Jo Bell Hosey rocked him.

"I told him," Miss Lena said, "when he was a senior and in my Spanish class, he should forget about playing football at Alabama and go to Vanderbilt to medical school, but of course he had to go fight—all of them had to go fight.

"He did go up to Nashville to work one summer and to look it over. Said he had particularly liked the Parthenon in Centennial Park, said it had changed his life. I thought that a rather odd thing to say."

Chapter 20

He would always come back home in time to preach and tend to business at Redeemer, but then after a few days he would leave. He seemed to have to leave. We would breathe easier.

On this trip, there was a small church up on Sand Mountain that needed him. Their preacher had left—"absconded with the church funds, and the church organist," he said, raising his eyebrows to Mother over his breakfast cup of coffee, as if we wouldn't know what "absconded" meant. I would ask later in a parachute meeting.

The members of that congregation desperately needed someone who would renew their faith, he said, someone they could depend on in their time of need. He told Mother he had to go, although he was tired and would not get back in time to do much planning for his sermon next Sunday at Redeemer. Sand Mountain was a long way away, but nevertheless he was needed. He bent down and kissed Mother. She stood up, her arms around him, trying to prolong it. He pulled away, gave her a final peck, picked up his cup, and gulped down the last of his coffee. She followed him to the door and watched him drive off.

Then she walked back into the kitchen, picked up her breakfast plate, and said to the remainder of us that she hoped we remembered the rule she had made in one of our meetings. We remembered and went to our bedroom to change out of our pajamas.

Her rule was that every time we went to Sunday school, we had to make a return trip to the library, "so as to keep everything on an even keel." Today she was going to teach us how to use the card catalog that stood on the left of Miss Delaney's desk as we came in the main door. With a card catalog, she said, we could find out anything that had ever been known to mankind—or womankind—since the day one. In particular, on this trip, we were to look into sign language, so we could talk with Dummy, because Dummy was not dumb and off-putting, he just spoke another language. She called from her room as she changed Roger's diaper: "Hurry and get dressed—we're off."

We walked to the library because he had to have the car for his church business. She said we needed to be walkers everywhere we went anyway. It was perfect for us, much healthier than riding in cars, breathing in all that carbon monoxide.

As we walked along—me pushing Roger in his stroller, Hercule holding Mother's hand, Jane trailing behind—she would tell us things so interesting, not to mention hardly believable, that we were not supposed to notice the heat and the distance to the library and the fact that my socks were getting wet from the perspiration running down my legs and Jane's hair, that she had kept in rollers all night to preserve, was now wilting down around her face like strands of warm spaghetti.

Once, she said, she had had an opportunity to have a car given to her, a brand-new Buick, with air-conditioning, from a man who begged her to come be vice president of his company, but she had said no, she would rather that we all walked and not be subjected to the fumes that a car gave off. She was biting her tongue, trying to keep a straight face when she glanced around to see if she still had our attention.

"Right," I said, lifting the stroller down off the curb. "You probably gave up a job that woulda paid you a million dollars a year and you woulda had three secretaries to do all the work."

"And they would have been men secretaries," she said. Even Jane laughed at that one.

It was so hot, the wheels began sticking in the road tar. She picked up the front of the stroller and helped me carry it across the street. "He was a nice man, and I would have made a wonderful vice president, but"—she couldn't help but laugh now—"I didn't know much about aeronautical engineering."

Jane had turned sour. She said she wished Mother had taken the Buick when it was offered, *if* it was offered, so we could take our chances on fumes, especially since she knew lots of people who had cars and they weren't developing any hacking coughs, *especially* when we had to walk to the grocery store in the dead of winter and it was pouring rain to boot. Mother sighed and said Jane might be developing some kind of a commonplace streak that we might need to work on.

I was to discover, years later, something of our mother's early life, devoid of all the spin—when she finally felt we could live without it.

Chapter 21

The object that had triggered Mother's memory of childhood was a toy model of a steamboat that someone had given Hercule when he was old enough to sit patiently and glue tiny parts of the paddle wheel together. I think she told us then only because she thought it might interest Hercule.

Her mother's maiden name had been Lee, a descendant of old Jim Lee, who founded the Lee steamboat line out of Memphis. Their boats had ruled the Mississippi River around Memphis in the late 1800s. The custom in that era had been to name their steamboats after the Lee children. The *Sara Lee* had been a favorite on the river, and Mother had in turn been named after her great-aunt Sara or the boat, "whichever you prefer," she had said as she watched Hercule glue his fingers to the tiny pilot's house.

The Lees had been known for the entitled, even haughty, look of their women. She told us that as a child she had had her hair arranged, pulled back off her face, the better to show off the Lee profile—the thin straight nose and high cheekbones. When she was five, she was taught to walk with her shoulders back and to affect an air of distant, formal cordiality when coming into contact with strangers. Looking back,

I think that although it was not the person she became, upon first meeting her that was who you saw.

She had gone to Miss Hutchinson's School, at first as a regular student and then on scholarship, because her father, the one who raised her, had lost the money that had been left to him by his wife when she died. Her father had been at the cotton exchange and couldn't resist investing in futures that had none and, too, by that time the steamboat business was giving way to the barge business.

She had been five and a half years old when her mother passed away, and she began to live in a world imagining life as it might have been had her mother lived. Eventually, she must have become the mother of those imaginings.

Of course, we never thoroughly knew her. We are introduced to our parents after almost half their lives have been lived and can know only what they tell us, and what they tell us is true only to their memory. She said she wanted us all to have the siblings she never had—sisters and brothers to grow up with, to make the long trek together.

After high school she entered Vanderbilt, one of the few women to do it at the time. She was very proud of going to Vanderbilt and moved to Nashville for good after her freshman year because her father had decided to relocate to Texas to make a new start, in the tradition, he told her, of so many others: Sam Houston and Davy Crocket, to name a few of the Tenn-Texans. And she would have joined him had she not met Jack. She might have been a Texan and lived an entirely different life had it not been for Jack.

She had not been interested in staying in Memphis anymore. It was a river town filled with so many old traditions that they were beginning to stumble over one another, imploding on themselves—in white upper-crust Memphis, anyway. Nashville, on the other hand, could claim to be older than Memphis, and in addition it was just discovering its country music roots, giving it an odd flashiness that somehow she liked.

Once she had asked Chief why their paths had never crossed, both of them growing up in Memphis. He had smiled sheepishly and said he had spent his youth down by the river in Pinchgut, the old Irish section that was mostly black now. She had only heard tales of the goings-on down by the river, had never actually been there, and had marveled that she would come all the way to Alabama to meet someone from that part of Memphis.

In Nashville, in the late 1930s, she had been timid and afraid in her new circumstances, without a family name for backup or money. She tried not to let it show when she was invited by a friend to her coming-out party. There she had met Jack. He had been assigned as her blind date—at least that's what she thought. Actually, Jack had asked to be introduced. He was home from the Citadel for the holidays. She had worn a black dress and flats, a custom she always followed with new people, fearing she might be taller than her date. At five feet eleven inches, she had been overly aware of her height. It had taken years for her to appreciate it.

Jack, she said, had presented himself in full dress whites. She had been so dazzled, it had taken half the evening for her to realize that she was indeed taller by several inches, but by then she didn't care. He had seemed to think that her every weakness was a strength: her height, the fact that she was very bright and didn't know how to hide it, and most of all that she was not from good Nashville stock and—the crowning blow—did not have family money.

Right after he graduated they had run away to marry. His family never forgave that, and they never forgave that she was driving the night of the accident, when he was killed. Neither had she, but deep down she knew she would eventually survive because she had survived her mother's leaving, and she told us that a child who survives her mother leaving, for whatever reason, can survive anything.

Daniel had come along and saved her life, literally saved her life and little Jane's. If she had ever believed in God's good graces, it had been the day she met Daniel. It was in Centennial Park near the Parthenon. For months she had been so distraught over Jack that she would go for days without sleeping. This particular Monday, she hadn't slept for two days and had dozed off sitting on a blanket she had laid out near the lake, watching Jane play with her toys. Fifteen minutes later, Daniel, handsome Daniel, holding Jane in his arms—the sun splayed behind his broad shoulders, giving him the look of a guardian angel—had touched her on the arm, returning her wandering child, who had toddled down to the water's edge. Immediately she had been struck by his kindness and his caring, for Jane and for her, and she had been eternally grateful. They had sat there on the quilt for hours, talking and talking.

On their second date, he had presented them with a puppy. "Centennial" had had a red bow around his neck and a collar with his name engraved on it—after the park where they had met. "And look, I've already taught him tricks." He grinned at little Jane, who had immediately run into his arms when Sara opened the door to their small apartment. Daniel knelt down, holding Jane, and picked up the puppy's paw, pretending to shake hands with him. "See, he already knows how to shake hands, and tomorrow I'll teach him to roll over." He winked up at Sara. "I told you I was a genius when it came to kids and dogs."

"Brilliant . . . I can see that," she said, laughing and touching the top of his head of thick wavy blond hair. He stood up, holding Jane in one marvelously muscled arm and the puppy in the other, and stepped in close—a starched button-down short-sleeved sports shirt, pressed khakis, the aroma of Old Spice—presenting himself like some gorgeously wrapped Christmas present.

She couldn't seem to stop grinning or stop looking into those beautiful blue eyes. She had caught his arm, the one holding the puppy, pretending interest in the dog, but really it was to steady herself. She was weak in the knees.

"The day after that," he said, "I'll need to teach Centennial to stand on his hind legs, and the day after that . . ." He handed the puppy to her and closed the apartment door.

"I think I might need to teach him a new trick for every day in the year." He tickled Jane's tummy. "Right, Janie?"

She had leaned up against the dining room table, holding the dog, not daring to mention that her apartment building didn't allow pets. "I suppose . . ." She cleared her throat; her voice was breaking and she was praying she didn't sound like a complete idiot. "I suppose . . . I'll need to think of some way to reciprocate." She wished she could stop grinning like some commoner. It was not the way she had been brought up.

He had insisted that they marry before he left for the war. Both were virtually orphans; he would be able to send her his army money while he was gone. She had been the envy of all her girlfriends. This six-foot-four, spectacularly handsome man, intelligent and so much fun to be with. The gods had smiled upon her. She didn't know why and couldn't possibly care.

After he had returned from overseas, it had seemed that he wanted to spread his caring like a blanket over everyone he came in contact with; he was obsessed with doing it. At first, she must have felt it had something to do with the war, with his gratitude at getting out of it alive. But there was a darkness that hadn't been there before, and there were the nightmares.

Everyone took time to adjust. She knew that. It was only natural. And she had changed, too. She wasn't the person she had been, either. She had thought that maybe she was the one who couldn't adjust. Maybe s*he* was the one who had been on her own too long. After all, he was kind to everyone, to a fault. Maybe she was just a little jealous of having to compete for his affections.

Chapter 22

Our trek to the library was about a mile. It took us down Main Street and then left on Walnut past the park. Mother wore slacks and a V-necked blouse and sensible walking shoes, not heels and a hat as one might have expected of the preacher's wife. Her excuse was that clothes needed to be loose fitting so we could get plenty of circulation to our brains. We were happy to go along with that theory. Following her lead, I had worn my cowgirl boots. Jane wore her boa shawl. Mother glanced at passersby, women out shopping in hats and gloves and heels. "It won't hurt his feelings, he's out of town . . . and besides," she mumbled to herself, "your father is holy enough for both of us."

I thought we looked elegant, and I presumed we must have when we came into the library and Miss Delaney couldn't take her eyes off of us. They widened ever so slightly before she went about her business of checking in books and collecting late fees. I had never really seen her do that much outside of stamping my book with a due date. That was about it. She had on occasion berated me for overdue books and magazines, in particular a *National Geographic* Jane and I had kept too long, perusing the naked natives of the South Pacific; four whole cents that one cost us.

From the beginning we had not gotten along with Miss Delaney, although she had told us she was good friends with Mrs. Brownlee and everybody else on Tripoli Circle and she knew our father when he was a boy. But then it seemed everyone had known him when he was a boy. I think she thought we were not respectful enough of her library, and perhaps we were not. Mother treated it—and therefore we treated it—as if it were our personal property, coming and going as we pleased, dragging out books, searching the stacks at will.

We took places at our regular table, the one we had used since we'd moved from Nashville. Nobody else ever sat at our table, and if they did, they wouldn't stay long. Roger had a tendency to slobber all over the tabletop and then slap his hand in it—if Mother let him out of his stroller, which she did when the unknowing showed up. She told us there was no finer thing than to have your own table at the library, and we had obviously commandeered this one. She said your own library table was better than a box at the opera or getting to go on vacations once a year, commonplace things. We already knew we were not that.

Having settled in, we proceeded to the card catalog and Mother explained how to look up information about American Sign Language, 201.3 through 201.10, "and don't forget the *World Books*." Then she sent us to search the stacks. The one who found the book most suitable to the subject got a prize.

Mother had gotten herself a new copy of the latest *Atlantic Monthly* and was reading at the table and watching Roger. Hercule had gone off to the children's section, sitting in one of those too-small chairs, looking at *The Little Engine That Could.* Roger was smearing a zwieback all over his stroller tray.

When we found the right place in the stacks, Jane and I grabbed several books, but Jane won because her book had a diagram of the basic American Sign Language signs.

Mother was thrilled with the picture chart—just what we needed. She asked Miss Delaney for some paper and pencils and we began to copy the page out of the book. After a while, Jane said she was getting sick of copying and why didn't we just check out the book and take it home with us? If we tried to check it out, Mother said, Miss Delaney would probably want to know why we hadn't paid our fine for the last book we checked out and forgot to return on time. "It should be of no concern to Miss Delaney that I haven't yet finished *Murder in Mesopotamia,*" not to mention that we hadn't yet got the money to pay the fine.

So Jane said, "Okay, while she's not looking, I could tear the page out of the book. We could take that home and have the real thing, especially since I am not good at drawing these fingers all curled up like this."

Mother looked over the top of her *Atlantic Monthly* to Miss Delaney, who was getting ready to take some returned books back to the stacks. I got the feeling she was about to tell Jane to go on and tear but thought better of it: we were all staring at her. "Keep copying," she said, and went back to reading her article. There were some things that were beyond the pale, even for us.

Chapter 23

On the way home, as we got closer to Tripoli Circle, we could see that there was some kind of commotion going on out in the Pruitt sisters' front yard. The chief's car was parked at the curb, and Jarvis, his assistant, was running around with a shovel as the Pruitt sisters shouted directions. Naturally Jane and I ran ahead to see what was up, me pushing Roger along in his stroller, bumping him over the cracks in the sidewalk, certain he would like it once he calmed down and stopped screaming.

By the time we got there, half the neighborhood was out, standing around yelling at Jarvis. Jane and I joined right in.

"He's there."

"No, he's there."

"You're slow as Christmas, Jarvis. Why don't you get him?"

And poor Jarvis was a pathetic sight, sweating and chasing around. By the time we got there, he had lost his deputy's hat.

Mother walked up holding Hercule's hand just as Jarvis finally cornered the rat and smacked his brains out with the end of the shovel.

"Biggest damn rat I ever seen." Chief was standing there, his hands on his hips and trying to stop laughing while he watched Jarvis raising his shovel up like he had just won the Olympics. "Ain't seen one that big since POW camp. That sucker's got some meat on him, good eating on—" Chief stopped short and looked around to see if he had been heard. "I mean . . . 'course nobody would want to . . . actually eat the thing." He coughed and told Jarvis to pitch it in the trash.

All of the rat chasing did not sit well with the neighbors. The minute the rat was disposed of, they jumped on the chief, saying it was his responsibility to do something. They did not—*did not*—want rats running about the premises, and "we all know where that particular rat came from," Mr. Oliver said. Mr. Oliver, postmaster and home for his noon meal, was not one to be toyed with—a government man, *federal*, and we in the South had learned our lesson about toying with that particular government.

Chief immediately began walking around to each one of the men and some of the ladies, too, shaking their hands, aware of next year's election. He told them he was doing everything in his power to get the place cleaned out, "when it really ain't even my job. It's more like the sanitation department's job. I'm just doing this as a special favor to all you folks here on Tripoli Circle." For the first time, I began wondering why he was doing it. If he got in the habit of doing time-consuming favors like this, he might as well run for trash collector instead of chief of police.

Just then he swept his hand out in a flowing motion and pointed to Mother. "*And*, I even got Miss Sara over there"—the neighbors looked to Mama, who stared back at them—"as my full-time neighborhood director of this project." Mother's eyebrows rose, because until that moment she, we, hadn't known that she was an official anything.

All this seemed to mollify the neighbors. They began to back off and say they truly did appreciate the chief going the extra mile, because if they had to wait on Jimbo Durbin over at the sanitation department, Mrs. Brownlee's house never would get cleaned out. They might end up with armies of rats running around. And they did much appreciate Mama being his neighborhood director of the project. Mr. Oliver even went over and slapped her on the back, saying it was mighty sociable of her, which was to my way of thinking, not a description that fit our mother.

"We got somebody as knowing as Sara here," Mr. Oliver said, "bound to get things done."

Mama blushed, another first. "Do you think so, Mr. Oliver?" she said.

"By golly, I know it." He nodded to the others in the crowd. They nodded back.

She mumbled that she was happy to do it, for the neighborhood.

As I watched all of this, it occurred to me that my mother might not be in perfect command of every situation—that she might in fact be shy and ill at ease with these people, in this small town. That considered, I quickly threw it out with other absurd thoughts I had had from time to time.

The crowd began to disperse. I glanced back at Mrs. Brownlee's house before turning to push Roger up over the curb, headed home. One of the windowpanes on the second floor was catching the afternoon sun, ricocheting it back out over Tripoli Circle like some picketed searchlight.

Chapter 24

The next day, we had gathered on Mrs. Brownlee's front porch to drink our tea. It was hot, but the oak tree branches gave us some shade and we preferred it to the stench that greeted us as soon as we stepped in the front door. Mother was explaining to Dummy with hand signs that he now had a new name. I wasn't sure he was all that delighted about it, but he liked Mother and seemed willing to go along. Vincent van Gogh was a famous painter, she was saying, "as you are when you paint houses." He seemed pleased with the comparison.

Next door, the Pruitt sisters were peeking out through lace curtains as Mayor Carl's car coasted to a stop at the curb. I knew only that the mayor had been in the war like everyone else, but now it was hard to imagine him, fat as he was, in an army uniform. While the chief was stout, the mayor was downright fat for his size. Chief, being a big man in the first place, could carry his weight. It gave him an air of authority, like a bull standing his ground. The mayor, at around five feet six inches, brought to mind a snowman with legs, little shoulders, and broad hips, even though his clothes were tailored to try to hide it.

He waved to us from behind the windshield and then swung open the door and proceeded to try to dislodge his considerable hulk. When he did make it out and straighten up, he looked rather dapper in his dark blue suit with the red tie and gray felt hat. Men had begun to leave off wearing hats after the war, but not the mayor. It was one of his campaign props, and the mayor was constantly campaigning. "Afternoon, Sara," and off it came, sweeping down to his side in a flourish. "And Chief . . ." He smiled at the chief, pointing the hat in his direction, nodding his head to each of us. "A tad hotter than usual for this time of the year." We all agreed that it was.

He walked up slowly, looking at the front of the house, running fingers along the porch railing as he stepped on its bottom tread. "Ah, the memories this old place brings back. I'm telling you, I can recall many a day . . . many a day, coming over here . . . sitting on this very porch with Sammy and Jonnie, drinking tea and shooting the breeze." He turned and walked back down the steps out into the yard, looking up at us as he backed away, arms outstretched. The mayor was one to employ the dramatic flair. He walked slowly back to us.

"She would bring us out a big pitcher of mint tea—made the best mint tea I ever tasted. Probably six or seven of us sitting around here"—he raised his hat again and pointed—"on this very porch, with our letter jackets on, most all the football team." The mayor walked up the steps, taking them slowly. It was hard to imagine him on a football team, short and fat as he was now. "Sammy, he was the ladies' man, you know, and Jonnie, he was her youngest . . . and had a way with words. My goodness . . . won the American Legion essay contest we had every year at school. Did you know that, Aggie?" Mayor chuckled and we knew a story was in the offing. "One day, right here on this porch . . . Did I ever tell you this one, Red?" The mayor was famous for his stories. This story, as it turned out, was meant to divert us from his real reason for coming.

Chief shook his head. "Can't say this one sounds familiar, Carl."

"Well, one day, we were sitting around here, after football practice, and Jonnie . . . I told you he was the youngest, didn't I?" We all nodded and smiled back at him, as one can't help but smile at a story the teller thinks is funny. It was only polite.

"Well now, Jonnie, he decided he was gonna bet us all he could walk across this here railing without losing his balance." The mayor put a hand down on the decorative iron railing that ran the length of the porch. It was probably six feet off the ground, and the railing had tiny arrow-shaped spikes running along the top. "Now, you might say to yourself, That ain't no big deal, but it was if you was to happen to slip and fall—in the wrong way." He winked at the chief. "Might come close to losing your manhood." All the men chuckled—it was expected—except for Vincent, who was looking quietly at the mayor and smiling.

"Well now, we went to egging him on, telling him we bet he might do it once, but two or three times? He never would make it back and forth that many times without falling. You see here"—he fingered the spikes again—"you had to balance yourself. And then Sammy, his brother, he chimed in. Sammy was Mrs. Brownlee's firstborn, you know, and quite the ladies' man. He says to Jonnie, 'You do it and I'll get you a date with Bretta James.' Well now, that did it, 'cause Jonnie had had his eye on Bretta for a year and hadn't got up the nerve to do anything about it." The mayor winked at the others, who obviously knew, but he had to say it out loud anyway: "Sweet Bretta and I will celebrate our fourth year of married bliss this coming November."

The mayor stopped abruptly now and looked at all of us, holding our glasses, glancing down at the empty tea pitcher Mother had placed on the slate floor. "You know, I could sure use a good taste of tea on such a hot day. Suppose you could get me a glass, Aggie?" I looked to Mother, knowing we had used the last of it.

"Carl," she said, "I'm so sorry, I just poured the last bit out for Mr. Z, but let me run across the street and get some more."

He smiled. He knew it was what she would offer. "I don't want to put you out. I'll wait right here while you and Aggie go get it. Won't move a muscle."

It must have been obvious to Mother that the mayor was looking for a way to dismiss us and this was the best he could do. Even so, she went along—the roundabout protocol of the day always won out over the coarseness of being obvious. "Carl, it won't take but a minute. I have some already brewed and in the refrigerator."

She picked up the pitcher and started back across the street as the mayor said, "Don't you want to go along, Aggie, help out?" I shook my head no, wanting to hear the rest of his story, not realizing I too was being asked to leave. "Well now, then, while your mother gets the tea, maybe you could go in the house and get me a . . . a chair to sit on. The old mayor has been working hard all day."

I said, Yes, sir, I would, and went back in the house to search for something sturdy that would accommodate the mayor. I hadn't let the front screen door close before the mayor had turned to the chief. "Any luck?"

Chapter 25

Chief sounded perturbed. "No, Carl. And I told you on the phone, I'd let you know if I did."

"I know, I know it, but you can't be too careful. We're both . . . we're elected officials, you know." He turned and looked up at one of the second-floor windows of Mrs. Brownlee's house, as if he might be seeing something . . . or someone. "This whole thing of her dying . . . it's brought it all back to me."

"Hell, Carl, that was war. Nothing to do with now."

The mayor turned and looked out over the lawn and watched Mother disappear into our house, and then he watched a blue jay light in the branches of Mrs. Brownlee's oak tree before he said in a barely discernible voice, "We coulda saved him, you know . . . Jonnie...that day. Did I tell you . . . I dream . . . sometimes?"

The chief was not a patient man, not with the mayor. "We all dream, Carl. Dreams don't mean shit."

The mayor had taken off his hat and was looking down at it, fingering the crease in the front. He looked up again at the house. "We thought he was over there tending to Sammy . . . we never knew he was on his last leg, too . . . did we?"

"'Course we didn't know. We been over this a thousand times. There wasn't a damn thing we coulda done about it anyway. He had that bum leg too long—poison probably went to his heart. That's what killed him."

"Do you think?"

"Hell, yeah. It's what I gotta think. And you too, if you know what's good for you."

The mayor looked up at the chief like a child begging for the right answer. "We were all so excited that day, 'cause our tanks were coming over the rise to liberate us . . . I was excited. Weren't you, excited? God, the Kraut guards were hightailing it, the gates were open, thousands of people streaming out . . .Weren't you? You had to be."

Chief took a deep breath and let it out. He crossed his arms over his big barrel chest, looking down at the iron railing, his head slowly nodding at what he was seeing. "Lying there in the mud . . . pencil in one hand and that damn log in the other." He looked up at Carl with a half smile. "Jonnie was always writin' in that thing." He set down his tea glass and got out a cigarette, chuckling to himself now. "There was the types that wrote about it and the types that didn't. I wasn't no writin' type." He offered the mayor a cigarette. The mayor shook his head. "Remember Baumgartner—guy from New Jersey—he spent hours writin' in one of those Red Cross journals they sent us. I guess they thought it would keep us occupied. Hundreds of them things floatin' around the camp. Remember Bloomfield, he drew portraits of the guys in his, charged a pack of cigarettes for each one." He took a deep drag and blew the smoke out into the yard. "Damn good portrait drawer, too."

"Yeah, but weren't you excited? . . ." Carl watched the chief's face, hoping for, and not getting, reassurance.

The chief said, "We didn't give him a thought . . . too hungry to give him a thought . . . I'll admit it. He crawled all the way over there to be next to Sammy. That's where he wanted to be when he passed, next to his brother . . . nothin' we coulda done."

The mayor was still staring down at his hat. "You didn't grow up with him. You didn't play on the same football team with him. You didn't sit right here on this very porch with—"

"No, I didn't," the chief interrupted, blowing out more smoke, "but I liked him and he was a nice guy. They were both nice fellows and I shoulda . . . we shoulda . . ." He looked across the street to our house, maybe watching for Mother. "And I sure did like their mama . . . before she started losing it . . . sweet old lady. We shoulda helped her more." Chief looked down at his cigarette. "Least we don't have to live with what Daniel…"

The mayor waited for Chief to finish and when he didn't he said, in a small voice, "He shoulda stood up."

The chief's head jerked around to glare at him. "Hell, Carl. That goddamn hindsight is always twenty twenty. If he had, none of us might not be here today."

I opened the door and began to drag out a dining room chair that had been in the foyer. The mayor rushed over to hold the screen for me. "Just what the old mayor needed, little lady." He pulled the chair over to the porch railing—and did not sit in it. He said to the chief, "'Course, I don't think it was anything about me . . . what he mighta written down . . . that day."

The chief saw Mother coming across the street with a glass and a full pitcher. "Button it up, Carl."

And he did, but not before he muttered, "Just don't want anybody ever thinking I didn't do all I could . . . to save them, you know."

Just as quickly, the mayor brightened and continued with his story as Mother came into hearing distance. "Well, to continue"—obviously wanting to end the story now, as he had already finished with why he had come by in the first place—"had to watch out for Mrs. Brownlee 'cause we knew she would have a fit if her baby boy was trying something so silly and dangerous as walking these spikes. So . . ." Mayor took a deep breath. "So, we settled on betting Jonnie he could make it three times without stopping, and as soon as his mama was out of sight, he jumped up on the railing and began to balance himself, walking across the tops of the spikes."

Mother handed him his glass of tea and he took a long swallow—and still had not seated himself in the chair I had wrestled out. "And just as he turned and started out on the third run across the spikes, we heard Mrs. Brownlee coming down the hall with refills for our iced tea.

"We was all doubled over laughing, Jonnie teetering on the brink and his mama coming and his bet to get a date with Bretta James going down the drain." Then he slapped his hat against his pants leg. "Lordy, was that funneee."

"So, what happened?" I asked, because no one else seemed that interested.

The mayor winked at me. "Just went completely limp and fell over in the azaleas, so his mama wouldn't see him when she opened the screen door asking where Jonnie had got to. Well now, Daniel, he steps forward, in front of the railing so as to hide Jonnie in the bushes, cool as you please, and he says with a straight face, 'Jonnie had to step inside to the men's room, ma'am.'

"And Jonnie . . . not being able to move a muscle, lying down there in the azalea bushes with a bunch of broken bones for all we knew, but by golly he wasn't gonna do anything to upset his mama."

The mayor put his hat on, adjusting it, changing the subject. "Bretta," he said to Mother, "has been after me to come over here and see if there are any antiques." His fingers absentmindedly flipped a few pieces of peeling paint off the railing. Then he brought his hands together, holding them over his big tummy. "You know . . . things y'all might want to get rid of, help defray the cost of a funeral and all." He tried not to glance up to the second-floor windows, seeing the sunlight catch in the panes. "Almost our Christian duty...don't you know."

The chief raised a hand to indicate the front door. Then he winked at Mama as he watched the mayor step inside. It wasn't half a minute before he was back out again, coughing, holding a handkerchief over his mouth, his eyes watering. "Lord have mercy, what is in that house?"

"Told you over the phone, Carl. Nothing in there but junk and more junk and a few friendly rats."

The mayor did not think that was funny. He headed to his car, still coughing and waving the handkerchief in front of his face. At the bottom of the front steps, he adjusted his hat and turned back to Chief. "You'll let me know if you find anything . . . might be interesting." The chief nodded.

Chapter 26

It had taken days of cleaning to clear out the downstairs rooms and gain safe passage to the second floor. This was interrupted time and again as Mr. Z and Vincent would unearth various burrowing critters—mostly rats, once a opossum—and chase them all over the house before hacking them to pieces with whatever was handy. If Mother and I happened to be present, I would jump on the nearest chair, delighted, holding high my tray of glasses—another story for the Pruitts. Mother would step up on the papers stacked on top of the sofa just inside the living room, balancing the tea pitcher and cookies, giving direction: "Hurry, Mr. Z—under the hunt-board in the dining room . . ." And then turn away at the final squashing. "Poor thing."

Now that Mrs. Brownlee was gone, now that there was nothing we could do to help her, I liked to think there must have been logic in her life. She had designated the stairs for old newspapers and catalogs—Sears, Roebuck mostly and some Spiegel, years of them. It would look to the outsider as if she were crazy, but as I went there day after day, there seemed to be a definite sense of order: bottles in the dining room, catalogs and newspapers on the stairs. The debris was stacked all the way up and down the steps, plus a few old clothes hanging on the banister, as if she had washed out a dress or a blouse, hung them there to dry, and then forgotten about them. But maybe not. Maybe it had been a perfect place to dry clothes, given the breeze through the hallway. I liked to imagine she had been happy living there in all the mess. It salved my conscience, pushing back the memory of a day when Marilyn McClure and I had snuck up and thrown pebbles at her screen door, trying to coax her out to sweep again in her slip.

There had remained a tiny path up the stairs only big enough for a small person to step through, if she was careful and held on to the railing. It had taken Mr. Z and Dummy a whole day just to clear the steps. I believed they were slowing down because they were beginning to like being out of jail and having iced tea brought to them every few hours, which was what Mama was doing now. They were beginning to feel at home with her, as most people did if she let them get to know her.

That particular day, the four of us were parked in the entrance hall, keeping the front door open to a breeze. It had been pretty much cleared out, and the smell, with the doors open and some of the dead varmints gone, was beginning to be tolerable. Faded hall wallpaper, printed with blue gray unicorns prancing among pink flowers and pale green trees, was cracked open at the seams and curled up around the edges. A small chandelier that had long ago lost its bulbs hung slightly askew over our heads.

Vincent had emptied two dining room chairs of all their junk, and Mother and I had placed the tea-and-cookie tray on one of them. Vincent had insisted that Mother sit in the other.

The rest of us were relegated to the floor for tea time. Mother and Mr. Z were lighting cigarettes, compliments of Mother. I was paying close attention to the process, as my plan was to start smoking as soon as I went off to college.

Mr. Z, Mama had discovered, was actually Mr. Zanino. "It's because people in this town couldn't pronounce it properly or wouldn't take the time to. From now on it is Mr. Zanino." She had made me repeat it several times so as not to offend: Za-ni-no, Za-ni-no.

At first, all I had seen in Mr. Z was an old derelict, hunched over and graying, shuffling through his chores. He would follow any instructions given to him by the chief with no comment, no interest—stopping to lean against a wall when the job was done, waiting for further orders. His eyes were not interested in seeing anything further than what was in front of him, until slowly he began to make some connection to Mother. Looking back now, I suppose their common denominator was that they both considered themselves outsiders, were inherently uncomfortable in the circumstances in which they found themselves.

After we had been over to deliver tea several times, he would begin to look up when we came, waiting for Mother or maybe the cigarette she would offer. From the first, they had had that in common and seemed to enjoy each other even though he was much older . . . my guess was fifty-five or so. On this visit he sat on the floor, smoking and rubbing his day-old graying stubble, his legs in frayed cotton trousers, stretched out in the sunlight streaming through the front door.

She asked him how he had come to live here, in this town. He looked up at her with slight surprise, smiled, and shrugged. "That is of no interest to women and children." He nodded in my direction.

"I will tell you about what happens when I am already here." And he proceeded to tell this story in broken English. He said that when he first came to our town, he naturally brought along his customs, and one of them had been to have a glass of wine on his porch after a hard day's work. He had rented a house on Pine Street, next door to the Church of Christ. The minister and his wife had come by to pay him a welcoming visit and bring him a casserole. He had not much cared for American casseroles, but he tried to be polite and in turn had offered the pastor and his wife a glass of wine he had just finished making in his basement. Mother winced, knowing what was probably coming.

He saw her look. "*Naturalmente, naturalmente,* zee rest, she is history . . . as you say."

"You couldn't know the county is dry," she said. He shook his head. "Or that Church of Christ members are famous for being teetotalers." He shrugged with his hands. "You should make some for me sometime. I would love it."

He grinned at her. "Then vee both end up in the hoosegow . . . and no one to bring me zee tea with ice in it."

After that run-in with the minister, he lost his lease on the rental house, not to mention his supply of homemade wine. His eyes began to water and his voice faltered when he told about pouring out the wine he had worked so hard to make, thinking it would be a treat for his new neighbors. Mother had looked away and quickly changed the subject, but it had been the first of many conversations they would have, sitting and smoking and passing the time during that summer.

Chapter 27

"So, what's new on the home front?" Mother asked. She also signed the question to Vincent, including him in the conversation as much as possible. This endeared her to him—that and the fact that she was also teaching Jane and me to sign. In turn, Vincent had developed the habit of bringing her things, little gimcracks he had found in the house while hauling off trash—anything he thought might interest her. When we would come over with tea, he would immediately dig down into his pocket and give her whatever he had found—a booklet of rationing coupons left over from the war, an old recipe book. This day, he had brought her an old picture from the newspaper that Mrs. Brownlee had framed. It was of all of them, the men, the boys, standing down at the train station, leaving for the war. My father was there and Mayor Carl, Mrs. Brownlee's two sons, Sammy and Jonnie, Moody Redd, Mr. Darby down at the cleaners, and several others I didn't recognize.

She would always thank Vincent as if it were such a treasure. Later, she would set it aside or put it in the trash with everything else. This time, it was a treasure. "I have never seen this before." She called me over. "Look here, Aggie, your father, he looks so young and lighthearted." Vincent reached over and pointed to the mayor in the group. Then he smiled and held his arms out around his stomach, waddling up and down the hall. She chuckled and signed back, "The mayor was almost thin back before."

Mr. Zanino, not to be outdone, began telling us what he had been up to, becoming more effusive than I had ever seen him—attempting, I believed, to make an interesting story of cleaning out a filthy, smelly old house. "Today, vee haaf breached zee moat." He gestured to the stairs. "And"—he raised a heavy black eyebrow—"it is so curious, what vee find."

Mother said, "More curious than that stuffed squirrel Vincent found yesterday?"

I had thought the squirrel would make a wonderful addition to my room, but no luck. "They're running around outside all over the place. Why would you want one inside—and dead? Besides," she had said rather emphatically, "we don't take anything out of this house. It's not ours to take."

She smiled at Z. "Tell us what you found, Mr. Zanino."

"Come, vee show."

So vee all traipsed up the stairs and gathered around the first door on the right.

"A door?" Mother squinted, searching its surface.

"Zee *locked* door. Vee haaf manage to get open all other, as you can see." He gestured down the hall. "All open."

Mother and I looked down the length of the upstairs hall at the doors, four or five of them. They were all open, a little, with newspapers and other assorted boxes and debris piled around them, blocking an easy swing. Dummy stepped past us to a hall table stacked with magazines and books and picked up a hammer that was lying on top. He raised it to show Mother.

"Well, why not." She seemed to have taken seriously the chief's directive to the neighbors that she was now his designated neighborhood assistant.

One blow with the hammer did it. The knob fell off and rattled down the uneven floorboards. We watched the door slowly swinging back. This in itself was surprising considering that all the other doors needed prying and cajoling to open beyond the few inches necessary to let a small woman pass through.

Chapter 28

We had come upon the boys' room, perfectly preserved.

The movement of the opening door swirled dust up through the lines of sunlight that streamed in the windows. It was like seeing some aging postcard—everything in its place, but slowly fading out to white.

Up against one wall were their twin beds, covered with matching spreads of a sporting theme. Faded quarterbacks and pitchers, track stars and swimmers, all caught motionless in midstride, forever winding up for the throw or held at the pinnacle of a leap or bursting out of the water to signal victory. A scruffy football lay on one bed up near the pillow as if one of them had been sitting there tossing it aimlessly. Café curtains, sagging from tarnished brass rings, were printed with the same heroes as the spreads, and above the curtains, turned inward, was a service banner slightly crooked, with two stars signaling two boys gone off to war.

On the wall opposite the beds, each had his own desk. Textbooks were stacked carefully to one side. Pencils were gathered in ceramic mugs festooned with the white-and-gold high school crest, souvenirs of their senior prom.

After a long moment of silent looking, Mother stepped inside. I came in behind, walked over to the window, and pushed back the café curtains to look down at our house across the street and years away. Hercule was in the side yard with our garden hose, filling the wading pool. Jane was close by, sitting on a beach towel she had just spread, soaking herself in baby oil.

"I should have done more to help her," Mother was saying. "If I could have done more to help her . . . I don't know."

I walked to Jonnie's desk and picked up a small silver medal. He *had* won the American Legion essay contest, just as the mayor had said.

Mother moved to one of the boys' beds, brushing at the dust before she sat down, running fingers over the dulled, faded cloth of the spread. "How terrified she must have been, both of them wanting to go . . . and then going."

Mr. Zanino had moved back into the shadows to lean against the far wall, watching her. The air was hot and musty, but not with the stench of downstairs. It was old air they might have breathed.

There were individual pictures of Jonnie and Sammy framed and sitting atop each desk. Sammy stood in his uniform, hat slightly to one side, hands on hips and grinning. Jonnie's picture was more formal—seated for his portrait, looking serious, the hat just so, uniform pressed, buttons shining. Mother placed the framed newspaper picture Vincent had given her beside Jonnie's picture.

Mounted on the wall directly above their desks was a gun rack with hunting rifles one over the other, and hanging from one of them a carrying case for cartridges—standard fare for the fall deer season, left as they must have put them there, oiled and cleaned and ready for a trip to the woods.

On a small side table still in their leather cases were a Purple Heart and an air medal. Beside that was a candle burned down into its small brass holder, the melted tallow having overflowed onto the tabletop. Mr. Z came over to inspect. "She need to watch. She burn up the house," as if she might still be downstairs.

"The Pruitt sisters told me both her boys were still buried over there," I said, idly looking around the room. "They said Mrs. Brownlee talked about bringing them back home, but she never did." I was getting bored now with the dust and the memories. It was hot, and I might need to go play in the wading pool with Hercule. My fingers began tapping on the desk, waiting. They caught the middle drawer handle and slid it open, not looking for anything, just idling, passing time until the others were ready to go. When I first saw it, I had no intention in the world of taking it, not a thought of it.

It was lying on top of some stray papers, a tiny light brown soft leather-bound booklet, almost doll-sized. *Journal* was engraved in small faded gold letters on the front. I picked it up and began turning tissue-thin pages. Dates and words in pencil flickered by: "Dec. 43, stalag, Jerry," all printed in the neat, cramped style of a boy.

"Let's not dig into the drawers in here, Aggie. We'll need to wait on the chief's permission for that." Mother had glanced up at me and then back to reading a school textbook she had found.

I dropped it in the drawer and began slowly pushing it closed, but then something, some odd notion, came over me—the intermittent belligerence of childhood, perhaps, or its size, so compact and fitting perfectly into my hand, or maybe some lingering spirit in the house wanting to make itself known. I had never before taken anything of Mrs. Brownlee's and would never again; but that time, at that moment, I picked up the little journal back out of its resting place, slipped it into the pocket of my shorts, and closed the drawer. I often think back to that moment, how it changed all of our lives.

Chapter 29

"What in hell is going on here?" Chief stood in the doorway, staring at us—at the room—caught off balance to the point of reaching out to touch the door frame, keeping himself upright to his horizon. For a moment, he must not have been able to understand where he had seen it all before, and then slowly it must have dawned. This room was as familiar to Chief as his own boyhood room. He had heard it described so many times on those cold, bone-chilling nights when he would sit with Jonnie and Carl and Daniel and the two fellows from Arkansas, wrapped in thin blankets that were not keeping the warmth in or the cold out—so miserable that they couldn't sleep but had to endure it, so they would talk of anything that came to mind. For Carl and Jonnie, it was a favorite subject. Their life had gotten just that far before the war came along—high school, the terrible cafeteria food that now they would give an arm just to taste again, the girls in their classes, teachers that they liked, football, always football, and this warm, safe room that Jonnie and Sammy would come home to every night, the smell of supper drifting up to them from their mother's kitchen.

"It is just as you see it. No one touches," Z said to him, watching his reaction.

Chief stepped in slowly, realizing now that he already knew this place by heart.

"I'll be damned if it ain't just like he said. Hell, Z, if this ain't the spittin' image." He turned to Z in amazement. "Will you look at this place?"

"The same as he tell us." Z nodded slowly, finding the handkerchief in his back pocket. I realize now, other recollections I didn't know existed must have come rushing back to Z. He began wiping at the sweat that had broken out on his face and arms.

I raised a hand in greeting to the chief, standing up particularly straight, hoping the lump of the journal I had just pilfered wasn't showing itself in my shorts pocket, too stupidly young to realize that their thoughts must have been light-years away from me.

Mother and Vincent were on the other side of the room, absorbed in the books stacked on Sammy's desk, missing the chief's revelation.

Chief walked up to Jonnie's desk, tentatively touching it. "Look here, Aggie." He motioned me over. "Jonnie said he carved his initials . . . let's see . . ." He pulled out the upper-left-hand drawer. "Damn if it ain't still here, just like he said. Look at that." He ran his fingers over a neatly carved set of letters—*JMB*—that had been cut into the bottom inside of the drawer, some idle mischief on a night long ago. "Middle name was McDavid. Did you know? Used to kid him about that." He smiled as he looked down at it, easing the drawer in and out. "Talked about how he'd come in every night and do his homework, sitting right here," thumping the top of

Jonnie's desk with his thumb and middle finger. "This here was Jonnie's," he said, telling me again.

He straightened up and looked around. "Said him and Sammy would get into it once in a while. Said one night . . ." Chief paused, walked over, and lifted the spread on one of the beds. "Hell, yeah, here it is. . . . Damn. Look here, Z. Here it is—" His voice broke, and he pursed his lips together, swallowing hard to keep it all down. He had come upon something he had only heard about, that he had only half believed at the time, and now here it was—a perfect retelling.

"Said him and Sammy got to roughhousing one night, fell on this here bed, ended up breaking the leg . . . and here it is. Said it made his mama cry and he felt worse than if she had give him a whipping." He stood quietly staring at the mended bed leg for a long time before he let the spread drop back down over it. He took out his handkerchief, wiping his eyes, not embarrassed, only remembering.

"I tell you what, Aggie . . . tell you what. Think to myself lots of times, what in the hell am I doing here and he ain't — and they ain't?" He looked at me for a moment, mystified by the randomness of it all. "They was younger, lots younger," and began stuffing the handkerchief into his back pocket. "Never did understand it . . . old boy like me."

Chapter 30

"She probably couldn't bring herself to change it . . . the room," Mother mumbled, barely aware of the rest of us, as she had found an Alabama history textbook on Sammy's desk and was engrossed. She lifted it up, flipping back several pages. "Will you listen to what they say in here about Reconstruction after the Civil War?" Not waiting for them to answer: "'The loyal white men of Alabama saw they could not depend on the laws or the state government to protect their families. They knew they had to do something to bring back law and order. This organization became known as the Ku Klux Klan.'" She stopped and watched the chief, waiting for some reaction, and when she didn't get any: "It doesn't occur to you that this might be a tad overdone, the loyal white men wanted law and order so they organized the Klan? In a high school history text?"

He looked at her as if he didn't comprehend. Moments before he had been years away, back in the war, in the POW camp. When he did catch up with her, he must have been disgusted by what he thought was her naive attitude. "I don't make judgments about situations I don't know nothin' about. Did enough of that in . . ." Chief looked at her for a long while without finishing and then dismissed her and turned his attention to Z. "Whatcha lookin' at there, Z? Find anything useful?"

Mother sighed, shook her head, and went back to her reading.

"Sammy and Jonnie and Carl . . . before." Mr. Z handed over the framed newspaper clipping.

"Yeah?" Chief began to pat his uniform, looking for eyeglasses. He found them in his chest pocket and fumbled with them, trying to get the wire rims around his ears. When he did, he looked over the top of them and noticed us watching. The glasses gave him a different look—knowing, intelligent.

"One of them benefits of army life," he said, his face flushing a dark red. "Tell me it was malnutrition caused it or I wouldn't be due for a pair of these here for another couple of years." He walked over to the window for better light, holding the picture up close to read the caption. "Wouldn'ta knowed any of them, if they didn't have the names wrote down here. Look there at Jonnie . . . just a baby, and Carl . . . he was a skinny son of a gun back then." He gazed down at the names, running a rough thumb over the glass, nodding, and finally placing it on a side table.

"They were the last of her family, you know. Last of the Brownlees. Been in this part of Alabama for generations, and they were the last. She had planned to send them off to the university when they came home, had it all figured." He walked over and touched the service banner in the window, turning it around so the front faced the street again. "A month ago I talked to her and she was fine. Still sad, she would always be sad, and hoarding everything she could get her hands on, but she seemed okay. If you can call being a recluse okay."

We were all listening now, especially me, because just then Chief hadn't been speaking with his usual indifference to the proper grammar. He cleared his throat. "Maybe I'm feeling guilty because I didn't pay more attention to her. . . . Hell, I *am* feeling guilty." Then abruptly back to Z: "Brought some cleaning supplies, Z. In my trunk."

Mr. Zanino nodded and left to go fetch supplies. The chief turned his attention to us and eased back into his folksy ways.

"Guess we better leave everything like we found it, 'cause we're gonna want to keep this here room just so." He sighed. "Gotta wait to get the official report from Birmingham, seems like poor old Miz Brownlee . . . I don't put much stock in it, but seems like there mighta been something unusual about her dying, so the Birmingham boys say. I'm gonna need to make out some more reports to the fellows down there and wait a little longer on some test results they think they gotta do." He slapped his hat against his pants legs. "I was a damn fool for ever getting them people caught up in this."

"Why would you keep this room in pristine condition and think nothing of tearing up the rest of the house?" Mother said, still fingering through the history book.

He seemed not to hear her. "Now I'll end up with a mound of paperwork. And for nothing." He glanced at Mother. "Probably this room is full of all sorts of papers and stuff. Y'all hadn't took anything out yet, have you?" I picked up the Purple Heart and busied myself with examining it, feeling the journal getting hot in my pocket, reproaching myself for having picked it up in the first place, and knowing it was too late now to put it back.

Mother didn't bother to turn around when she shook her head no. She was still interested in the various books that were scattered about the room.

Chief pointed to Dummy. "See that there big dresser sitting out in the hall? Clear all them old newspapers off the floor and pull that thing in front of this door. Wouldn't want no pryin' neighbor kids messin' with what looks to me like a real nice-kept room, sorta a memorial to her boys."

Dummy looked at the chief, unsure of his instructions. He turned to Mother. She began to explain in sign language, walking him out to the hall and pointing to the chest.

The chief rested hands on his gun belt and waited. Vincent nodded and, after we were all out of the room, began to push the wardrobe to the door, inadvertently leaving a small space when he had finished, one that someone my size might squeeze through. The chief didn't seem to notice that. I thought at the time the gesture must have been more for show than security.

Mother put an arm around my shoulder and was turning me to leave when she thought better of it and stopped. I stood paralyzed, waiting. All along she must have seen me take the journal.

She reached into her pocket and took out the drawing of sign language pictures we had made at the library, unfolded it, and held it out to the chief. “You might take the time to try to understand him.” I breathed again.

Chief looked at her from across the hall, tapping his fingers on the grip of his gun. Then he walked over to us, close enough for me to smell his Old Spice. He stared down at Mother, lifting the paper out of her hand. “I’ll think on it,” and turned to leave.

We could hear him call to Z as he took the stairs two at a time, “If you see anything outside the boys’ room you think I need to look at, save it. We gotta keep going to clear this place out. Neighbors are still raising the roof ’bout the rats and flies, and I can’t say as I blame ’em. It ain’t accordin’ to the code, but the boys in Birmingham, they don’t have to live round here.”

As we crossed the street back to our house, Mother said, “I know it’s a temptation to want to look in every nook and cranny over there, but we have to resist it. Chief seems very possessive of what’s in that house.” We walked on in silence, waving to the Wilsons as they passed in their Ford.

“What was it, anyway?”

“What was what?”

“What was it in the desk drawer you were so interested in?”

“Nothing.” I didn’t look at her. “Just some old journal, kind of a diary thing, probably Jonnie kept it in high school.” I told her I had read only a sentence or two, that all it had said was that the weather was cold and rainy. Even now I can remember how the journal felt in my shorts pocket, touching my leg each time I took a step toward home.

Of course, I had read more than I had told her, and in the future I would read much more—randomly opening the tissue-thin pages, leisurely dipping back into another time, when I could get a few moments alone with it. That's how it began with the journal—a passing curiosity more than anything else. When I first picked it up, I felt I was reading the musings of someone close to my own age. Looking back, he was in fact still a boy when he began keeping it.

Oct. 22, 1943

It was flak that brought us down, Ma—not some sharp-shooting Jerry. We were just past the IP and couldn't do anything about it, had to sit there and take it—three engines gone. I caught my leg on a sharp edge of metal as I was pushing out over the side.

Everybody was scrambling—the ship was almost in a nosedive.

Carl and I made it down, which is a wonder, none of us having ever used a parachute before—pulled the ripcord and prayed.

And we were captured right off because of my bum leg and Carl not wanting to leave me behind—figure Daniel must have waited until everybody was out before he jumped. Don't know where he is or if he made it. Farmers, right out of the fields, gathered around us with pitchforks— If it hadn't been for two fellows who showed up in uniform, we would be goners. —JMB

Oct. 24

We were stacked in cattle cars like cordwood for two days. No food, but worse, no place to use the facilities. We came off that train smelling like the stockyard at auction time.

I kept thinking about the Hershey bar I left on my bed back at the base in England.

P.M. —Kraut medico took a look at my leg— It's somewhat better. —JMB

Oct. 25, 1943

We finally got some food today—soup and German black bread—Kriegsbrot, they call it. Did it taste swell!! They're taking us to another location, but I don't know where.

Nov. 5, 1943

We are in a stalag deep in Germany. The barracks are lined up in rows. Not very well built or insulated and cold as a . . .

It's cold, Ma. Krauts gave us a couple of blankets and we each got a Red Cross Capture parcel: food, a few clothes, toothbrush, cigarettes, etc. Must be over a thousand of us in here and more coming all the time. Each compound is surrounded by double barbed wire and rounds of concertino wire in the middle of that. We're not getting out of here anytime soon. The Brits are over in the next compound— more Americans next to them. I have seen some others too, Italians, French, etc. Our barracks have six fellows to a room —triple-decked bunk beds and mattresses made of wood chips.

Well, it's softer than the German ground!

Nov. 7,

One good thing, officers are not required to do much menial labor. With my bum leg, I would be in a lot of trouble. Other POWs (enlisted men) come in and do chores—sweeping up, etc. Our room has an older gentleman, must be in his forties, from Italy. He seems to have been in camp several months, we think. Mr. Z doesn't speak much English, and I, of course, have no Italian. We are teaching him a few words of English and he in turn is teaching us his language —or trying to, anyway. I'm not so good at languages, Ma. Some of the fellows are making plans to tunnel out.

Only way you can escape around here. After our run-in with the farmers, I don't think trying to get on the outside is such a good idea. There is a whole carton of Lucky Strikes in my Red Cross parcel.

Think I'll take up smoking—nothing else to do.

Nov. 13, 1943

In the middle of the night two goons manhandled a fellow into our barracks–dumped him on the floor. Backed out like they were scared of him, and when Carl lit a match, lo and behold it was old Daniel himself. We grabbed him and almost smothered the life out of him, we were so happy he made it. He is taking the one empty bunk we had left in our room. Said he was hiding in the bushes when we got caught–watched the whole thing. Then he wandered in the woods for days, looking for the underground, stealing chickens from farmhouses and roasting them when he could find a good hiding place to start a fire–said it reminded him of when we used to go to the river camping in the summertime, fishing off that old boat we restored, living off the land.

He was that offhand about it. He said starting a fire was his undoing. Somebody saw the smoke and next day the Krauts found him. He came in with bruises and cuts all over. He said he wasn't giving up without a fight, and he must have had one from the looks of him. First thing he said to me and Carl, "You boys doing okay?" I couldn't help but grin at that one. I know he doesn't like being here any more than the rest of us, but it sure makes me feel better knowing old Daniel is going to be around.

P.M.

It's night now. The beam from the searchlight in the guard tower of our compound sweeps past our window every few minutes, so strong it seeps through the cracks in the walls. Snow is piled up on the windowsills, more than I have ever seen, which isn't saying much since it very seldom snows in Alabama. —Never can get warm. JMB

Chapter 31

He had come in from yet another trip up to Sand Mountain. We were all sitting in the dining room, waiting for him to serve each plate with a piece of fried chicken and then pass it to us. When he was in-house, we always sat down together at the table for meals. Mother took a plate, passed it on, and asked, "What was the chief like, when y'all were in the prisoner of war camp?"

When he was away, it was an entirely different proposition. We ate on the screened porch, serving our plates in the kitchen, going back for seconds as we felt like it. After a meal out under the porch fan—Mother had said one was more likely to be imaginative if one was cool— we would sometimes leave our glasses and plates right where they were and put on a play. She said it was a play. We, having never been to such a thing, were happy to go along. Most of the time the plot would take the loose form of a movie she had seen—*It Happened One Night*, which was one of our favorites. Jane and I would take turns being Clark Gable, really the more robust role. Claudette Colbert was such a ding-a-ling, Jane said. "No self-respecting woman would want to play her." Mother smiled approvingly.

It was frowned upon for members of the First Redeemer to go to movies, so we were rather naive on that score, too—except for those times when he was out of town and she would let Jane and me walk downtown to the Saturday cowboy movie. This rather cloistered life was perfectly fine, Mother said, because she would rather we develop our theatrical skills than sit in a dark, stuffy theater all the time.

There was always a valid pretext for our way of living. Jane was beginning to look askew at these explanations, and therefore I was beginning to wonder, too, but not often. Our mother kept us too engaged to do much wondering.

Father looked across the table at her as if he hadn't heard what she had said, so she asked again. "You know, was Chief a rabble-rouser or did he pretty much toe the line when y'all were in the war together?" He looked at her again but still didn't answer, just served another plate and passed it on to Hercule. "We were over at the Brownlees' today," she said. "He was telling us . . . you know . . . a little bit about what went on."

It was not until he took up his knife to butter a biscuit. "I don't remember that much about Red's personality back then. I really don't. . . Nice fellow."

"What do you mean, you don't remember that much about Red? You've known him for years." She looked baffled, or maybe it was hurt I saw—that he would feign such ignorance to his own wife, as a man might if he had a mistress he was hiding from her. "You told me he was in prisoner of war camp with you." This happened every time she tried to talk about the war. He would react as if it were his experience and she had no right to ask, as if he wanted to keep it all to himself—no funny stories, no sad stories, no stories at all. "You went through the war with him," Mother began again, more frustrated now.

He saw her exasperation and sighed. "He didn't live here while we were all coming up, is all I meant. He moved here after the war, after we all told him what a great place it was to live."

"I know, but you said you had known him when you both were prisoners of war, that you were both in the same camp. I just assumed—"

"Did you decide back then that you wanted to be a preacher?" Jane interrupted just as Mother might have gotten him to say something interesting, other than what I had already begun reading about his war when I could get a moment alone, without Jane or Hercule to interrupt—and most likely snitch. I was beginning to take a passing interest in the journal, probably more than anything else because it was stolen property. However, I did feel that as blood-and-guts high adventure, it wasn't much. The last time Mother had let us sneak out to a Saturday movie at the Majestic Theater, at least twenty Indians had met their Maker in the course of the hour-long feature—and with no more concern on the part of the cowboy hero than a rousing expletive (dad-blasted polecats). So far, the journal paled in comparison—no bombs blowing everyone to kingdom come, no machine guns mowing down hundreds of Krauts. How important its contents might be to my mother had not yet occurred to me.

He stared at Jane for a moment. He was doing that more and more lately—staring when one of us would ask a question before he would answer. "It was after the war, Jane, that I was saved."

We went on eating. Mother changed the subject, going on and on about this new card game she was going to teach us as soon as she finished the book about how to play it: canasta.

One day earlier in the summer, I had been sitting on the front porch steps with him, helping him oil the lawn mower. Looking back, I realize it's the only time I can remember being alone with him. To this day, I try to forgive myself for what I said to him as we sat there. Even as children we were beginning to invent our own version of the war, add to it, change it to suit our needs, as every generation does. It is impossible not to. I slapped at a mosquito perched on my forearm. "Allen Silverberg said you weren't even in the war. He said all you did was sit around in a prisoner of war camp and wait to get rescued." I glanced at him and then quickly grabbed a piece of grass to begin making a whistle, waiting for him to disagree. When he didn't, I looked over to him and there were tears in his eyes. Fear shot through me. For a moment I stopped breathing. It was like feeling the slight rumbling of a coming earthquake. "Are you . . . ?"

He saw me looking and grabbed for his handkerchief, pretending to blow his nose. "Allergies, working around this grass," he said. I thought it was so and felt the shot of adrenaline that had just rushed through my body subsiding.

My father in tears over anything other than allergies was not possible.

I got back to the subject at hand. "I told Allen Silverberg he was just jealous 'cause his daddy was only a supply sergeant and you were a captain in charge of a whole airplane."

He held the handkerchief over his eyes for a moment, rubbing them, then put it away slowly and went on oiling the mower. He didn't say I was being unkind to Allen Silverberg or that really he had done much more than that. His put down the oil can and his hands came to rest, one on each knee, elbows stiff. He was looking down at the steps, and I waited. I wanted some little something to throw back in the face of Allen Silverberg the next time we got into a one-upmanship. "He said you got Red Cross packages sent to you with all the food and games you needed and he said you could play all the baseball you wanted."

His head began to nod, as if what Allen Silverberg had said were fact. And of course it was, fact.

"Well?"

He lifted one arm and put it around my shoulder. "Aggie," and pulled me close, "we did get Red Cross packages and they did have games in them—and food."

"Oh." I tried to nod my head as if it were some interesting bit of information, all the while trying to think of how I would slant it to my good use, history being an argument for either side to knit into the flag it waves. And then—I can still feel his arm slipping from my shoulder—I pulled away from him so as not to hear more. "Probably it was because you were an officer and his father wasn't even one." I stood up and walked away. . . . I stood up—and walked away. I have relived that moment for years—my one chance to connect with him. Perhaps now it is finally fading as my own children grow older and I see the bone-hard necessity for forgiveness. I like to think he forgave me, even as he could not forgive himself.

Toward the end of dessert—we were having sugar cookies and strawberries—Jane said, out of the clear blue, because she hadn't discussed it with me beforehand, "When am I going to see the light and get saved?" I almost dropped my napkin. I did drop my fork, on the plate, loudly. She pretended not to notice. What was she talking about? Jane saw the light every Sunday at Redeemer, like everybody else: the light on Sunday morning in Sunday school, the light at eleven o'clock service, the light at Sunday evening worship service, the light at Wednesday night prayer meeting. How much more light could she see? I was baffled and beginning to think Jane was up to no good and was doubly insulted because she was not including me in her nefarious plans. And if she wasn't including me, it might mean she thought I was too young and should be classified in the Hercule category—triple insult.

Just for that, I decided then and there, I was not going to let her in on the reading of the journal. She didn't deserve it. And with that snap decision, I lost any perspective I might have gained with the two of us sharing its contents.

Our father perked up immediately. "Don't worry, Jane sweetheart; you'll know when you do. Maybe"—he glanced at Mother—"I'll take you with me out on the road sometime. You can visit my other congregations with me. Would you like that?"

Jane nodded enthusiastically. She didn't look at me, just casually flipped her head back, getting the hair out of her eyes. Recently I had noticed she had changed its style from a ponytail to a wavy curtain that hung down dramatically over one eye.

That night, to make myself feel superior to Jane more than an interest in the journal itself, I took the flashlight from under my pillow.

Nov. 15, 1943

Yesterday, we got only four Red Cross boxes, and Daniel, being the senior officer in our room now, divided everything and gave everybody equal shares. There's me—Carl—Daniel—a fellow from Memphis, and two from Arkansas. Daniel gave his share of gum to me. I'm saving it for later when my mouth starts tasting like horse manure. When morning appel comes (it's what they call roll call and it's twice a day), Daniel and this fellow from Memphis—name's Red—they help me to make it outside so I can stand at attention, trying to look like I'm not hurting much, but my leg is still pretty bad. Daniel says I should go back to the German Doc, but I'm not having any more of him. Heard if you aren't fit, they send you off to a hospital and you might never be heard from again.

No thanks, to that! JMB

Nov. 18, 1943

Last night the dogs caught somebody trying to tunnel out. Sergeant Bronitz, the Kraut in charge of security in our compound, he put the two fellows in solitary for two weeks. Told Daniel they would be in more danger escaping than staying inside. If they did manage to get out, they would probably get torn to bits by the local citizens.

Can't say as I blame the Germans seeing as how their land and houses are so torn up now from our bombs. Reminds me of the stories Grandpa used to tell about when the Yankees ravaged our land. Course Daniel is already talking with the senior officers in other barracks and making plans to tunnel. The Brits have three going right now.

I told him to hold up, I don't want him leaving without me or Carl. Carl says he'll help, but he isn't interested in escaping. We have a small stove to heat our room and to cook with, but not much fuel. Breakfast from the Krauts is tea, lukewarm and a piece of hard black kriegsbrot—dinner is soup, potatoes and turnips in it.

Mostly we cook our own food from Red Cross parcels.

JMB

P.M. —Just after appel.

Whenever I get feeling low, seems to help things to write a few words. We're locked up for the night. The guard tower light is swinging back and forth through howling wind that is pinging sleet against the wall next to my bunk and I am thinking of how I used to walk home after football practice, turning into Tripoli Circle with the sun settling down into the trees, getting a whiff of your pot-roast, Ma, cooked with onions and potatoes and carrots, the swell aroma of it all floating out on the evening air to meet me.

November 22, 1943

Ma, guess who shows up today? Sammy. Your Sammy boy!! We were all out by the main gate, watching the new batch of prisoners come in.

Must have been over three hundred in this bunch–different ones of us yelling when we saw somebody we knew and generally smart-talking all the fellows as they came in, "What kept you?" or "Forget your plane?" Stuff like that. I spotted him walking in by himself, carrying his capture parcel–blond hair catching the sun. Damn, I was glad to see the fellow. There must be over four thousand in this camp now. We're busting at the seams.

Sammy is in our same compound but two barracks over from ours. Sure good to see old Sam. He was shot down a couple of weeks ago and managed to stay loose for a week when the Krauts caught up with him at a farmhouse where this good-looking gal said she would hide him out in her basement. Sammy always was a sap for the girls, but this one turned him over to the first Kraut that walked by.

Said he was so hungry he could eat shoe leather. We said we didn't have any to give him. So he opened up his Red Cross parcel and ate half the stuff right off the bat. Then found a pencil and pad in there and started writing to Bretta James. He was sweet on her in high school. Everybody was sweet on Bretta—even me. Carl said he'd give his right . . . arm to have Bretta James say hello, much less get a letter from her. "You gotta know how to treat 'em," says Sammy. Same old Sammy.

Chapter 32

The next morning, after he had left for another preaching trip—there was a little church over in Waterloo in need—Mother looked down at her empty second cup of coffee, picked up her breakfast plate, and said that today she was going to teach us how to use the microfiche apparatus that stood in the corner of the library. "So jump up, get dressed, and we're off." She said everyone needed to know how to use the microfiche, and to teach us, she was going to have us look up . . . "oh, let's just pick a subject at random. How about anything that had to do with any of our troops overseas during the war—you know, that would have appeared in the local paper?"

Jane and I gave each other a look, not fooled about how random that was, but we would go along with it. Every time we saw an article that had to do with army troops from our town, or every time we saw a picture of a person in uniform, we should report it to Mother—for no particular reason, she said. It was just an academic exercise.

Miss Delaney was not happy with this arrangement—that the microfiche should be used by public persons, at a public library—but she went along with it, eyeing us from a distance at the checkout counter. Hercule was fascinated and said that he too wanted to learn to scroll the microfiche. Of course, Mother had insisted that he try his hand. As soon as she had gone back to our table to tend to Roger, I explained to Hercule that the microfiche, if you touched it in the wrong way, would electrocute you and fry your fingers till they fell off. He left to go to the children's section to read *The Little Engine That Could*, again.

Mother had gotten herself a copy of the latest *Saturday Evening Post* and was reading at our table while Roger had his daily orange juice.

We hadn't been at it long before Jane found something she hadn't expected. She was teary-eyed when she told Mother to come have a look. It was a picture that had appeared on the front page of the paper in 1946. Mayor Carl was standing in front of a train down at the depot. He's shaking hands with a man who looks a little like Mr. Z, only thinner and in strange, ill-fitting clothes, holding a suitcase in his other hand.

> Our wonderful town welcomes into the fold Mr. Alphonso Zanino, from this day forward better known to all of us as "Mr. Z." He arrived yesterday from Italy, by way of New York. Seems Mr. Z got to know some of our local boys (the newly elected Mayor included) when they were overseas fighting the Germans. Mr. Z was put in a P.O.W. camp right after his country—Italy—surrendered and came in

on the side of our boys. Mr. Z had the misfortune of losing his whole family in the war—a wife and two girls, ages twelve and fifteen. That was before he was captured and spent considerable time in a Prisoner of War camp with our men.

The bright side is that they sponsored him to come over to our country and start a new life in good old Dixieland, and we welcome him with open arms and hearts.

WELCOME to AMERICA, MR. Z.

Mother studied the article for a long while, reading it over several times. "I never knew that. Your father never mentioned this to me." She looked up at me. "But neither did Mr. Zanino. I guess . . . too painful."

Chapter 33

The chief was driving up to Mrs. Brownlee's when we came walking home from the library. Mother called as we passed by and told him we would be right over with drinks. Because I pushed Roger all the way home, I got to help. Jane didn't argue. She seemed more interested in reading the *Seventeen* that had just come in the afternoon mail. Her Christmas present that year had been a subscription. It was completely lost on me why she had wasted her one present on something like that. I had asked for, and not received, a Great Dane, which probably would have eaten more in a day than we would have consumed in a year. The idea had occurred to me after hearing Mother tell us the story of *The Hound of the Baskervilles*. A gigantic ferocious dog to fend off all comers had seemed a grand idea. I had received instead, a chemistry set, with one of the test tubes missing. Santa had discovered the Salvation Army thrift store.

Chief was out in the kitchen when we got to Mrs. Brownlee's, standing at the door to the back steps and looking at the door frame, running his finger along the edges of it.

We set the tray of glasses and pitcher of iced tea on one of the counters. The smell in the house was getting more tolerable or our noses were getting immune. In any case, we decided it was better to be in the shade of the house and have the smell than sit outside without it—it being hot enough to fry an egg on the sidewalk, which Hercule and I had succeeded in doing once.

Mother stepped over to look at what Chief was up to. "Just wondering why there would be fresh paint around the frame of this door and no place else." He bent down to look at the edge of the door. "Do you know if anybody was doing any painting for her before it happened? Sometimes hobos, passing through town, they'll come by looking for work, but I hadn't seen any down at the bus station lately." We all knew that the person most people in town hired to do their painting was Vincent, when he was sober. Chief seemed to be making a great show of inspecting. I think now that he might have been trying to divert our attention from what he thought was obvious. "I imagine," he said, straightening, "that whatever happened here was probably an accident."

We were in the midst of serving everyone tea when the mayor dropped by again. We could hear him before he was in the front door, calling to the chief, "Hey, anybody home? Where are you, Red, buddy?"

Chief sighed. "In here, Carl." And before the mayor could walk back to the kitchen: "I told you before, Carl, there ain't nothin' in here."

In my eyes, the mayor was ancient, as anyone over twenty was decrepit to me, but in fact, Mayor Carl was the youngest mayor ever elected to the office in our town. Some said it was payback for his war service—the town trying to show everybody how much they appreciated all the men who had gone. Others said no, it was the football game—the fabled football game.

He took off his hat as he came through the doorway, dressed in tie and white shirt, damp around the collar and underarms. His dark pants had settled in just below the belly. As always, he was smiling, bound to please, nodding to Mr. Z as he passed. "You're looking fine today, Z—looking fine on this beautiful day."

We all knew the day was more hot than beautiful, but that was the mayor. "Now, Chief," he began, "I'm not after nothing. I know you'll take care of everything," holding up his hands, his rosy soft skin glistening with the heat. I watched him, trying to imagine how he could ever have run somebody through with a bayonet—any of them, Chief or our father. What could make our smiling mayor mad enough to want to kill anybody? Standing there in the steam of the summer heat, and having read more of the journal, I tried to see them in another place and time, freezing cold and high above the earth, our chubby mayor grimly letting loose a load of bombs on the hundreds of soldiers below. It was laughable.

"I told Bretta," the mayor was saying, "if there was something over here worth having, she never could get the smell out anyway." He sniffed the air and brought out his handkerchief. "Just thought I'd drop by—doing my duty." He raised the handkerchief to his mouth but thought better of it and pretended to wipe his face. "Some of the neighbors been complaining to my office again."

Mayor Carl turned around and walked back out in the hall, looking up the stairs to the second floor. He had taken off his hat and was twirling it around absentmindedly, then using it as a fan. "So, Chief, how much longer you think this is gonna take?"

Chief looked perturbed and leaned one hand up against the door frame, the other resting on his gun belt. "Well, take a look at the place, Carl. And the boys ain't been slackin' neither. I could spend the town's money and hire more people to come in, instead of using convict labor, but that would mean more hands messing with everything." He walked over to the tea glass Mama had set out for him, took it up, and drank it down. "Wouldn't want that, would we—people messing with bygones?"

The mayor was still out in the hall, looking up the stairs as if he might have heard something, fanning himself with his hat, perhaps getting ready to go up, but he sniffed the air and turned back. "No, we wouldn't want that," he said. "What's done is done."

December 1, 1943

Damnedest thing–here we are in the middle of a war and yesterday the Krauts come in. "Weee hauf the surprise for you. One of our national heroes vill do us the honor to visit our camp tomorrow.

This person you vill know immediately"–as if we were in a kindergarten and the teacher was getting ready to give us a treat. All day long fellows were going around the camp taking bets on who it might be–guessing movie stars or sports people–one fellow even thought it might be Adolf himself. Guess that shows how much we have to do around here. Well, come the next afternoon about two o'clock, in drives Max Schmeling the famous German prizefighter–probably the best known fighter in the history of the Krauts. And get this–he is all smiles, with spit-polished boots and uniform and medals, and the Krauts are showing him off like he's Jesus. And to top that off, our guys are–some of them, anyway–not me or Daniel or Red, but some of them–Carl couldn't resist. He was rushing around trying to get Max Schmeling's autograph.

And not a day's ride away, our fellows are killing their fellows– Seems strange to me.

December 13, 1943

One of the Brits' tunnels was discovered last night—goons used a high-powered hose to wash it out. The Brits lost two men who were working down there. Goddamn shame. I'm getting so I swear like everybody else around here—Hope I lose the habit before I come home, wouldn't want to let fly in front of you and the neighbors, Ma. We hear things are going badly for the Krauts in Italy, and Z told Daniel things are not looking good for them on the Russian front either. Z gets all the scuttlebutt as he can move around more easily on cleaning detail. Daniel says discovering the tunnel won't stop us. He says it is the duty of every soldier to try to escape. I also want to think along those lines, but my leg is not quite back up to normal yet. PS—Started hiding this in my boot for safekeeping.

December 24, 1943

I am hoping that the Pruitts or Mr. Oliver helped you put up the Christmas tree, Ma. We made one here by stacking empty cans from our Red Cross parcels. Kinda cute, but nothing like the one we have at home and will have next year.

December 31, 1943

Tonight we are going to celebrate the New Year—won't be long now!! We hear Berlin itself is being bombed.

One of the men from Tennessee, who has had some experience in making whiskey, is brewing us up some wine—we are calling it that, anyway. He has been aging it since I got here—had over fifty of the fellows contribute the raisin and sugar rations from their Red Cross parcels and he added some other stuff. Reminds me of those stills we used to run across out in the country quail hunting in the fall.

Jan. 1, 1944

After lockup last night—we hid Sam in our barracks—we opened the brew and everybody, especially Sammy, got roaring drunk.

In the midst of it all, Sammy was standing on a table, proclaiming to the world that he was God's gift to the women. Well, this fellow from California took exception and they got into one hell of a fight, busted up the table and the California guy picked up a baseball bat and by the time he finished wielding that thing, the whole place was a mess, especially Sammy's head—damn near knocked it off. Good thing he is from hardheaded stock—ha, ha. This morning he is throwing up nonstop and I have one heck of a headache myself, even though I didn't drink that much of whatever ended up being in that stuff.

Jan. 4, 1944

Krauts made us sleep out in the open stockade for three nights, "if we cannot act civilized," they said. "That's a hell of a note," Red said to the goon who told us our punishment for tearing up the place. Red got a rifle butt to the gut for that one.

It's a wonder we all didn't freeze to death out there—my toes have turned purple. I am hoping they will clear up and I'll get some feeling back in them. Don't think I'll be trying any Kriegie wine again soon. "It was a damn fool idea," Daniel says, wasting our good raisin and sugar rations brewing up that mess, especially since we didn't get any Red Cross boxes this past week.

Chapter 34

The mayor turned to Mother. "How's Daniel getting along, Sara? Still saving souls?"

Mother didn't turn from pouring tea. She was used to people outside the church asking about our father. "He's fine, Carl. I'll tell him you asked."

Mayor Carl kept fanning himself, the thinning hairs on the top of his head lifting with the breeze. "Never saw such a change in a man. Used to be, before the war, he was cheeky as all get-out. Quarterback of our high school team, you know, the year we won the region championship. Did Daniel ever tell you about that?" He looked at us eagerly, hoping.

Mother did not think much of football, and when she was silent I, thinking myself tactful, jumped in. "I don't know about it," I said, trying to make my eyes big and surprised, as I had been told women were supposed to do with men. "He never told *me* about it." And truly, he had never said anything to me about winning the regional championships. Not that our household seemed to set much store by football, but on Friday nights in the fall everyone in town was down at the stadium, cheering. At least I had heard that they were down there. Church of the Redeemer frowned on the short skirts of the cheerleaders. I had never actually seen a Friday night game.

It was the entrée the mayor wanted. He grinned at me as if I had just said I would vote for him as soon as I came of age. He leaned back against the refrigerator. "Sara, I could use a sip of that tea if you have any left over." Mother immediately apologized quickly pouring him a glass, using the one that I had brought for myself.

He took a sip, wet his lips, and looked up at the ceiling, getting himself in the mood. A good storyteller must be in the right frame of mind, like a good athlete before a competition.

"Well, now"—he winked at me—"it was years back, right here in town, right on our same field, the one we still play on Friday nights in the fall. Every time I go to a game—and I don't miss any, you know—every time I go, I can see, in my mind's eye, I can see us running down the hill from the locker room into the stadium, breathing that cold rainy night air, our breath streaming behind us. Something special about night air in the fall . . . man, oh, man."

He smacked his lips, remembering it like it had been a delicious meal. "We had done so well during the regular season, we had home field advantage—don't you know—for the championship." The mayor breathed in deep, smelling again the sodden night air. "I was playing end. Daniel was quarterback. Sammy"—he pointed up in the direction of Sammy's old bedroom—"he was playing first string end. Jonnie, his brother, right upstairs"—he pointed his finger again—"he was our running back. Friday night, still drizzling on and off—the field lights were having to shine through the fog—gave the whole thing sort of a magical feeling." He winked at me again. "We should have known miracles were going to happen that night."

Z grinned, put his hands together, and rubbed them back and forth fast, as though he knew what was coming next. "Go on, go on, Mister Mayor."

"Well now, by the second quarter everybody but me was muddy, like they had been wallowing in a pigsty. I was a scrub, been sitting on the bench for two years. My uniform was spanking white—bright yellow and white—school colors, don't you know. Never had played much, maybe a minute or two the whole season."

He downed the rest of the tea and set the glass on the counter, looking through us back to the stadium. "It was a gut-wrenching, devil-take-the-hindmost kind of a game—against the Russellville Tigers. They would score and we would score and they would score and then we would. Field goals—three to three, and then they made a touchdown, ten to three. Then we made a touchdown, ten to ten. At halftime, I remember, Jonnie came off the field, and he had so much mud on his face guard—they had just invented face guards that year—so much mud, he had to take off his helmet and wipe it with a towel just so he could see out. He was only a sophomore and our running back—muddy, muddy, believe you me. Everybody was slipping and sliding all over the place. Moody Redd came out with a sprained ankle. David Springer had a broken arm. Practically nobody left on the sidelines."

The mayor smiled at us. We smiled back at him, at how much fun he was having in the telling. Chief had folded his arms, leaning up against the counter; so had Mother.

"Now . . ." The mayor stretched his hands out and crouched, getting ready to start another play, as if he might rush across the kitchen and tackle somebody. "There we were, on the thirty-five yard line, down to fifteen seconds left to play in the whole game. The regional championship was on the line, and brothers and sisters, it was starting to rain again, and the score—did I tell you they had made another touchdown and we had come right back? The score, it was still tied, seventeen to seventeen, and we had the ball." He stood up for a moment, taking himself out of action to do some explaining.

"Now, you might say, why didn't y'all kick a field goal, that close? Well, I'll tell you, brothers and sisters, Joe Van Bibber, our kicker, he was out with a broken big toe—happened in the second quarter."

Mother burst out laughing on that one. This did not sit well with the mayor. He frowned. Mother coughed and tried to look serious, saying she was sorry about Joe's toe.

The mayor went back to his story, running his tongue over his lips. "Well, pardon me, ladies, but it was one *hell* of a moment. And to top it off, if Sammy didn't get hurt on the next play, lying flat out on the thirty-yard line. Had the breath plumb knocked out of him so bad, took two of our boys to drag him off the field." The mayor searched the field, eyes squinting under his helmet, the rain pouring down so hard he could barely see, still hunkered down.

Suddenly he stood up and put his hands on his hips. "And what do you think that did?" He looked at me and I shrugged, not knowing because I thought we were ready to charge. "I'll tell you what that did, little lady. All during the game, first one and then another of our team had been knocked out and bummed up and broke to pieces, because that team from Russellville, buddy, they had come to play, let me tell you—butting heads the whole time." He stopped, unbuttoned the sleeves on his dress shirt, rolled them up, and jabbed himself in the chest. "Me," he said, still jabbing. "Me, they had to send *me* in."

Chapter 35

"Here I was, hadn't played a total of three minutes the whole season, and they were sending me in. The coach kept going down his list of names on this wet old sheet of paper he had in his hand, and finally he turns to me. 'Okay, Carl, go on in there, boy. We got to have eleven men on the field, and if you ever had balls, ever in your life, now's the time to prove it.' Sorry, ladies, but you can't tell the story without saying exactly what the coach said to me at that particular moment in history."

Now Chief was laughing outright, and so was Mr. Z. Mama grinned and I did, too, thinking I was supposed to.

"Well, I can tell you, brothers and sisters, I was about to mess in my pants I was so excited and scared. . . . Hell, I was scared silly. I remember the band playing so loud I couldn't hardly hear what was going on, and when I stepped on the field I think my feet sunk down in at least a foot of mud." Chief raised his eyebrows on that one. "Well, six inches, anyway, couldn't hardly get my shoes out of the gunk. And stick out—you talk about the dot on the domino, just by being out there with that clean uniform on, I was screaming scrub, scrub, scrub, and everybody knew it."

The mayor folded his arms, and then he lifted his right hand and pointed to us. "And that, brothers and sisters, was the genius of it—*the genius of it.*" He shook his head slowly and rubbed his chin. "That Daniel was brilliant, I'm telling you right here and now, the boy was a genius. We had one time-out left, and Coach called him over to the sidelines and he told Daniel the only thing to do was to try to give it to Jonnie 'cause he was our star runner. 'Course, everybody knew that, and so did the other team."

Now the mayor pushed back his rolled sleeves. "Well now, folks, me and Daniel were walking back on the field and Daniel says to me, he whispers to me, 'I'm gonna tell everybody in the huddle that I'll be giving it to Jonnie and they'll know it and so will the other team.' And then he looked at me. 'But when I snap the ball you run to the end zone and I'm gonna pitch the ball to you, Carl.'

"Hell, nobody passed much back then. It was like a trick play. 'What?' I almost shouted at him. Hell, I did shout at him. 'Are you crazy, man? I'm a scrub.' And he said, 'And that's why, Carl. Everybody will think you're nothing to worry about. They aren't even going to bother with you. Just get to the end zone, stand there, and I'll pitch it into your arms. Just hold your arms out and catch it, simple as that. Don't think about it, just catch it.'"

The mayor put his hands on his hips. His eyes had gone moist. "He said to me, 'I have faith in you—you can do it, man.'" Mayor Carl was almost overcome. "My whole career . . . Hell, I'm mayor of this town today because of that night. In a split second, I coulda been the goat or the hero, either one, but Daniel, he gave me a chance." He sniffed and got himself back in the mind-set of the game, seeing himself crouched down on the line, hands out, ready to sprint. "Well, to make a long story short . . ."

I looked over to Mother because this was *not* a short story, but she was smiling and so was the chief. "Daniel snaps the ball, and half the Russellville Tigers start after Jonnie and the other half start after Daniel, and he dips and dodges and circles around"—the mayor's short, fat legs dipped and dodged and spun around out into the hall, with his hand back ready to throw the ball—"because it took me some time to get to the goal line even though it was just a few yards away." He stopped and walked back into the kitchen. "I'll admit it—never was the fastest thing on two feet.

"And when I got there and turned around, there wasn't a person within a mile of me." He stood in the kitchen end zone, holding his hands up, ready to catch the ball. "So Daniel pitches the ball up in the air and the whole stadium goes stark silent, seeing who he's pitching it to and thinking I was never gonna catch it, not in a million years. I am standing there with my arms out and it seems like it took five minutes for that ball to float down to me."

He stopped right there, overcome, and took out his handkerchief to wipe his eyes. I think also to wait for somebody to ask—so of course I did. "And what? What happened, Mr. Carl?"

The mayor held his hands up, watching the ball come spiraling down into his arms, then jerked them down into his chest. "I caught it." Big grin. "Only damn ball I ever caught in my life, but on that night, on that wet old misty night, years ago, I caught it. Almost dropped it—it juggled around in my arms, but I held on and there was nobody around to push me. Just stood there holding the ball and suddenly there was this deafening roar and the band was playing and everybody was cheering and the team was running over and jumping on me—cracked a rib in the pile-on."

Chief laughed out loud on that one.

"For years I pretended it was from somebody pushing me during the play, but really, it was after the whistle had blown." The mayor stood there smiling, remembering being on the bottom of the pile and knowing that now—in our town, in his world—he was forever a hero.

"Funny, isn't it, how in a split second, one thing, one thing in your life, can change it forever—for the good or the bad." He looked over to the chief, and their eyes connected for a moment, and then he looked away. "Funny how that can happen."

Chapter 36

He turned to Mother. "Daniel never told you that story? He almost got kicked off the team for not following the coach's orders."

"He did tell me, once long ago, before he went overseas, but"—she smiled back at the mayor—"he never made such a good story out of it as you do, Carl."

"Well . . ." The mayor came over to take me by the shoulder. "I like the kids to know what a great player their daddy was."

For a moment, just for a moment in the silence, as we all stood there I thought I heard a sound coming from upstairs—faint laughter or maybe Jonnie, opening up a desk drawer to start his homework, or Sammy, home from practice and dropping his cleats on the floor—until I heard Vincent dumping a load of cans out on the street. We hadn't realized he had left, I supposed not knowing that much about football and not hearing a word to boot.

"Well, I better be getting along." Mayor Carl looked down at me. "We owe your daddy a lot, and we'll never forget it."

Mother stood fingering the empty iced tea glass as the mayor took his hat off the countertop and told us good-bye.

We could hear him out in the hall speaking to Vincent as he passed. "That was a nice story," and she turned to the chief. "Had you ever heard it before?"

"Oh, I'd say about fifty times. Everybody in prison camp heard that story at least once every week." He walked over to the back door. "But that was one of his better versions," and pulled out his pocketknife, studying the splash of green halfway up the door. "I think it musta been old paint after all. She probably started to paint it herself, trying out a sample, and didn't finish for some reason."

As everyone got back to work, Mother and I gathered up our tea glasses. Dummy and Mr. Zanino were passing down the hall with armloads of old cans. They were concentrating on the library or what used to be the library. All the shelves were jammed with foodstuff: tattered boxes of Quaker Oats, rat nibbled, scores of soup cans, boxes of cornflakes . . . none of it worth saving. The tops of the cans were beginning to rust at the seams, liquid oozing up through the cracks. Mother grimaced as she paused in the doorway on our way out. "You know, there's a name for this, a name for this condition—one who neurotically collects things."

I thought she was talking to me, and I was about to say no, I didn't know somebody who collected trash had a name, other than crazy. But just as I was about to say it, Chief piped up from the kitchen door, "Hoarding. It's an obsessive-compulsive kind of thing."

"What did you say?"

"Obsessive-compulsive, couldn't resist hoarding. The old girl was a classic case. Newfangled term they use now for people like her."

"How in the world did you know that?" Mother was incredulous, as if she had just heard one of the Pruitt sisters' cats reciting the alphabet.

"You ain't the only one knows how to use the library, Sara."

"I . . . I didn't mean . . ."

Chief pretended not to notice her surprise. He was busying himself with the paint sample he had just carved out of the back-door frame, taking out his handkerchief and carefully wrapping the wood piece and then sticking the whole thing in his pocket.

He came out into the hall, still holding his pocketknife. "Sara," he said, "how do you think it'd look if I went around town talking like you? I'd get my butt run out on a rail, and I'd deserve it, too. People don't want no chief of police that don't sound like a chief of police. Probably wouldn't get one single vote in the next election." He clicked his knife shut and slid it in his pocket. We watched as he opened the front screen and disappeared out into the yard.

"You might get *one*," she called after him.

January 15, 1944

Things are not looking so swell—weather is cold and rainy. The tunnel the others were working on was discovered—goons sneaking around with their dogs after midnight—and the damn shame of it is they were almost done, not ten more yards. We all worked on it practically every night after lockup. I was serving as lookout and damn if I heard the Krauts and the dogs—snuck up on me. Daniel said I shouldn't blame myself.

There wasn't anything any of us could have done anyway. Daniel and a fellow from Sammy's barracks, the two working down in the hole at the time, got solitary for a week, but have to serve it later. Seems there are so many POWs being caught trying to tunnel that the solitary cells are filled right now.

Haven't received any Red Cross packages for over a week. Sure could use the food.

Jan. 18, 1944

Daniel is back at it, but Billy and George (the Ark. Boys), they say they have had enough digging what with the thin rations we are getting now—constantly hungry—watery soup the Krauts serve helps—when we get it. Went without supper again last night. We haven't had a regular breakfast or dinner for some time now. Billy and George joined the theater group putting on a play for everybody's entertainment. Carl says he believes he will join the theater group also—says theater was always one of his strong points. That's the first I ever heard of that!!

Only Red and Daniel are still willing to "work."

Jan. 20, 1944

Z comes rushing into the room after lockup last night. Don't know how he got inside our barracks after hours. "Guards, they come, they come." I was hardly awake and didn't know what he meant at first but he kept pointing to the floor under my bed and saying "zee guards."

I got everybody up and out of the dig just in time. When they came we were all in our bunks, snoring away, Daniel had even managed to jerk on some pajama tops. We owe one to Z. He saved our hides tonight.

Jan. 21, 1944

They found it today—Daniel and Red got 10 days in solitary.

Chapter 37

The next day, as I was riding my bike past the sisters' house, I slowed, thinking they might want to know the latest. But to my surprise they had something to tell me, and I hurried back home to give Mother the lowdown.

"Did you know, Mama, that the medical men in Birmingham have now said Mrs. Brownlee was done away with, as in murdered, as in there was foul play, Mama, just like we thought in the first place."

Mother didn't look up from rolling out dough for supper biscuits. "I wouldn't put too much stock in what the sisters say if I were you. I don't think they have a pipeline to the chief's office."

"Yes, they do, it's their nephew Jason Pruitt. He works down in Birmingham for the state, and he called them last night and said not to tell anybody 'cause it would be out soon enough, but it looked like foul play and what were we doing up here in our sleepy old town?"

"This whole state is one sleepy town," Mother said. She tapped the biscuit dough six times with the end of an iced tea glass and then began lifting the circular cutouts onto a cookie sheet. She hadn't responded, at least not with the surprise I had expected—wanted. But that afternoon as we served tea, she mentioned it to the chief.

"Damn if I should ever have sent anything off to Birmingham to begin with. Stuff from down there—it's not a hundred percent anyways, it's just a guess. Hell, they got some little trainee, doesn't know what he's doing."

"So you're telling me that they think it could have been something other than a natural death?"

I'm telling you that this whole damn state is like a sieve, couldn't keep a secret if you was to bury it in a hole. It mighta been—*might have been*—blunt force trauma to her head, but so what. She coulda fainted dead away and hit her head on something, which is more'n likely. Them Birmingham boys ain't got nothin' better to do with their time. If it wasn't an election year, damn if I ever woulda sent anything down there in the first place."

"But you said there was nothing for her to hit her head on, from what you could see."

"Jesus, Sara, you been reading too many mystery stories. You sound like . . . what's her name . . . Miss Marple?"

Mother blushed. The chief saw it and grinned. "Oh yeah, I saw you was a big mystery fan, all them books stacked on the side table out on your porch. Didn't figure a brain like you for such light reading, but I knew it couldn't be the children, and it sure ain't Daniel. If it don't have one of the Three Wise Men in it, it ain't likely to get Daniel's attention." He watched her, enjoying her embarrassment. "Well now, it ain't a sin, sitting round reading mystery stories. Next thing you know, you might take up *romance* stories."

Mother snapped back, "I don't see you reading Voltaire, Red. I'll read whatever I please, thank you."

The chief laughed out loud. "Wooh, didn't know you was so sensitive 'bout your readin' habits. Guess I need to get me a copy of that Voltaire next time I'm in Huntsville, just so I can keep up." He leaned back against the wall, drinking his tea, grinning like he had a fish on a stringer.

"It's . . . I know it's not . . . instructive, but it keeps the mind occupied . . . for a short time." Mother tried to busy herself with pouring more tea, although there was not much left to pour, everybody else having finished and gone back to work. We could hear Vincent dragging around boxes out in the hall. She handed the glass to me, grabbed a napkin, and pretended to wipe up a spill on the countertop.

"Well now, reading mysteries, it's just like us boys going hunting, something to do to take your mind off your everyday cares. Nothing wrong with that." He set the glass down, picked his hat up off the counter, and turned to me. "Ain't that right, Aggie?"

"Yes, sir . . . I guess . . . but what about poor Mrs. Brownlee? Have you forgot about how she mighta been murdered?"

"Listen, Aggie honey, this here was just a old lady turned funny and died, bless her soul—nothing more to it." He put his hat on and squared it. "I'll tell you what's a crime, it's a crime the rumors that are spreading all over this town—ridiculous stuff. Why, the other day, somebody had the gall to ask me, had I found a dead body in the basement? Do you believe that?"

I busied myself with drinking my iced tea, having almost forgotten I had started that one. He turned to Mother. "Sara girl, she was in this house for a week or more before we found her. She mighta hit her head and then got up and walked all over the place before she died. Can't tell nothing from that."

"Well"—Mother was delighted to leave the subject of her reading habits—"*I* can't tell anything, but if that's what you think, why are you digging paint samples out of the door frame?"

"I'm just gonna take that sample down to Moody at the hardware store, see if . . ." He stopped himself and pointed a finger at her, blushing himself this time. "And see if he has a color like this here for my kitchen—been planning on painting it."

"Oh, right." Mother couldn't help but laugh.

I was beginning to feel comfort in the relationship that was building between them—the chief and my mother—not that, as a child, there is anything you can do about adult dealings one way or the other, but there was a sense of security that came from knowing someone was there, some other adult. And that summer I somehow felt it was becoming more and more important that we have some kind of help, although I wasn't sure why. For a child, absent the adult's power of reasoning, everything is intuition.

Chapter 38

For the next three days Jane was the one to go to Mrs. Brownlee's and serve the tea, despite my protests. Mother had insisted. This abrupt change of plan had been precipitated by the Girl Scouts.

The day before, Marilyn McClure, down the street, had come over to ask if Jane was going to Girl Scout camp this summer. Everyone their age was going, Marilyn said, even some kids from Church of the Redeemer. Delighted to know that Scout camp might not be on the quarantined list, Jane hurried in to ask, and Mother had said of course she could go . . . until Jane said she wanted a uniform like all the rest—the official hat, the official dress, the official socks. In a word, Jane wanted to look normal.

The idea of mimicking the masses was repugnant to Mother—but probably more important, in the current circumstances, there was no way she could afford a full Girl Scout uniform for Jane.

Better than some passé mirror image of the person next to you, Mother had said, we would all go to the thrift store to find Jane something that was more chic and stylish than your basic old uniform—something she could take to camp and show off, a stunning hat or perhaps a colorful scarf.

Somehow, the very mention of thrift store and Scouting in the same breath seemed to be the confluence of all that had been bothering Jane of late—the final preteen straw. She let loose the floodgates. *"That was not,"* she yelled, "*not* what I had in mind." The Girl Scout uniform had become the very symbol of sameness that Jane was hankering after. She wanted, she said, "a regulation uniform like everybody else in the world had," and nothing—not a scarf, not tacky shoes, not a pink boa—would do outside of the real thing.

I was sitting on the screen porch, watching this, chewing my fingernails, and looking from one to the other.

Mother lowered her reading glasses—she was in the middle of *The Murder at the Vicarage*—and said that perhaps Jane needed a change of scene, a look into all the fascinating and mysterious things that were going on over at Mrs. Brownlee's that were unique to any experiences the other girls in the neighborhood might have.

Jane stared at Mother, completely nonplussed—as if she had been talking to a Chinaman—before she turned and walked outside to the curb to tell Marilyn that she had decided, after all, not to attend Girl Scout camp.

This all meant Jane would be the one on tea duty for a while. She would get to be the one who knew what was going on at Mrs. Brownlee's. I would babysit while they were gone, and to top it off, when Jane came back, she didn't even make a halfway decent story out of it—just said they were dragging out trash and it was hot as Hades over there.

"Jane," I said, "I have been sitting here on these front steps, waiting for you for over half an hour—and that is all you have to say, 'hot as Hades'?" Jane gazed through me into another world and left to do who knew what. No wonder the Pruitt sisters always asked me to tell them what was happening on Tripoli Circle.

Later on that same day, Mother and Chief were sitting on the porch with afternoon tea when Jane came stalking in, aggravated as usual. "This blouse looks awful." She waved an wrinkly cotton blouse in the air. "I will never again buy anything at the thrift store and that's final." As if she could actually give ultimatums to Mother. To me, even the thought was laughable.

"People like . . . like old Tot get their clothes down there. Those are the kind of people who get clothes down there."

Without any outward sign of annoyance, Mother turned from the chief to Jane. "And who, pray tell, is old Tot?"

"Mr. Tot . . . Tot. Everybody knows Tot, don't they, Chief." Jane had heretofore pretended not to notice the chief. Now she needed him for backup.

"Sure, Tot Curtis, down at the Trailways station—colored janitor works down there." Chief was not surprised that there was yet another local Mother knew nothing about. "Everybody knows Tot, or knew him. He left on out of here last winter, going up to Chicago. Said coloreds could find better work up there. Can't say as I blame him."

Jane had her hands on her hips, still holding the blouse. "See, Mother. He used to wear an old worn-out army jacket all the time, like the ones hanging on the racks at the thrift store. Must be dozens of them down there—"

"Jane," Chief interrupted, "that wasn't no jacket from the Salvation Army thrift store, that was his genuine jacket. Tot got that in the war."

"Colored people were in the war?" Jane was taken aback. "Like you and our father were in the war?"

"He was in the South Pacific. Built airfields . . . wounded in a air raid. Ever see that medal he always wore on his jacket? Didn't you notice?"

"A person"—Jane was not deterred by the facts—"wouldn't want to look like Tot, going around all the time in an old torn army uniform."

Mother put down her tea glass slowly and leveled her gaze at Jane. "I would say, Jane, that *a person* who would think like that would be a snob . . . and snob?" Mother pointed to me.

"Proud, or vain . . . or arrogant." I grinned at Jane.

"Which of course you are not," Mother continued, "because my children might be a lot of things, but they would never be snobs. Not in this house. So it must not be you we are talking about. Remember, your father wore that jacket. Half the town wore that jacket—proudly wore that jacket."

"Motherrr . . ." Jane rolled her eyes, sagged her shoulders, clenched her fists, and left—and left me seeing old Tot in the midst of an air raid in the South Pacific, bombs crashing down, planes on the runway splintering, and old Tot coming to the rescue. It had never occurred to me.

March 4, 1944

A little break in the weather today so everyone, including me, got to go outside to get some exercise. I mostly sat in the sun because of my leg. Some of the fellows got up a baseball game with equipment the Red Cross sent in—bats, balls, gloves—our barracks against Sammy's barracks. Those fellows have a great pitcher—fellow from Michigan—played for the University before he enlisted. Well, that told the tale. Nobody much could hit him. Daniel came the closest, going 2 for 4. Carl played center field and kept saying the sun was in his eyes each time he missed a fly ball.

After a while it got to be a joke—hit it to center and you had a home run. We started laughing and couldn't stop, which did not sit too well with Carl, but I got to give him credit, he was trying and it sure was great comic relief. Tonight, some of the boys in barracks seven are putting on a play— Carl and the Arkansas boys participating. I'm looking forward to it, but it won't be as funny as that game this afternoon. Haven't had any Red Cross parcels for weeks now, but Daniel had told us to save back some stuff because he was afraid this would happen as our Allied bombing gets worse and the Krauts aren't running trains except to transport their troops.

Tonight we pooled what was left of our packages and Carl prepared a kind of meat loaf made of moldy "Jerry" potatoes, mixed with kriegie bread and a couple of cans of salmon and some dried milk—not bad. Don't know what we'll have tomorrow. We're running out of anything to eat.

Around midnight:

For the first time tonight we could actually hear our planes—big groups of bombers overhead—up high. Brits say they are theirs. I don't care whose they are as long as they keep coming.

March 15, 1944

Around noon we heard some of our own bombers. Some of the fellows watched out the windows, said the sky was full of them— up at really high altitudes so they couldn't see any markings. Red says they were B17s, maybe part of his old squadron out of Memphis, where he joined up with a group of fellows who were on the police force with him.

That's how come he's so old—32. Said everybody in his group joined together right after Pearl Harbor. He wasn't going to be left out.

P.M.

Daniel has decided that we should stop trying to tunnel out. We're bound to be liberated soon (he didn't mention, or get shot by the Krauts), and nobody has energy left what with the food shortage. Yesterday I traded my last pack of cigarettes for a share in a can of Spam that Daniel got off a fellow in barracks G. Cigarettes from me, toothbrush from Red, a bar of soap from Carl. Daniel chipped in half a Hershey bar. We are making do the best we can, but it "ain't easy, McGee." All have lost considerable weight. Krauts are having the enlisted men begin to build slit trenches—knowing there will be more planes soon and more air raids and we'll need a place to go when it starts. Never thought I would see the day when I'd be worried about being bombed by my own fellows.

April 19, 1944

We have a new commandant, name of Von Guten—rolled in here with a motorcade this morning like he was Adolf himself. Mean-looking little son of a bitch. Must not be more than five foot four. Strutting around at appel and he spied Daniel who is six four if he's a day and white blond hair—Daniel looks more like the "Master Race" than Herr Commandant ever did. Right off he took a liking to Daniel—asking him questions in flawless English, like where he was from and did he have German ancestors? Daniel stood there at attention the whole time—later we were kidding Daniel *and saying maybe we could get an extra Red Cross box out of it. Last time they were distributed, we got three for the six of us in our room.*

Daniel divided everything down to cutting the last piece of gum into six pieces. I am cinched up to the last hole in my belt buckle. What I dream of now is some of that swell pecan fudge the Pruitt sisters make.

Red came in the barracks today, holding up a dead rat he had managed to corner. Held it up like some prize piece of steak. Carl said he would be damned if he was gonna eat that. We boiled him and Red wasn't gonna give Carl any. Daniel ordered him to.

Not much meat on the thing.

Chapter 39

We waited supper on him. When he finally came, the streetlight at the end of Tripoli had begun to lay down shadows in the grass. He looked so exhausted, Mother could not have had the heart to fuss over something as small as being late.

He had been helping a family out in the country, he said. Their house had burned down. They had the clothes on their backs and that was it. We prayed about it for the longest time. Jane had seemed particularly touched by our father's prayers for these people—sitting there, her hands clasped together, tears running down her cheeks. I was so hungry that I wasn't paying much attention to him. Hadn't she heard this before? Hadn't she been sitting at this same table time and time again, listening to prayers for other families? I didn't understand what was different about this family. Finally it began to dawn on me that perhaps it was not the prayer, but the listener. I was beginning to be afraid that Jane was hearing something I wasn't—that I was missing out on something, as if we both were looking at a see-through mirror and she was the only one seeing through.

This person was a sharecropper up on Sand Mountain. His whole house had burned down. He didn't even have any furniture now, and he was such a good, faithful church member. It was almost a sin, our father said, "that some of us have so many worldly goods and others don't have a thing and all because of a twist of fate, something that was nobody's fault, something that just happened, something you couldn't do anything about." His voice seemed tense and urgent. "It's hard for me to understand God's message in a thing like that," he said. "Perhaps it was a test from God—for the family—for me."

Gloom settled down on us like stifling midday heat. He told us they had been having a good year, this Sand Mountain family. They were bringing in a good cotton crop, were planning on adding a few more acres next year, were thrilled with the Lord's bounty, and then just like that, one night some sparks from their cooking fire jumped the grate and caught the living room curtains, and they ended up barely getting out with the children and their lives. Now they didn't even have a table to say grace over or a sofa to sit on. "How"—his fist clenching—"can we stand by and not want to help others who aren't so fortunate?" He looked to Mother and almost demanded, "How could *any of us* not want to help these people?" Sweat broke out on his forehead. Mother watched him, her face softening with sympathy for this family or for our father—I didn't know which one.

Meanwhile, I was watching the sofa in the living room, hoping he wasn't having the same thought I was afraid he was having. I liked that sofa. I used it all the time in the winter, to sit and read comics. I determined to go sprawl out on it after supper and read a book, to give him the idea.

After the prayer, after we had started in on our roast and potatoes, string beans and tomatoes, Mother said she was so sorry about the family on Sand Mountain and their house burning down, and she wished she could right every wrong in the world, but she couldn't and neither could he—that sometimes you had to leave things up to providence.

He let the butt end of his knife, gripped hard in his fist, slam down on the table. *"No,"* he said. "No, that's the trouble with the world now. You can't just let things float along, not making a decision. That's the real sin. That would mean we were no better than the lowly creatures of the earth and God has made us superior to them—*superior*," he insisted, raising his voice. Poor Hercule, his little mouth trembling, was trying to eat his string beans, not knowing why suddenly he felt like crying. Jane was stirring her mashed potatoes into a circular well.

Mother reached over—she had taken to sitting next to him at dinner and had put Jane at the other end of the table—and put a hand on his arm, which seemed to calm him somewhat. He tried to smile at her. Hercule lifted his napkin and wiped the tears out of his eyes.

When we had finished, she stood and began slowly gathering dishes so we could have dessert. I picked up my plate and Hercule's.

Jane threw her napkin down, jumped up, and ran to our room to get—as it turned out—her plaid jumper. It was her favorite, the one she always wore on the first day of school. She brought it back and said for him to give this to the little children who got burned out. She took it off the hanger and began folding it carefully. When she finished, she placed it on the table before him, an offering.

This seemed to please him when nothing else had. He gave Jane a hug and said there was a girl in that family, one about Jane's age, and she would surely love having such a fine jumper, and he hoped the Lord would provide them with other clothes and furniture, somehow. Right now they were staying with neighbors and had only the clothes on their backs. We watched him, trying to drink his iced tea, the glass shaking all the way to his mouth. I was pretending—we all were—that it was shaking because he was so touched by Jane's gift.

Chapter 40

Mother began to hurry things along, telling us we could go on outside and eat our sugar cookies she had made for dessert—it would keep the crumbs out of the house—and to take the parachute and cover the swing set to make a fun play place and have a good time.

Jane didn't want to do it. She wanted to stay close to him and hear more about the poor starving family up on Sand Mountain, but Mother dismissed us.

So we left, and for dramatic effect, Jane got a candle and lit it under the parachute. It was dark by then, and we knew it would attract a crowd. It gave off a peculiar glow, the light through the silk. In the past Jane and I had not cared about outsiders, but now it was different with Jane. Sure enough, Marilyn McClure came over and then Allen Silverberg from next door—all of us sitting under the parachute, covered over by it, the tree frogs beginning to tune up.

It was only intermittently that we could hear them arguing as they sat on the front porch. The soft light of the table lamp next to the glider cast out their shadows, almost to the front steps. It was not a yelling argument—it never was with them—only the low, steady sounds of one and then the other, one and then the other, one and then the other, because when two people agree there is an end to it.

Allen Silverberg said, "They say your daddy's gone crazy—got himself into the snake-charming business, one of those churches up on Sand Mountain where they have rattlers and copperheads and cottonmouths during the church service, and they sing and chant and dare them to bite so they can prove the Lord will protect them. My daddy says he hadn't been sane since he came back from the war, and now he lets 'em crawl over his shoulders, just daring them to bite."

I replied to Jerry Silverberg that he should take that back immediately, the part about our father being crazy, or I would pick up the candle and set his hair on fire and burn his whole body to a black crisp. And so he did.

Even with that he persisted, having the nerve to ask me if I had ever been to see the snakes. I was on the verge of grabbing the candle and maiming Jerry Silverberg for life when Jane piped up and said that no, she hadn't been to see the snakes up on Sand Mountain yet, but if there were snakes, she was going with our father the next time he went, because if he tended to a church like that, there must be something good about it.

June 21, 1944

Planes come over almost every day now. We can't help but get excited. Some so low you can practically see the names. Old Jerry is getting more and more nervous. I guess they are afraid we'll get out of hand somehow. Yesterday, one of the boys in Sammy's barracks made the mistake of going to the door to look out during an air raid—probably wanting to see the type of plane, if they were ours or the Brits. A guard, in the tower, saw him move in the doorway and shot him—without a warning, just shot him dead. Fellow from Indiana—Greeley. He was catcher on his barracks' baseball team. Greeley was catching the day Carl kept missing all those fly balls in the outfield. I remember he laughed so hard. I am likely to remember him like that, instead of the other.

Daniel was over in that barracks when the raid started and was standing just inside the door talking to Greeley when he got shot. He reached to catch him as he fell and held him while he passed.

Nineteen they say he was. Daniel came back to the barracks with blood all over him. Later he changed his clothes but left the dried blood splatters on his face. Looked like war paint on an Indian chief.

Even the guards steered clear of Daniel today.

June 22, 1944

The Brits have a radio hidden in their barracks, so we sometimes get the news even before Jerry. We know that our boys have been on the continent for over three weeks now, but we haven't seen or heard a thing from them. We eat a cracker—one cracker—with a mug of tea for breakfast.

The Krauts bring watery turnip soup for dinner—if we're lucky—and a lot of days, that's it. Herr Guten said we should be happy with what we get. Most of the rail lines have been bombed out and there is no way to get the Red Cross packages to the camps. That's what he said. I don't know if we believe him. He told Daniel any prisoners found trying to escape from now on will be "shot on sight—no more solitary confinement— no more tunneling as sport."

Sept. 11, 1944

Daniel is so thin his pants are bunched up around his waist, his sweater looks three sizes too big. Carl is telling us he is sure even his feet are shrinking. Red said Carls brain may be shrinking but his feet sure aren't.

We lie on bunks talking mostly about food, trying to pass the time, waiting for our fellows to come and get us.

Red tells about the black beans and rice his mother cooks and how, when he was a kid, he would sneak out and go hear the coloreds playing music up on Beale, eating fried catfish and hush puppies in the joints up there. Says he wants to go back to doing the same thing he was doing before– policing, only in a small town where nothing goes on so all he'll have to do is hand out parking tickets and stop the little old ladies from jaywalking.

I told him he should think about coming back to live in our town: football in the fall, fishing the river in summer– good-looking gals everywhere. I tell about how Sammy and I used to race home on our bikes after football practice and how I could smell what we were having for supper as soon as I turned onto Tripoli. Course that brought to Carl's mind his great football exploit and we heard that story again. Says when he gets back home, he is going to go sit at the Friday night games and do nothing but eat dogs–lots of catsup–and never leave town again.

Daniel tells how to cook quail, wrapped in bacon, over a campfire like when we used to go hunting down by the river, come first frost. Used to, we would talk about girls.

Chapter 41

The next day, Mother waited until he was gone before leaving the house to take tea across the street. Z and Vincent probably thought she had forgotten, but I knew she was waiting for him to leave, making sure he didn't cart off some of the furniture when he left. He pulled out of the drive about the same time the chief was parking in front of Mrs. Brownlee's. They gave barely discernible waves to each other as their cars passed.

After he had gone in to check on Vincent and Mr. Z, Chief came back out and stepped across the street to us. She invited him into the kitchen while she brewed up a pitcher to take over.

He must have sensed something was not right but didn't comment about how late it was or how hot the day was for his workers, just sat down and pulled out a pack. Before he could get one lighted, she pounced.

"What happened over there, Red? I know it has to be something connected with over there." It was an accusing tone, as if Chief were responsible. "I've asked him time and again. He never will talk about it, constantly brushes me off." She took one of Chief's offered cigarettes, put it in her mouth, took it back out again, and laid it on the table, not knowing she had done any of it. "Since he came back, he's changed . . . hasn't he?" She asked the question and stood there looking at him momentarily before she turned away, opened the Frigidaire, and got out some lemons, shutting the door hard. "Or am I losing my mind?"

Chief took a speck of loose tobacco off his tongue and blew out smoke. "Sara, you're married to him. You know him better than anybody."

She paused, holding three lemons in her hand, looking down at them, almost whispering, "You're the only one I can talk to about him." Chief moved uncomfortably in his chair and kept quiet.

"You and Carl were the ones in the prison camp with him, side by side for over a year."

"Yeah . . ." Chief shrugged but still didn't offer anything else, taking a deep drag off his cigarette. Finally he said, "All we wanted to do was to get back here and get on with our lives."

She must have known by now he wasn't going to revisit it either, none of them were. And I, having read more pages of the journal, was not of an age to understand the deep turmoil caused by blood-splattered clothes or boiling rats for food.

Still she persisted with the chief, getting nothing in return. "I look back and think surely he wasn't like this before." She placed the lemons on the counter, almost talking to herself now. "I know he wasn't. We didn't have that much time to get to know each other before he shipped out, but I never would have . . ." She didn't finish, rattling her hand around in the knife drawer, looking for one. "Back then, there was not one mention of this . . . this passion for munificence."

Chief hesitated, looking down at his hands before he said, "I always thought you two were married sometime before that . . . what with Jane and all. Woulda had time to get to know each other. Not like a lot of these other war brides."

Mama stopped what she was doing and slowly started shaking her head before she turned around to face him. "The first thing you pick up on is not that I am worried sick about my husband, but that I might have been having sex outside of marriage?" She turned and slammed the knife down through a lemon, and then she burst out laughing. "Red, you thought I might be a fallen woman."

"No, no . . . no . . ." He couldn't say it enough times. He even stood up out of his chair, face crimson, to say it again. "No, ma'am . . ." He sat back down slowly. "No, ma'am, didn't mean that at all."

She let Chief squirm in his chair for a bit before she told him, "Jane is my child by my first marriage. Didn't Daniel ever mention that?" She turned back and began to slice the lemons against the cutting board. "My first husband died in a car accident before the war." I could hear the whack, whack, whack, as the lemon slices fell on the cutting board, then a pause before she said, "I was driving the car . . . a rainy night."

I could see part of the chief's face through a crack in the drop-leaf table I was under, in the dining room, pretending to play house. He was staring at her.

"And I was driving," she said again. "We were hit by a drunk driver, but it was my fault. I should have seen him coming. The whole thing was my fault."

Before this moment, when I had heard the story of her first husband, as told the way she wanted us to hear it, it had seemed dreamlike and romantic. Hearing it now, I felt a rush of pity and was thankful Jane wasn't sitting with me.

"Daniel never mentioned that to you?" She walked to the sink and began to fill the kettle with water, all the while shaking her head slowly. "I can't believe he never mentioned that to you."

The chief had no place to hide, so he mounted a defense. "Listen, maybe he did, maybe he didn't. When you're starving to death, some things tend to get lost in the mix. What do you think we were doing over there, sitting around over a cup of tea and playing bridge?" Chief blew out smoke and flicked ashes into a saucer that was sitting on the kitchen table. "I just don't remember," he said, staring down at his cigarette. "He always talked about his beautiful little daughter, so naturally I assumed Jane was his firstborn." Chief pushed back his chair and stood up, becoming more and more agitated. "Hell, you think we were concerning ourselves with things like that?" He stubbed out his cigarette and picked up his hat. "We were damn near starving to death and thinking we might get our heads blown off to boot."

Rather than get upset with him, she seemed salved with this show of emotion. "Will you please sit back down?"

He hesitated but did sit down. She returned to making her tea and said in a quiet, even tone, "I had just lost Jack when I met Daniel. He was God-sent. He loved Jane from the very first—used to ride her around on his shoulders and they would sing Jane's little songs." She took the top off the sugar canister and held it a moment, remembering. "They were so precious together." Then she lifted the canister and poured a shower of sugar into the tea pitcher. "Now, he's losing all sense of reason. It's like he's desperate to . . . to, I don't know, absolve himself. He never talked about being a preacher before he left. Now he comes back . . ."

At that moment, hearing all of that, it flickered across my mind that my mother might be frightened. But just as quickly I dismissed it as preposterous. It was like saying President Truman might be frightened, or John Wayne might be frightened, or the pope. Besides, in all of this unease over my father, there was no room in my mind for a frightened mother.

"I'm not saying I have anything against being a preacher," she was saying, "if that's how he feels, but this . . . this is beginning to go beyond anything reasonable."

The chief was sitting very still, not moving a muscle, staring at the floor the way men do when they are embarrassed to be hearing something they would rather not be hearing. I don't think she noticed, too relieved to have another adult to listen. "I thought"—she jostled a little more sugar into the tea—"when we moved back here, he would feel more comfortable, more at home. He felt like the offer, coming out of the blue like that, to preach at Church of the Redeemer, he felt it was divine intervention." She put the top back on the sugar canister. "I don't know what I thought."

"Maybe I shouldn't't've suggested it." He was still looking down at the floor, probably thinking out loud. Immediately his head shot up. There was a stricken look on his face, and he began to backtrack. "Don't say I said that. Don't you never tell Daniel we had anything to do with that."

"You?" She turned to look at him.

"Well, it was me and the Pruitts. They were asking me one day who might be good to take Brother Hardy's place. Hell, I don't know any preachers. Thought Daniel might like it. Me and Carl thought so." He was holding up his hands now, trying to mend his carelessness. "Don't you go telling him. Men can't stand things like that—especially Daniel. In camp he was always doing for us and never took a word of thanks." He was almost begging her now. "You ain't gonna tell him, are you . . . are you?"

"Of course not, if you don't want me to, although I don't see any great harm one way or the other."

"You ain't a man."

"Thank God."

Chapter 42

"Look at you and Carl . . ." She turned to the chief, who had settled back down in his chair. "It's been over five years now. You've readjusted, put on weight . . ." She blushed when she realized what she had said. "I mean, mostly Carl has put on weight . . . a little on you. I didn't mean—"

"Nope, that's all right." He held up his cigarette hand. "I been fat and I been thin—real thin. And if I got to choose, I'd rather be fat, believe me."

"Well, pleasingly plump."

"Yeah, right." Chief grinned now and patted his tummy.

"And that's my point. Look at Daniel. He's still so thin, he doesn't fit into any of his clothes. I thought he was gaining, but lately he hardly eats anything . . . and he doesn't sleep three hours a night, always in his office working."

"Lucky, skinny, him." Chief took a deep drag. "Nobody likes to talk about it, Sara. Daniel was the officer in charge. He had to make some . . . some hard choices. It was a mean time. People want to forget it and get on with what they're doing. It was years ago now."

There was silence then. I could hear more lemons being cut for the tea, and I could hear Hercule running around in the backyard shooting his cap pistol. Chief took another deep drag and blew a stream of smoke up to the ceiling, then tapped the ashes. The next time he spoke, his tone was suspicious. "Have you been reading some of that nonsense over at the Brownlees' house? Is that what this is all about?"

She stopped what she was doing. "What nonsense? What, over at Mrs. Brownlee's?"

Chief fiddled with the hat he had laid on the table, picking it up, watching it fall. "I don't know . . . letters, things he mighta sent back, things he mighta wrote. Jonnie was a big writer, wrote . . . things down. Could be all sorts of stuff over there. If you find anything, don't pay it no mind." He picked up his hat and pushed his chair back, getting up, ready again to leave. "Look, we were prisoners of war, for God's sake. Didn't have control over anything. What happened over there—nothing we could do about it, nothing. It's history now."

Mother grabbed some fresh mint, twisted the leaves to bring out the flavor, and tossed them in the tea pitcher, then mashed them against the bottom with her wooden spoon, mumbling, "And what is history but a fable agreed upon . . . as they say . . . as they act like around here, anyway."

Chief nodded slowly. "Old Bonaparte knew what he was talking about there, didn't he. What's done is done, and it ain't never coming back in the same way it was lived . . . and just as well."

Mother stopped what she was doing and turned to him, mildly amused. "You knew I was quoting Napoleon?"

"Well, hell, Sara, I ain't a complete ignoramus, ya know." He sat back smugly, took a deep drag off his Lucky Strikes, and blew the smoke straight up in the air, grinning, so pleased with himself. "Miss McDonald, tenth-grade world history. She was a fool for the man."

"I am *talking* about"—Mother would get back to her present predicament—"the fact that this morning he wanted me to let him have the living room sofa to take to a family in need out in the county." I could hear her slicing away again. "And what are we supposed to sit on, pray tell?"

"Oh, *that.*" The chief looked relieved. "Old Daniel always was one to feel like he was responsible for the whole shootin' match."

"Responsible for what? *What?*" She grabbed all the lemon slices and dumped them in the tea. Vincent's mouth was going to pucker when he got a taste of that batch.

"Maybe he's just a sensitive fellow."

"That is not the word for it. Obsessed, manic, fanatic, might be words for it, but nothing as bland as *sensitive.*"

"I'll see what I can find for him down at the thrift store, and I'll let him borrow my truck, if he wants to take some furniture to those people"—he laughed again—"that's not yours."

"I suggested that, but he said it wasn't the same thing as giving our furniture. It wasn't as Christ-like."

Chief was in the dining room now, his big black shoes standing next to the table I was hiding under when he called back to her, "Don't you worry none 'bout that sofa, I'll fix it. That's no big deal."

"It isn't your sofa," she shot back.

Chapter 43

The children of Tripoli Circle had begun to borrow pieces off the pile of junk that was accumulating out front on Mrs. Brownlee's curb. They needed it to make things: stick bats for street baseball, scooters, playhouses for their dolls, forts for the ongoing war games, stick horses for the cowboys among us. A giant toy store had suddenly appeared on the curb and was too much to resist. Debris was being spread all up and down the full length of Tripoli Circle.

Finally—Chief must have badgered them—a larger than regulation garbage truck came and hauled off some of the trash. Not all of it, but enough to make a dent. There was far too much for one load, but it did help, and the neighbors were almost cheering as they watched it drive off.

Dummy was still bringing Mother things he thought might interest her: an old brooch, a picture of Jonnie and his brother when they were children—about the age of most of the children on Tripoli Circle now. Mother would sign, "Thank you," and I believed she was also signing to him that she would like to see any letters he might find. At least I thought that's what she was signing.

A day later, he walked up to her all smiles and handed her a letter, small and written on thin paper with CENSORED stamped across the front of the envelope.

"What? What's in it?" I was standing there watching her as she read it, imagining what it might describe. I saw American tanks, flags flying, rolling over the snow-draped countryside, guns blazing, and in their wake, dead Germans squished flat like pancakes lying in the snow. "What? Tell me."

She didn't answer.

"Is it about the parades they were in when they marched through the streets of Paris and the beautiful girls throwing flowers at them?" She kept reading. "Or is it about them coming home on the ships, seeing Miss Liberty for the first time, people cheering for them? What?"

She finished and folded it up. "It doesn't say anything much." She was tucking it back in its envelope.

"It couldn't *not* say anything. You've been reading for five minutes."

Mother lowered her head and looked at me through her eyebrows, strands of dark brown hair falling in her face.

"Well?"

"Did you inherit your morbid curiosity from me—God is paying me back—or did it skip a generation and come from your uncle Ashton?"

I was not going to fall for that one. She had done that before, insert somebody like a person named Uncle Ashton in the conversation so then I would ask, "Who in the world is Uncle Ashton?" And she would get me off on another one of her stories, which were, I will admit, fascinating. But not this time. I would ask about Uncle Ashton later, if I remembered to. I didn't say a thing, just stood there looking at her until she gave in.

"It's from Jonnie, saying that he is somewhere in England and the weather is cold and that he got to visit London one time. See this black stamp on the outside? That means the censors looked at it before Mrs. Brownlee read it. See all these little holes in the paper?" She took the letter back out of its envelope and held it up. There were so many places cut out, it looked as if someone had been trying to fashion a string of paper dolls. "The censors did that, so it wouldn't have much detailed information in it. I've been standing here trying to decipher it, but I can't, not in this condition. I remember they did that to a lot of the letters your father sent me. I never could figure out what they said. I burned them all in celebration the day I found out he was coming home, so sure we would be together again and he would tell me everything that happened to him, to all of them. The letters would be redundant." She handed it to me. "Now I wish I hadn't."

She turned to begin pouring tea. "Take it and put it in the boys' room upstairs, if you can get in there. I guess if it belongs anyplace, it belongs there."

I took it upstairs and walked by the dresser guarding the door—someone had moved it out so there was plenty of space for an adult to enter now—and tiptoed into their room, but I read it before I put it in the desk drawer.

Feb. 3, 1943
England

Dear Mother,

In your letter you asked about the length of our missions. For the first mission the group only went to but you realize it is nothing but the which are being thrown at you. are darn accurate—consoling thought.

When we left the target the fighters we encountered were into one side as we were coming into the target moving in. After we were clear of the flak area of the target they started to were attacking. was on the rear of our formation. If I had only known those fighters were attacking at our rear, I'm afraid my maps would have been neglected for a while. By the way, those fighters were the latest thing in fighters. You probably know that they carry a Some of them have as many as four to a plane. One

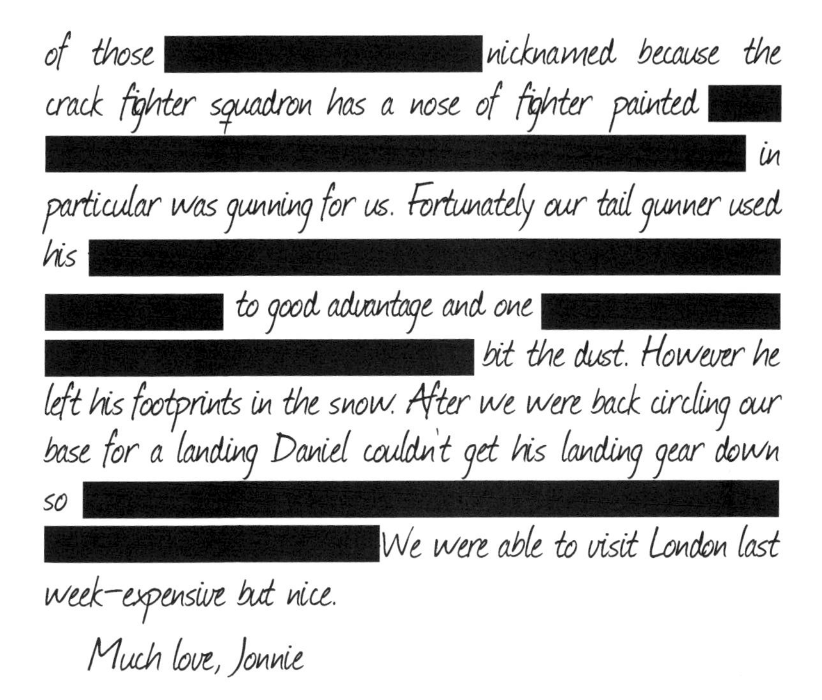
of those nicknamed because the crack fighter squadron has a nose of fighter painted in particular was gunning for us. Fortunately our tail gunner used his to good advantage and one bit the dust. However he left his footprints in the snow. After we were back circling our base for a landing Daniel couldn't get his landing gear down so We were able to visit London last week-expensive but nice.

Much love, Jonnie

I read everything I could find at Mrs. Brownlee's, not that this one made a particle of sense to me. The Pruitts had a right to know. I put the letter in Jonnie's desk and passed back out of their room, wondering who had moved the chest that the chief had said must be left in front of the door.

Chapter 44

Later that day, when we were over with our second serving of tea, Chief walked in just as Vincent was taking a ring out of his pocket, another trinket he had found to show Mother. He was handing it to her when Chief took two quick steps forward and grabbed it out of Vincent's hand. He snatched it so quickly that poor Vincent almost lost his balance backing into the corner, with Chief poking him in the chest, saying if Dummy found anything, *anything*, it should go to him and only him. Dummy was nodding furiously, trying to accommodate, not sure why things had suddenly turned sour.

Mother was horrified. She rushed to Vincent's aid, locking her arm around his waist and pulling him to her. "Red, for heaven's sake, what has gotten into you? Will you look at him?" Vincent's face was wrinkling up as though he might start crying—one minute happily going about his work and then suddenly he was a pariah.

When Mother put her arm around him, it must have been a signal to Vincent that she was on his side. Suddenly he didn't care what the chief thought. He reached out and grabbed Chief's hand, the one with the ring in it, and began to crush it. The two of them stood there locked in a silent, motionless wrestle.

The chief was the first to call uncle. "All right, okay, Dummy, you made your point." Dummy evidently felt he had not made his point and kept squeezing. Chief's knees were beginning to buckle. "Let go of my hand—before you break every bone . . ." And when Dummy didn't, he shouted, *"And I have to keep you in jail till the cows come home, dammit!"* Mother reached out and gently touched Vincent's hand, and he began a slow release.

It was just as well, because out of the corner of my eye I could see that Mr. Z had grabbed up one of Jonnie's old baseball bats resting in the corner and had stepped forward a few feet. Mother held Vincent's hand until it was down by his side. He was still confused, looking from one to the other. She led him to the sofa and told him in sign language that it was okay and that he should sit down. She would get him a glass of tea.

She turned back to Chief, explaining that it was all her fault. "It was simply a way for me to interact with Vincent, for both of us to practice our signing." That was her excuse, anyway, although the chief probably knew it was another pretext for her to search out information about what their war had been like. She said, "From now on I won't do it, if it's going to cause such a ruckus." She reached down and picked up the ring that had fallen on the floor. "And this is nothing, *nothing* to fight over." She opened her fingers. It was an old Captain Midnight decoder ring, one you could get simply by saving up cereal box tops. This one was so used and scratched, even I would not have wanted it.

Chief was rubbing his crushed fist, still disgusted with both of them. "Do you want Dummy to walk out of here with something in his pocket that doesn't belong to him? How do you think that would look?" He shook his hand out in the air, trying to get the circulation back. "There's trouble enough with that fresh paint on the back door and everybody in town knowing Dummy does all the painting around here, and rumors flying in every direction."

"Red," she said, "that's laughable. Nobody would suspect Vincent, even if there was something to suspect—"

The chief cut her off. "*I'll* decide what's laughable and what's not. You haven't lived around here as long as the rest of us. You don't know what's gone on, or what the hell *is* going on. Stay out of things that don't concern you."

He turned and walked away, still shaking his hand.

She followed him out into the hall. "I *know* he wasn't doing anything wrong, and if he was, it was my fault." She brushed past him and went to the kitchen, jerking up the tea pitcher and pouring some in a glass. She grabbed some ice cubes out of the thermos we had brought them in and plunked them in a glass. Tea spilled out on the counter. She shoved the glass into my hand. "Take this to Vincent." And I did, but I hurried back into what I guessed was a fine argument brewing.

"You can be so insufferably insensitive sometimes, Red. Vincent is a sweet, lovely man. Just because he can't speak you think—"

"Me?" he shouted back at her. He walked over to the counter, grabbed some ice cubes out of the thermos, and

began rubbing them on his swollen knuckles, grimacing as he rubbed. "Listen, Miss Know-It-All, you wanta come with me sometime down to the Trailways station, at one in the morning, on a Saturday night, when old Vincent in there has had one too many and decided he wants to tear up the place, because it's where his mama abandoned him when he was twelve years old?" He saw the look that brought to Mother's face. "And he proceeds to rip up one of the nailed-down—yeah, *nailed-down*—waiting room benches and decides he is gonna heave it through the plate-glass window?" He threw the ice cubes in the sink. "And I end up with two of my deputies in the emergency clinic before we can stop him?" He gingerly wiped his wet hand off on his pants. "Oh, yeah, he's a sweetheart all right . . . when he's sober." He turned and walked back out through the hall, calling to Vincent and Z as he passed out the front door, "You fellows get on back to work, the show's over."

I hopped up on the counter beside the tea pitcher she was fumbling with. "I guess we showed him."

She dumped what remained of the ice in tea glasses, grabbed the pitcher, and jerked up the tray to leave. "Why does everybody around here know more than I do—about every damn thing?"

Chapter 45

Late the next afternoon, he appeared at our front screen door saying he had come with a peace offering. He stepped just inside the porch where we were all seated—Mother reading *Treasure Island* to us. He held out a brown paper bag. She hesitated but then put down her book and stood up to take it and pull a bottle out of the bag. Turning it over to look at the label, "German wine?" and then began to smile—and then to laugh. "Where in heaven's name did you come across German wine, Red?"

We all watched as the chief's face went crimson under his tan. His free hand moved up to touch his collar. That's when we saw he had on a tie, and Chief didn't usually wear a tie. It wasn't knotted properly, the way our father wore his, but it was a tie and it was on the chief. We were flattered. It was not every day the chief of police came knocking on your front door with a tie on and a bottle of German wine.

Mama's grin got wider. "Is this confiscated evidence you and Jarvis took off some poor unsuspecting fellow traveling through town and not knowing we are in a dry county? Why, Chief, shame on you."

The chief stepped forward and took the bottle back, slid it down in the brown paper sack it had arrived in, not looking at Mother. "I'd never do that, Sara." He hesitated before he added, "And I'd think you'd know that by now." He turned to go—as all the while Jane and I were staring at him. He paused when he put his hand on the doorknob. "I was over in Huntsville this morning on business and picked it up." The sack and bottle were almost hidden now, under his big muscled arm that was covered in crisp starched uniform. "The place is full of Germans since Von Braun and his crew came in over there. You can get a pretty good vintage, at a legal package store." He blushed when he added, "Thought you might be used to having something like wine, and I felt downright guilty 'bout yesterday, you not knowing Dum . . . Vincent's history and all. I can see how you'd think like you think . . . about Vincent . . . among other things."

Chief pulled open the screen door and stepped out onto the front steps before Mama said a word. It was that long before the shock wore off. "Wait a minute, Red, wait, please." She walked over and touched his arm. "How rude of me, how terribly rude of me," and began pulling him back inside. "I thought . . . I don't know what I thought." He didn't look her in the face but let himself be drawn back in on our porch. "You were trying to do something nice for me and I was acting like . . . I guess I've forgotten how to act."

"I coulda been a mite rough on you yesterday, when I went to fuming about Dummy—Vincent, I mean—bringing you things. Guess that's only natural, you and Vincent and the sign language and all." He swallowed hard. "And listen, I didn't think about it till I was halfway here with it, but maybe . . . maybe drinking wine is against your religious persuasions."

"Me? Red, kindness is never against my . . . persuasions. I'm just too slow to realize when it's being offered." She held tight to the chief's arm, reaching up to take back the paper sack of wine.

She noticed the rest of us watching her—Jane with a critical eye. "Why don't you two go check on Hercule and see if the baby is still asleep and"—she turned to Chief—"I'll get two glasses and we can sample this lovely present."

"Daddy wouldn't like you drinking spirits."

"This is not spirits, Jane." Mother put an arm around her shoulder, turning her toward the living room door. "This is a drink to friendship, which I didn't have the good graces to recognize."

I grabbed Jane's arm and started pulling. "Mama knows what she's doing." I was one for keeping on the good side of the law.

After we had given passing glances to Roger and Hercule, we took our places under the bedroom window to see just what Mother *was* doing.

"What if he comes home and sees her," Jane whispered. "He won't like her drinking wine."

"He never comes home during the day."

Chapter 46

"By the way," Chief was saying, "it don't mean much, but seeing as how you were so concerned about Vincent, I'll tell you that yesterday afternoon I took that paint sample down to the hardware store, and Moody, he said sure enough, it was the color of a can Mrs. Brownlee bought from him a while back. Wanted to test out the color to see if she liked it. Said it took her three hours to decide on that one color. Poor old soul."

Mother was pouring wine into two orange juice glasses she had retrieved from the kitchen, filling the chief's and giving herself a few sips. "I'm glad," she said. "That was sticking in the back of my mind, and after what you said about him yesterday, I was beginning to wonder." She handed him his glass. They both sat awkwardly, holding their glasses before half raising them in a self-conscious salute to each other. After she had taken a drink, she complimented him on his choice, even as I saw a slight wince when she swallowed.

He didn't notice and seemed pleased with his gift, settling into a sociable mood. "Last time I had a glass of wine—if you could call it that—was over there in the POW camp. 'Course, that ain't to say I ain't had some hard liquor." He took a deep drink. "This here sure is better than that stuff we had back then. Some fellow thought he knew how to make it, and we volunteered all of the sugar and raisins from our Red Cross parcels for him to give it a try." The chief took another drink and finished his glass as if it were iced tea. She poured again. "He told us he could cook us up a batch." The chief shivered involuntarily. "You talk about a gut buster." He began a rather lighthearted account of their night of drinking homemade wine when he, when they, were all in the POW camp together during the war, making it sound like some raucous fraternity party. And I began to feel a growing sense of unease because I had already read about that in the journal—the journal that I was stuck with keeping hidden now that I was a common thief.

Chief was having a fine time with his story. His account of the winemaking turned out to be nothing like what I had read. The whole time he was retelling the story, she was keeping his glass full, not that I thought a little wine could faze the chief, but it did seem to be making him more expansive.

"Hellfire, you shoulda seen us dancing on the top of that table. I think somebody had a lamp shade on." Chief was blatantly improvising, but Mother didn't know it. Maybe he didn't know it. He mentioned nothing about the nights they had spent in the snow after their drunken brawl. She filled his glass again and put a few more drops in her own. The chief saw it but didn't seem to care. He was on a roll, or maybe the wine was giving him license.

"I'll tell you," he was saying, "I got a call at five this morning to go break up a catfight between two ladies down at the marina, and I been going flat out since then. Ain't had a damn bit of nourishment, so this here is tasting mighty good." He finished off another orange juice glass.

She must have decided he was mellow enough to ask. "Did Daniel drink any of it that night . . . when you were there?" She was tentative, trying to ease into the subject without having him shy away from it. It didn't work.

"Can't say as I remember." He shook his head as if to clear it. "That whole night is a blur." She poured them both another glass, putting just a splash in hers and filling his to the brim.

He changed the subject, asking about how she had liked living in Nashville, saying he had visited there once. It was a dandy place. He liked "the Grand Ole Opry . . . opera."

She poured the last of the bottle in his glass and tried again. "Do you remember, was he ever manhandled by the Germans? Was there any one experience that was particularly traumatic?" Chief had begun gazing out through the screen porch, across the street to Mrs. Brownlee's, his eyes on the verge of closing.

"Red?"

"What?" He perked up and drank down the last of his wine. He had consumed almost all of the bottle in the short time they had been sitting there. "What were we talking about—paint colors? I told you I found out about that, didn't I?"

She couldn't hold back a laugh. "Yes, you told me what Moody, down at the hardware store, what he said." She gently placed a hand on his shirtsleeve and spoke slowly and distinctly. "I-was-asking-you-about-Daniel's-war-experience."

"Paint colors," he said, staring straight ahead, his eyes trying to narrow in concentration. "The war . . . it's like . . . you went and took some goddamn balloon filled with paint colors and you threw it up against a wall . . . paint shooting out all every whicha goddamn way. White snow in there . . . and blood red . . . and brown barbed-wire rust. Things . . . just busting into each other." He brought his hands together in a loud clap. *"Pow!"* And then let his hands drop slowly into his lap, staring at them. "And you go asking me what happened? How did we get here, all the way back home . . . and sitting here now, looking at them crazy paint colors on that goddamn wall?" He shook his head, mystified at what the wine was letting him see.

I myself was blinking back confusion, having lost my way in his tipsy verbal maze. "Can I sit here . . . ," he began again, choosing his words carefully, thinking he was making perfect sense. "Can I sit here . . . and look at all of that and tell you how it got there?" He leaned toward her slowly and said in confidential tones, "Hell, yes, I can. I can tell you what I saw happenin', but it ain't gonna be like what he saw happenin' . . . even if we did see the same goddamn thing." He sat there in a slight stupor and thought about it a minute, then shifted his weight back in the rocking chair and suddenly heaved himself forward and up out of it, swaying toward the screen door, then turning around, almost losing his balance. "And I'll tell you one more thing."

"Please do," she said, raising her orange juice glass to him and trying to suppress a grin.

He flung an arm out toward his imaginary paint-splattered wall. "To some people, that wall is a beauty to behold, like some fancy modern art picture that cost ten million dollars . . . 'cause you got out of it alive, 'cause you got home safe, and you thank God every day. . . . But to them others . . . they can't take eyes off it. To them . . ." His arm dropped to his side and he sighed, slowly turning his head back and forth, viewing the wall from all angles. "It's like looking straight into the innards of hell."

He stood there, head held high, waiting for the gravity of his pronouncement to sink in. In the meantime, he realized he still had the orange juice glass in his hand, so he walked slowly over to place it, with exaggerated care, on the side table. Then he headed back to the door.

"Why, Chief," she said, laughing in spite of his gloomy pronouncement, "I had no idea you were a man of such subtle metaphors."

"Yes . . . well, ya never know, do ya," nodding his head in agreement and pulling open the screen door—lurching out, missing the first step, but regaining his balance and his dignity as he walked away across the front yard. Chief was finished with the war.

Chapter 47

Jane had made up her mind: she was going with him to one of his preachings up on Sand Mountain.

Mother had fussed, but Father, and then Jane, had turned against her—Jane saying there was nothing weird about it if her father was going, and our father saying there was no possible way Jane could come to any harm. He would make sure she sat in the back; it would be a good experience for her. Besides, Jane said, hadn't Mother herself told us we should have all sorts of experiences in life, just like she had?

Even though the whole idea of snakes made me weak in the knees, I would have gone, just to keep up with Jane, if anybody had asked me. Nobody had.

Jane, I decided, was still brooding over the episode with the Girl Scouts and their uniform ways. In any event, if I was going to be left out, I most certainly was not going to approve.

She had taken to sitting around listening to "Cold, Cold Heart" sung by Tony Bennett. Her friend Marilyn had let Jane borrow her record player for the time she was gone to Scout camp, and the only record Jane had was a forty-five of "Cold, Cold Heart," so we heard it over and over and over again—I think an admonition to all of us. I much preferred

"Mule Train" by Frankie, Lane if anybody had wanted to know. They hadn't.

They had left very early in the morning to get all the way to Sand Mountain by preaching time. That being the case, we were made to wait through the whole day and late into the night to find out what had come to pass up on the mountain.

We did have the tea delivery to keep us occupied, and that helped.

Chief had asked what our hurry was. Didn't we want to snoop around like we usually did? Mother scowled at him and we scurried back to the house, not being able to leave the baby and Hercule without a sitter for more than a few minutes. We sat on the porch all day, reading our books—hers *The Murder at the Vicarage*— me *The Black Stallion.*

In the early evening we put Roger to bed, then Hercule. The light atop the pole in the middle of Tripoli Circle had long since come on. The glass in its four panes was so muddled with age that there wasn't much more than a faint glow. One by one, the houses on Tripoli Circle began to bed down, lights blinking off.

By ten o'clock we had tired of reading, eating, and playing innumerable games of gin rummy. We simply sat silently, watching the street, listening to the tree frogs come into full throat. Along about midnight I went to bed, only because Mother had insisted. I didn't go to sleep, at least I thought I didn't go to sleep. What if Jane had been bitten by a snake or our father had been bitten or Jane had gotten religion and started speaking in tongues, and I wasn't there to see it? My worry over their fate was not outweighed by my angst over possibly missing out on something.

I woke up when I heard the car wheels hit the gravel in our driveway, no telling what time. By then, all the houses up and down the street were black boxes. I snuck out of my bedroom to the back kitchen window and watched as he pulled the car up into the garage. Mother was standing out on the back steps, the light glowing from her cigarette.

Jane got out and came inside, brushing past Mother without a word. Father opened the door, went around to the trunk, lifted two long boxes out, and took them upstairs to his office.

I ran back in time to be there when Jane came into our bedroom. "So what happened?" I whispered so as not to wake Hercule. "Were there snakes? Did you get the Holy Spirit? What? What? What?"

In the half dark, Jane flung herself on the bed and pretended she was instantly asleep, clothes and all.

I snuck back down the hall to see what he was doing—what she might do *to* him. When she met him at the back door, she said that it had gone far enough, this religious obsession or whatever it was. She had been thinking about it all day, and she could not have him endanger their children.

And our father, in a voice I had never heard before—joyous, bubbling over—grabbed Mother and gave her an extravagant hug. "It is not endangering, sweetheart, far from it. It's a lifting up of the spirit, it's . . . it's a new birth. It's a surge of life and new hope. I can't explain how peaceful it makes me feel since I took up handling."

"*Handling?* Do you mean you actually touched snakes?"

"At first I did it just to insert myself into their congregation, but now . . . the Lord has taken over. I have let go to His will . . . whatever that may be. It's the most peaceful feeling I have had in years."

Mother began rebutting, about snakes and the happenstance of *their* will. He wasn't concerned, he said, it was in the Lord's hands now. He was free. I had never seen him so euphoric. On that night, the part of him that usually seemed crushed with responsibility had somehow disappeared—washed away, if only temporarily, by what I suppose was the promise of venomous retribution. He grabbed Mother around the waist, putting his fingers over her mouth and then bending to kiss her before she could protest again. "Remember"—he smiled down at her—"the time we went dancing in that Miami nightclub, right after I finished my flight training, right before I shipped out? You made a special trip down there just to see me graduate." He began to twirl her around. "You were stunning in that yellow dress—and could you ever cut a rug." She was laughing now, in spite of everything. "Wait a minute." He took her hand and pulled her out to the screened porch. I watched as he turned on the little radio that sat on the side table and tuned it to one of her favorites, a station we could only get at night when the signal was strong: *Music from the Blue Room*, high atop the Roosevelt Hotel in New Orleans. Leon Kelner and His Orchestra had just begun to play "Sentimental Journey." "I love this one," he said, and he pulled her close and they began dancing there on the porch. "Remember, babe? Every fellow in the place was envious of my gorgeous wife." Her eyes were closed, and her hair cascaded backward as she rested her head in his shoulder. She was lost in him, completely overwhelmed by him. In the soft yellow light of the porch lamp, he was smiling as he kissed the top of her head. She must have felt that maybe, at long last, she was getting him back. She melted in close as they moved slowly around the baby's playpen, stepping over scattered Lincoln Logs, back to what they had been, before time and the war had changed everything. I remember that I could smell the honeysuckle wafting in through the porch screen, and I could see the moon passing behind feathery summer clouds as they danced on.

Chapter 48

After that song and two more, he took her hand and they walked into the hall to check on us. I hopped in my bed and pulled up a sheet and heard the rustle of Jane's as she did the same. After a moment of checking, the door to our room closed and they went into their bedroom, closing their door.

Our curtains ruffled slightly as a hot breeze wandered in the window and out again. I had counted to one hundred slowly and was about to get up and go over to her bed when Jane sat up and then stood up and tiptoed to the door. She turned the knob so slowly, I couldn't hear it.

"Where are you going?"

"Shut up, I'll be back."

I sat there and waited, looking out the window into the night. Lights in the Olivers' house clicked on in the kitchen. Mr. Oliver was getting up, making coffee before he left for the post office to sort the morning mail.

Minutes later she tiptoed back in, holding something in her hand. She came to my bed because her bed was too close to Hercule's. When we wanted to talk at night, we used mine. I thought maybe this meant she would tell me what had gone on, but no, she wanted to use the flashlight I had under my pillow for night reading.

"Give it to me," she whispered. She was carrying the Bible, the one we kept in the bookcase in the living room. She took the flashlight but couldn't hold it and turn the pages at the same time, so she made me hold the light while she looked. It shone on the pages, a weak little beam, as she flipped through.

"What are you looking for . . . and at this time of night? Did you get religion up there or something? What? Did they have good stuff to eat? *What?*" When she didn't answer, I began jiggling the light.

"Cut it out. I'm looking up something."

"What?" I jiggled again.

"They say there is a place in the Bible that tells why they do that."

"Why they do what?"

"Why they take up handling snakes. They said it was in here, but I didn't believe them."

I shone the light right in Jane's face to see if she was serious. She pushed it back down to the book. "Did you see them? Did you see the snakes? Live ones? Poisonous ones? I don't mind a corn snake or a racer, but moccasins or rattlers—nothin' doing."

"Yes, poisonous ones." When I lifted the light to her face, there were tears. She was biting her lip and searching frantically through the pages.

"You didn't get bit, did you? You're okay, aren't you?" When she didn't answer, I grabbed her arm. "*Jane?*" Her arms slumped, leaving the Bible at rest in her lap.

"What happened?"

"I don't know, I don't know . . ." Her voice was a wail. She threw up her hands and let them flop down on the Bible. "There was so much going on. The people were singing and the piano was playing. We were in this old building that used to be a Texaco station. People had tambourines. This lady gave me one, and before I knew what I was doing, I started shaking it, like I was one of them." She gnawed at her lower lip. "At first it was fun . . . I think. Father was up front and I was way in the back where he told me to sit. These men and a lady, too, they had snakes in long boxes up on the altar . . . and after a while, they got them out." She looked at me and held her hands up as if she were handling. "And they lifted them up and . . ." She took my flashlight hand and pointed it back in her lap, beginning to flip through the pages again. "And he took one, and he held it up."

"He did? Our father did? Did it bite him?"

"No. He said the Lord kept him safe this time."

Then I asked what I didn't want to ask, but I knew I better. "Those boxes he brought back tonight, the ones he put up in his office—are they . . . ?"

"Yes."

"Full of snakes?"

"Yes."

She had found the page she wanted and was running her finger down a column. "He says there is a place in here that tells about this stuff . . . about snakes and true believers. He said it was wonderful not to have to carry the burden any longer—to put his complete trust in the Lord."

"You know what Mama thinks about that."

She dismissed me. "I don't want to talk about it."

But I persisted. "'The Bible is a wonderful group of stories that are meant to guide us in—'"

Jane snapped back. "Mother *only* says that when we are under the parachute having a meeting. Never out in the real world." Her finger stopped. "Here it is." And she picked up the book to get a closer look and read to me.

"Mark 16:17: 'And these signs shall follow them that believe: In my name shall they cast out devils; they shall speak with new tongues; they shall take up serpents and if they drink any deadly thing, it shall not hurt them; they shall lay hands on the sick and they shall recover.'"

She eased the Bible back down in her lap, staring at it. "It's true. It's in there, just like they said. So it must be true."

Chapter 49

It was almost a daily occurrence now—the chief coming over to our house for a glass of afternoon tea, as if he might be some sort of a family member. Jane was getting suspicious; she had not informed me of what, just that we should keep an eye on him. Men and women in our town, Jane had explained, men and women of the same general age, needed to be related to each other or married to each other in order to associate with each other on a casual basis. It was an unwritten rule. She said probably it was written down somewhere, she had just not run across it as yet.

This day he sat on the front porch in his usual rocker and took out his usual cigarette, but he didn't look right. He seemed agitated, sitting there clearing his throat as if he might get up and make a speech.

Mother brought out an ashtray and tea for both of them. I believed she was beginning to like these afternoon visits. It appeared to me that she had begun to time the baby's nap so as to coincide with the chief coming. I had been lying on my bed next to the window, reading *Black Beauty* and waiting. No one would think anything unusual about me being on the bed. In the summer, everyone rested in the middle of the day so as to stay out of the heat and not catch polio.

"Got two rooms to go, upstairs," Chief was saying. "Might be able to get to the attic in another couple of days, then the garage."

He took out his Zippo and began flipping it. "Might not though, 'cause Z has served his time and he'll be getting out in another couple of days. I'm gonna try to talk him into staying on and let the town pay him. Don't know if he'll go for it, but I think he might since he ain't got a job right now." He thought about it a minute more, flipping his Zippo open and shut. It was obvious he wanted to say something, but he didn't seem to know how to start.

I snuck another look through the curtains. "Is there something on your mind, Red, besides the obvious?" Mother gestured toward Mrs. Brownlee's. A large garbage truck had just pulled up and two men had gotten out and begun pitching trash in the back.

"Daniel in town?"

"No, why?"

"Well, this is something I wouldn't ordinarily take up with a woman . . . that is, it ain't none of my business, woman or no." Chief pulled the handkerchief out of his back pocket and started wiping his face. Then he got up and gave a jerk to the cord on the overhead fan, turning it to high.

"What is it?"

"Well now, seems like I was downtown this morning, at the bank." He sat down again, rubbing the stubble on his chin. "I was downtown cashing a check and Bill Mitchell came up to me." He stopped there, got up out of his chair again, and found the flyswatter we kept on a peg next to the front door. He unhooked it and chased down a fly sitting on the screen, not bothering a soul.

"So," Mama said, watching him step on the fly after he had given it a good swat and it had taken a nosedive. "What did the president of First National Bank want with you?"

Chief sat back down but obviously was not comfortable. "Well now, he was asking me, since he knows I'm around in these parts a lot lately and I know you and Daniel and this is a small town and everybody knows everybody else's business." He raised one hand. "Now, if this ain't none of my business, you just tell me."

"Well, I have to know what you're talking about to know if it is or it isn't your business. Will you settle down and tell me what's on your mind?"

Chief swallowed hard and wet his lips. "Okay, well, now here it is . . . Bill Mitchell was asking me, this morning . . . while I was at the bank . . . minding my own business. I didn't bring it up 'cause as I said, it ain't none of my—"

"*Red!* For heaven's sake."

Chief took in an outsized breath and let it out. "Okay, he was asking me if this house was in your name or was it in Daniel's name, because he says Daniel is bound and determined to take out a mortgage on it, and if he recalled correctly, it was in your name. Lot of men do that, in case something happens to them, then the house is in the wife's name already. Told Bill he needed the money for one of his churches. Seems one of them needs a new roof, and there's a family over in . . ." He stopped and looked down at his hands. "Needs some help."

She stared back at him.

The chief began to backpedal. "Now . . . now, you tell me if it ain't none of me, but . . . but Bill, he said he wasn't sure you knew 'bout it, and it sure would be a shame if you didn't know 'bout it, since Daniel has a hard enough time making ends meet as it is, and if he goes and puts a mortgage on the house—which he can do in this state—it could be a real hardship if somebody was to have to pay it off . . . and they didn't know they had it in the first place." Mother still hadn't said anything, and the longer she sat there with her mouth open, the faster the chief talked.

"'Course, now Bill said it wasn't any of his business, neither, long as Daniel had you sign on the note. Told Bill he'd bring in the paperwork tomorrow—said he already had it done."

Chief lifted both hands. "I said wasn't any of my business, and Bill said the same. Your business is your business, but this being a small town and all . . ." His voice trailed off. He was staring at Mother's ashen face. "And people wanting to help . . . Bill, he was in the navy . . . in the Pacific . . ."

Chapter 50

More telling than Mother's white face was the fact that she hadn't said anything, and Mother always had something to say.

"Look," he said, "I told you, it wasn't none of me." Chief clasped his hands in his lap, looking out at the front yard, seeming to be afraid to look her way, and when he did he leaned over and touched her knee. "You all right? You're looking kinda peaked."

"Wait a minute, wait a minute, this can't be right. He told you that *we* were getting a loan on *this* house? This house is the only thing we own free and clear. We used all the insurance money I got when Jack was killed in the car accident. Are you sure he meant Daniel, *my* Daniel?"

Chief slowly nodded his head.

"He has gotten to the point that he's mortgaging the house?" She almost shouted when she said it. "This house?" Then she did shout. *"This house I am living in . . . now?"* Her finger was jabbing wildly at the glider cushions. "No, no, no, this is *my* house."

Chief, as if he had to reconfirm it, "House on Tripoli Circle, that's what Bill Mitchell said."

Mother lifted her hands to her face. "I'm living a nightmare. He has gone completely out of his mind."

Jane came running out on the porch from the kitchen, holding a spoon full of cake batter. "What's all the shouting, Mama? You okay? What's up?"

Mother jerked around, staring at her, and stopped whatever else she was about to say. Slowly she brought her hands back to rest in her lap. "I'm fine, Janie. I was just surprised by . . . something Chief said." Then she noticed Jane was holding the spoon dripping with batter. "Watch, sweetheart. Don't let it drip."

Jane shrugged, turned around, and went back to the kitchen, holding her other hand under the spoon. "Pineapple upside-down cake for supper," she called back. "You're gonna love it."

Chief said in a lower tone, "We just figured—me and Bill—we just figured, since he's been acting so . . ." Quickly Chief held up his hands. "Nothing wrong with getting religion, I know that, but it seems to me . . ." He let his arms drop and watched his hands rub up and down on his trousers legs. "Nothing wrong with that, mind you."

"What *is it*, Red? Why is he like this? What happened over there? Now he seems bent on swallowing us all up in his misery. I'm beginning to be afraid that—"

The chief interrupted her even as he shifted uneasily in his chair. "No more than went on with thousands others of us. We fought a war, a lot of people died, and then we was put in a prisoner of war camp, and then we got out at the end of the war and we come home. Hell, it was like that with fellows all over the country. Matter of fact, people thought we had it made. We wasn't getting shot at, we was sitting out the war in a prison camp."

He took a drag off his cigarette and blew out a long line of smoke. "Maybe it wasn't something happened over there to make him act out. Maybe it's something since then, when he went to seminary, something like that." He looked down at the floor when he almost whispered the next thing. "You two get along okay?"

That did it. She jumped up from her chair like she had been stung from behind. "Now you're accusing me? *Me?*"

"I ain't—"

"Now I'm the one responsible? I can barely make ends meet as it is, with the little left of my own money, and now I'm responsible for the way Daniel is acting? The woman is always somehow responsible, is that it? Of all the colossal nerve."

Chief was already up out of the rocker, edging away from her, his back to the screen porch walls, feeling for the knob to open the door to escape—never taking his eyes off her. "And I admire that," he said, "keeping body and soul together. I admire that, yes sir, I do." He held up one hand. "Sorry, sorry, I didn't mean nothing by saying that. Ain't none of my business, like I said before, and I'm terrible sorry if it seemed like I was interfering." And he was out the door.

"You men," she shouted after him. "You got us into that godforsaken war, and now you come back here acting like nothing happened?" She picked up a book and threw it at the screen door.

Suddenly she must have remembered. She rushed out after him and caught him by the sleeve before he could get off the front walk. "Wait a minute, just wait one minute."

Chief stood still, like he might get a whipping if he didn't. She let go of his shirt and began to smooth it down, patting his big chest, catching her breath. "Now, Chief—" She cleared her throat. "Now, Red, I'm sorry if I was abrupt . . ." gulping in air, trying to calm herself. "I would appreciate your mentioning to Bill, next time you are at the bank, that I have no intention of taking out a loan on this house—*ever*. And I have no intention of signing any papers to that effect—*ever.* And I will be down there to tell him that to his face as soon as I can get loose."

The chief looked relieved that she hadn't gotten tougher with him. "You bet I will. I'll go on down there this very afternoon"—backing up another step—"and I'll mention you want to talk to him"—he held up a hand as if pledging—"but nothing else. I ain't saying *nothing else*, 'cause it ain't none of—"

She grabbed his sleeve again, trying to pull him back toward the house. "Come back and sit down. I'm . . . I'm sorry I said that about war, too. That was stupid."

"It's all right, Sara." Chief wasn't budging. "I gotta go and . . . and check on . . . on the men."

She reluctantly let loose of his sleeve, following him to the curb. "And another thing, Red. Why don't you do something about that ridiculous church that handles snakes? Surely it's against the law. People could get killed out there in the country."

He patted her arm as if she might be a senile old lady. "You're wrought up 'bout everything today, ain't you." She jerked away from him and started back toward the house.

Chief called after her this time, "It ain't in my territory, and even if it was, you know we got freedom of religion round here. Ain't that one of them things we fought the war for?"

Jan. 3, 1945

More planes today. Twice in one day. Hoping our boys will be coming soon. We're out of crackers—ate our last can of Spam a week ago. During the last air raid Sammy started shouting and running over to our barracks to tell me about a gaggle of Liberators coming in at a distance. For that he got a rifle butt in the face from one of the goons. Bloodied him up pretty bad and knocked out two teeth. I ran out and tackled the SOB which resulted in me getting a rifle butt in my leg—same place I was hurt before. I couldn't do anything but roll on the ground, it hurt so much. I must have passed out because when I came to Daniel and Red had brought both of us inside. They patched Sam up as best they could. Daniel told him that when we get home a dentist will fix him up with false teeth so the girls won't even notice it. He smiled at that one, and you should see. He looks like a hillbilly. I am another problem. Seems like that rifle butt reopened my old leg wound that was just about healed. Now my leg is swollen up twice the size of the other one and I seem to be running a little fever too. Well, it keeps me warm, Ma. Ha, ha.

Feb. 1, 1945

Daniel and Sammy and the others came to look at my leg. It's starting to fester really bad, throbbing so much I can hardly get my mind off it. The fellows said to Daniel, maybe he could go and talk to Herr Guten, since he likes Daniel so much, all the time calling him into his office to report to him, "as if that's what he really wants," Red says. Might be a chance he could get me some medicine or better yet something to eat. Sammy said, "Maybe we should tell the Krauts and they might—just might—take you to the hospital and fix you up." Carl says we should leave the Krauts be. We might get in trouble if we rock the boat. Faces were beginning to swim before my eyes, like I might be underwater.

Red up and hops off the bed and sneaks in a knife from the barracks next door. He used his Zippo to sterilize it and then he cut on my leg to get the poison out and let it drain. Daniel was against it, but Red didn't ask if he could do it, he just did it. The others went along, I guess – don't remember much about it. They had to hold me down, but it was worth it. Now it doesn't throb like it did and on the whole I feel better – so don't worry. Bombers again last night. Soon.

March 10, 1945

Daniel doesn't have a Bible, but he knows lots of verses and he's started telling them to us because we are sort of losing heart, what with our troops on the continent for some time now and nobody has come for us as yet. The radio the Brits had has been confiscated so we don't have any news, except what they see fit to tell us. Maybe our troops are too busy with other things or can't find us. Daniel and Red take turns helping me out to appel. It is all Carl can do to walk by himself. I think the Krauts must have swiped them—the Red Cross packages, I mean.

Only watery soup for days.

Chapter 51

A week after Jane had done it the first time she took off again, after Mother had told her once was enough to experience interacting with those *unusual* people. She had not mentioned the obvious, that now our father seemed to be one of those people.

They had left early in the morning, before any of us were up. I found the note on the kitchen table saying she was going with him to another snake preaching. That's what her note called it, "snake preaching."

After breakfast Mother stood at the sink swiping angrily at the dirty dishes, her back to us. I kept myself busy, pretending not to notice. When we finished in the kitchen, I took the parachute out to the side yard and draped it over the swing set for shade. I had brought along a Nancy Drew and sat with it, keeping one eye on Hercule playing in the sandbox and one on the other end of the street. Around noon, we ate a tasteless lunch and afterward went creeping about the house, as if any noise might be the thing that would implode the whole place.

A few nights before this, I had heard them—not clearly, but enough to recognize key words like bank and poorhouse and mortgage—and had known they were not said pleasantly. Perhaps pleadingly, but not pleasantly. That next morning, she had had Jane and me babysit for an hour while she walked downtown, "to take care of some things," she had said.

In the afternoon, I came in on the porch, keeping an eye on the street, trying to imagine them up there in the hill country, snakes slithering about and Jane coming too close or Jane getting the Holy Spirit and coming back a changed person—a better person than me. I didn't like either possibility.

We took tea over and came back. We didn't linger. Mother was probably too proud to mention Jane's whereabouts to any of those at Mrs. Brownlee's. And what would she have said, that Jane had found religion or that Jane was in mortal danger and that her own father was the one who had put her in harm's way? In any event, I imagined that the anguish we felt could not possibly be passed on in the telling of the particulars—in hindsight, somewhat akin to the retelling of their war stories.

"You want me to shell the purple hulls, Mama?" It was getting near suppertime and she hadn't lifted a hand to start it. She said she did. She had taken out *The Murder of Roger Ackroyd* and was rereading it, lying on the glider. Every once in a while she would look out at the street and then sink back into her book, smoke rising from her cigarette hand as she turned a page.

Hercule was in the side yard building a whole city in the sandbox, and the baby was asleep, and the day dragged along because this time Jane hadn't asked her. More than the imminent danger of the snakes—maybe we were losing her to whatever brand of religion our father had cobbled together to salve his conscience, if that was what he was doing.

I finished shelling and put the peas on and they cooked for the rest of the day, and we had supper and the sun went down, and Mr. Z and Vincent finished up across the street. We put the baby to bed and then Hercule, and the hours dragged on minute by long minute.

She had finished her book and started rereading it when headlights at the end of Tripoli Circle washed out the lightning bugs that were sprinkled across the front yard. She slammed the book closed and sat up abruptly. "Do you know who did it in *The Murder of Roger Ackroyd*?" She didn't look at me, not wanting an answer. "It was the person you would least expect."

"Are you going to get mad at him and fly off the handle and spank Jane, after you told her not to go?"

"What kind of slang is that, 'fly off the handle'?" She threw the book on the glider and went to the screen door.

"Become annoyed, irritated, exasperated, was all I meant."

I never found out what she would have done because by then our car had turned into the drive and come to an abrupt halt. Another car, unfamiliar, pulled in behind it. A stranger got out from the driver's side of our car, rushed around to the passenger door, opened it, and our father slumped out against him. He was that sick from the snakebites.

Chapter 52

The two drivers and their friends carried him inside to the bed. A dazed Jane followed behind them—an automaton, rigid, holding his coat, her eyes red-rimmed from crying. I walked along beside her, trying to search out anything that might look like a bite. "Did you get . . . ?" Slowly she turned her head, no.

The Lord, the strangers told Mother, had seen fit to test her husband tonight, and if He wanted Brother Daniel to come home, then he would die, but if He wanted him to stay here on earth with us, then he would live. It was up to the Lord.

"No, it isn't," she said, jerking down the bedspread as they lowered him, "it's up to Doc Trousdale," and she was going to have him over immediately. The men were not pleased with that, saying it was in the Lord's hands and she shouldn't interfere.

Our father was on the bed, half-conscious but listening. When he heard Mother say she was going to get the doctor, he tried to lift his hand. "No," he whispered, he would not see a doctor. It was up to the Lord to save him or not save him, and with that he was sick to his stomach, vomiting all over the bed sheets. Mother told me to get a pot out of the kitchen for him to use, and by the time I got back with it, she was laying down the law.

It wasn't up to him, she said, her voice brimming with ridicule. How ridiculous of him to think the decision to get a doctor or not get a doctor was up to him. It was up to the ones who had to wash the sheets and clean up after him and take care of him. It was up to the people who *loved him*, standing over him, spitting out the words. But by that time he was lying there incoherent, groaning.

That was it for Mother. She practically ran the strangers off the premises—ushering them out without even offering iced tea, which was the same as insulting them.

Hercule, awakened from all the commotion, was standing in the doorway with me, holding my hand and watching. I nudged his shoulder—our cue for him to ask, because I was afraid to and so had put him up to it. "Is he gonna die?"

"It looks like that's what he has in mind." She grabbed the spread from the foot of the bed and threw it to cover him. "Dying in the service of the great snake gods." She stood there, looking down at him, rubbing her forehead, not crying because she was too angry to cry or too afraid. "What in the world are you thinking? *What?*" stomping her foot in frustration and then brushing past us to the telephone.

Doc showed up with his black leather bag, looking rather disheveled, the cowlick on the back of his head standing straight up as he had been sound asleep when she called. He and his family lived in a house at the head of Tripoli Circle, so it had not been too far to come. He shooed us away, closed the door, and was in there for a considerable time. When he came out he said there was not much he could do because it had been hours since the snakes had bitten him, and, "What in the hell was he thinking? I've known Daniel since he was our quarterback, since he was a kid growing up not three blocks from here. Back then he was one of the most level-headed kids I ever saw."

Mother didn't answer except to say that she was tired of hearing about what had been.

Doc pulled his coat on over his pajama top and said we would just have to wait and see.

There wasn't any use taking him to the hospital, he said. He had done all that could be done.

He would be back tomorrow morning to check on him.

For the rest of the night, the three of us, Jane, Hercule, and I, sat out on the screened porch and watched people come and go. We had no idea how they found out about our father, but somehow people began to know and began to come. Mr. Oliver, from across the street, brought over some of Mrs. Oliver's soup. He said he was up early and saw our lights. The Pruitts brought fried chicken. Redeemer members began to appear with food and prayers. Each time somebody passed by, we got absentminded pats on the head.

"You could have stopped him, you know," I said to Jane, because I was mad at her by this time—going off by herself, letting the snakes get at him. She was the oldest one of us. The oldest was supposed to keep things sane.

She was still intermittently sniffing, wiping away tears, and trying to rock the baby, who was now wide-awake with all the commotion. Still, she had enough energy to be mad back at me. “How could I stop him?” she snarled. “He said the Lord had brought him to that place. He told me, ‘Sit in the back of the arbor,’ and then he went up front and started praying, and then all these men got the snakes out of their boxes. I never saw so many, not even down at the creek in the spring. He took out one and held it up and then another and then another . . .” Her voice escalated with each snake. “He must have had five snakes in his hands.” The more she said, the faster she rocked. “What was I supposed to do?” She stopped on a forward rock to glare at me. We were practically nose to nose. “Did you want ’em to bite *me*? Is that it? And besides”—her eyes narrowed to ensure that I understood she was in no way complicit in the matter—*“he was pray-ing.”* And she rocked back because the baby had started crying again. After he was quiet, she looked over to me and said in a softer, more thoughtful tone, “He does believe in God, you know. He does.” She rocked and patted, rocked and patted, now with her eyes closed. She had said all she was going to say on that subject.

The night breeze rustled the leaves in the side yard. A half-moon had come out and was tangled in the limbs of the oak tree over in Mrs. Brownlee’s front yard. Jane slowed in her rocking. “I guess…you know, if you believed like him, then things . . . Girl Scouts, outside things . . . they wouldn’t bother you.”

I was fed up with hearing about the Girl Scouts and their uniforms and their camp. “Well, if you did, Jane, if you believed like that, nothing else might matter ’cause you’d probably be dead as a doornail by now"—I leaned forward—"from *snakebites*."

She sneered back at me, baring her teeth, almost hissing.

Just then Mother came to the porch to see a church member out, and after that she turned her attention to Jane for the first time that night—not reprimanding. I was mildly disappointed, as I felt she deserved at least a lecture. Mother gave her a kiss and a hug that seemed to calm Jane a bit.

"You think the Lord wants him to die?" Jane whispered.

"I'll tell you what I think, Jane." Mother brushed Jane's hair back off her forehead. "It has absolutely nothing to do with what God wants and everything to do with using your God-given common sense. If the Lord wants anything, that's what He wants—for us to use the common sense He gave us and stay away from things that are liable to harm us. Your father seems to have forgotten that." She rested her open palm on the top of Jane's head like a prayer cap and looked at all three of us sitting there, waiting for some explanation, some reasonable justification.

"He was not like this before," she said. "I swear he was not like this before," knowing we had never really known him before the war. She kept her hand on Jane's head for a moment more and then turned to go. "Stay here, I need to check on your father." At the door, she turned back to us with a strained smile. "Don't worry—we girls can handle this."

I was not so sure anymore.

Chapter 53

And this, to me, was the astonishing thing. By the next morning, he was well enough to eat some of Mrs. Oliver's chicken soup. Two days later he was up and walking, albeit gingerly, around the house. All of this had Jane deciding she might become a nun.

He didn't seem that happy about it, telling us that the Lord must not have wanted him to come home yet. He would touch the place on his arm where the big copperhead had taken a bite, or he would look down at his left leg, which was swollen to twice the size of the other one. Jane believed it was the cottonmouth that had struck there.

The whole thing had seemed to me like some strange magic show. Mother and I were sitting in the kitchen when I asked. "The snakes"— raising an eyebrow, wanting to see if she thought so, too—"it was a miracle?" Mother put her elbows on the table and began to rub her forehead with her fingers, still weary from all the goings-on.

"Well, it coulda been," I said. "Look at him. He was eating Mrs. Oliver's chicken soup the very next day."

She stopped rubbing her forehead. "Of all my children, I thought you had the most common sense."

"I'm just saying it mighta been, that's all."

She rested her arms on the table, picked up a pack of matches, and began turning them over and over. "And it might have been that those snakes had already been milked of their venom or that the snakes, this time of year, don't have that much venom." She reached for her pack of cigarettes. "Or it could have been a miracle. You decide for yourself." She picked up her cigarettes and matches and got up to leave. "Or those people out there in the country are perfectly normal people who go around with snakes in their car trunks . . . or you might come to the conclusion, through logical reasoning, that those gentlemen were slightly off their collective rockers." She was in the dining room when she said over her shoulder, "The larger point is that it should never have happened in the first place."

One good thing came out of it. Jane said she was never asking to go back there to that place again. At least one person's prayers had been answered.

On the third day after he had been bitten, Chief came by to see how our patient was coming along. Mother walked him into their bedroom, where our father was lying there resting, contemplating, I imagined, what the Lord wanted him to do now that He didn't want him home.

Mother pulled in a dining room chair so Chief could have a seat. Then she brought one in for herself. The three of them sitting there seemed inordinately ill at ease.

Chief said he knew some little snake sure couldn't get old Daniel down, must be the smart care Mama was giving him . . . things like that. They sat there in silence after they had said all there was to say about the weather and what a good nurse Mother was and the chief had complimented Father on all the flowers church members had brought over.

Soon as he had stayed the required time and was getting up to leave: "Oh by the way"—he looked down at the floor—"got the final report back from Birmingham today, about Mrs. Brownlee, and everything is fine, like we thought all along. Just takes a long time for them boys to figure out the obvious."

Chief said that we could go on and have some kind of a funeral now and wanted to know if Daniel felt up to preaching the sermon. Without asking the date or time, our father said he was sorry, but he was going to be busy traveling that day and Chief better get Joe Hartwell over at the Methodist church to do the preaching. Chief looked down at his hat, turning it in his hand, saying he would be happy to, if that's what Daniel wanted. Mother sat there looking first to one and then the other, not commenting.

Mrs. Brownlee's funeral wasn't much, weighed against other funerals of my childhood. I felt that I was an expert in judging them, as Church of the Redeemer had a large population of older members and they were, on a regular basis, being sent off to their reward.

All of Tripoli Circle came to pay last respects, along with Chief and Mr. Z., Vincent, and the mayor and his wife. That was about it—no others from town.

I remember not being that impressed with Reverend Hartwell's sermon, accustomed as I was to a preacher who used ever-increasing volume to impart his message. Reverend Hartwell didn't raise his voice one time during the proceedings—somewhat of a cold fish, was my opinion.

For the most part, people must have remembered the Mrs. Brownlee who was out on the sidewalk sweeping in her slip, the old lady who had filled her house with refuse and memories, having forgotten the one who raised two boys after their father passed away and then sent them off to die for their country.

We sang, "Be still, my soul, when change and tears are past. All safe and blessed we shall meet at last . . ." And I was sorry he hadn't been able to come. It was his favorite hymn.

Chapter 54

As soon as he was able, he had hobbled out to the car, using a cane Mr. Oliver had brought him. Mr. Oliver said it was one his father had used after he came back from World War I. Our father said he had to go, he was needed. It was just as well; he couldn't seem to sit still in our house, wandering from room to room, this uneasy presence that made us all uncomfortable and watchful.

Some days before he left, I had decided, in the tradition of the Pruitt sisters, that a nice cup of hot tea might do the trick. According to the Pruitts it seemed to have supernatural powers, as they always said, upon handing me a cup when I visited, "This is strong enough to make you stand up and be counted." I had not quite understood that logic, but hadn't Miss Marple, Jane's namesake, hadn't she had tea on a regular basis, too? In my mind it seemed only logical. I would make him a cup of tea. He would drink that cup and then another and then another. He would then "stand up" right before my very eyes—change back into the person he had been long days ago on the morning of our trip to the river, before he had awakened from his sleep on the quilt, morphed into another person, and I would be the one who had made it happen. I would be the hero.

Mother had watched, not commenting, unaware of my brilliant idea as I marched into the kitchen and began to boil water. I set two teabags in the cup letting them steep until the tea was probably strong enough to pour over pancakes. I walked into the bedroom, presented it to him, and watched closely as he took a sip, and then another, waiting for something to happen.

"My, Aggie, you certainly make a . . . a stout cup of tea." He *did* give me a smile.

"I thought you would like it," my confidence growing. "The Pruitts say it'll make you want to stand up and be counted." He looked at me for a long moment and then slowly settled back on his pillows, thanking me as he put the cup down on the bedside table. Nothing. He looked the way he had always looked. And he hadn't asked for a second cup. As a child, I had come as close as I could come to remedying the situation. I took my teacup and left, deciding it must have been the pecan fudge the Pruitts were talking about, completely unaware that I could not have chosen more inappropriate words.

The afternoon after our father had left town, limping out to the car on his cane, Chief dropped by for a visit, all the while keeping an eye on the goings-on across the street. Vincent and Mr. Zanino were carrying out boxes and bags from the second floor—third bedroom on the left.

"I read a letter the other day that Vincent had found," Mother said. "And I had Aggie put it back in the boys' room. Just thought I'd tell you. Wouldn't want you to think I was stealing."

"Very funny." The chief fumbled for his cigarettes. "What was it, a V-mail?" He was watching Mr. Z piling trash on the curb. "Those things were tiny and hard to read . . . and to write, too."

"No, it wasn't V-mail, it was a regular letter, but so cut up she could not have gotten much out of it."

Chief seemed to relax and lean back in his chair. He nodded with a long "Hmmmm," as he lit up.

They both took sips of tea. Chief studied his Lucky Strike. She held out the cookie plate to him. "And Jonnie, the one who wrote the V-mail, how did he die?"

"Jonnie? He didn't fly with me."

"But wasn't he in camp with you?"

"Yeah, but he didn't fly with me."

"You told me that, but how did he *die*?" She was watching him closely. There was no way around her question.

The chief took a breath. "Well, he, uh . . . it was the day we got liberated. He'd been sick a long time, had a leg injury, wouldn't heal . . . died on the very day our troops came into camp to liberate us." Chief put out his cigarette butt in the ashtray and began fumbling for another one. "Nothing nobody coulda done about it. Died right there on the ground next to . . ." He looked up at her. "Our troops were coming over the hill, the Germans were deserting the place, and he had to die the very hour we got liberated. . . . Damn shame."

"And Sammy, his brother, how did he die?"

Chief stood up quickly and held up his hand to stop her—shouting across to Mr. Z as he walked toward the screen door. "Z, don't you know you got to have them things in boxes? It'll make the biggest damn kind of a mess if you don't. Throw everything in that piano crate."

"With all zee clothes?" Z shouted back.

"Why, hell, yeah, Z—the whole thing is going to the garbage dump. Trash people ain't coming back for a week to do the next pickup." He turned as he was closing the screen door. "Thanks for the tea, Sara."

"But wait . . . I want to know about Sammy. What happened to him?"

Chief looked back at her and just as quickly looked away without an answer—saved from giving one by Mr. Z.

"I won't . . . vill *not* do it," Z was calling from the curb.

"What do you mean, you won't do it? What's so complicated about that? You pitch the stuff in on top of them clothes." Chief was halfway across the front yard now, out of the porch shadows and back in hard sunlight.

"*No!* You take zee perfectly good clothing and you throw dirty cans all over? Somebody can use nice clothes. I won't do it—is wasteful."

Mr. Zanino had folded his arms tight against his chest and wasn't moving. "What would people think of me? In Italy, these clothes, they would be a treasure."

Chief stood before Z, fingers tapping his gun belt—Italians, always ignoring the practical solutions. Finally he reached down and pulled a folded cardboard box out of the rubble, unfolded it, and set it down by the curb. "Does that meet up with them Italian scruples of yours?"

Mr. Z looked down disdainfully at the box—Americans, so wasteful, so unworthy of their place in the world. Slowly he unfolded his arms, picked up a can with two fingers, and let it drop in.

Chapter 55

"Ya see, the thing about it is . . ." Chief lowered himself onto the glider and cleared his throat. He had come back over late in the afternoon. "We got most everything cleared out—all the way up to her bedroom." He leaned forward, elbows on his knees, looking past the dried grass in our front yard, his gaze traveling to the second floor of Mrs. Brownlee's house. "Right up to there," he said, pointing.

She nodded.

"Ain't seen a rat in two days, which to my way of thinking is a good sign."

Mother rocked slowly and nodded again in agreement. We had come to expect a preamble to any subject that was about to be discussed. We were waiting for the chief to get on with what he had actually come about. I was sitting on the floor with an odd assortment of crayons and a Captain Marvel coloring book, about to color his cape blue. The chief rubbed rough hands together, nodding to himself. We waited.

When we had first come to town, Mother would get aggravated at how slowly the conversations were in getting to the point. Now she had settled into the pace, especially the chief's. He was looking down at the floor, seeming to contemplate. "Now, Vincent and Z . . . they done gone and flat-out balked on me." We had come to notice that the more the chief wanted to make a point, the worse his grammar got.

"Is that right?" Mother was not disturbed by the unseemly sentence structure. I think she was getting used to it. She continued rocking Roger to sleep. Roger would get fussy if he didn't get his afternoon nap. We thought he was cutting more teeth. "Flat-out balked on you about what?"

"Well now, that's the problem," rubbing his chin. "I'll just come right out with it."

"Good."

"It's about cleaning out a lady's private things, her undies and such. Z and Vincent, they say it ain't decent and they ain't gonna do it. Say it's almost like they was perverts or something."

I stopped coloring and looked up at Mother. She had stopped rocking and had bowed her head, pretending to kiss Roger's hair to hide the grin. "What?"

Chief cleared his throat again. For all of his rough ways, the chief, like most of the men of his generation, still had a rather Victorian way of looking at things when it came to the opposite sex. "I done told 'em it was childish—they ain't nothing but garments, a few panties and some corsets, mostly scarves and blouses, things like that up there in that dresser. And the dresser is one of the few things I can take on down to the Salvation Army thrift store. It's in that good of a shape. But they say they don't care, they ain't gonna."

Mother began rocking again. I couldn't help it. I started laughing, until she gave me a look. I bent down to concentrate on Captain Marvel's cape.

"And you want me to do it—clean out poor old Mrs. Brownlee's things so you men won't have to?"

Chief sat back, visibly relieved that the solution was so obvious and he wouldn't have to delve more deeply into the subject. "Sure would be a help." He even smiled at her. "All you gotta do is clean out that one dresser. The rest of the room is pretty much clear, but the dresser . . . well, the fellows looked into the top drawer and they was a bunch of corsets and panties. They wasn't gonna touch it, especially Z. Funny thing, he pulled open the next drawer and it was full of scarves. Musta reminded him of something. Shot past me in the hall. When I went down to see what was the matter, he was sick to his stomach out there on the back porch steps. Whatever it was kinda snuck up on him."

Mother stopped rocking. She was particularly fond of Z. "Something in the past, do you think? During the war . . . his family?"

"Either that or he's coming down with the stomach flu."

"You didn't ask him?" Mother was patting Roger's back. He was sound asleep now.

"Well . . . uh . . . no. I asked him if he was feeling okay. He said he'd be fine, to just give him a while."

Mother stared at Chief. "Well? Is he better?"

"Said he was. You know how something can trigger a recollection. And he's sure got more than his share of 'em . . . recollections, that is."

"Red! For heaven's sake, you could have been a little more sympathetic than to just ask if he was okay. The poor man lost his whole family."

Chapter 56

"Yeah," Chief said, "never was sure if the Germans done it with their bombs or we done it with ours. In any case, one bomb got the whole kit'-n-caboodle. That's about all he ever said to us, and when we offered to bring him back to this country after the war, he seemed happy to come, get away from it all." Chief took out a cigarette. "Sometimes I wonder if we did the right thing."

"Good Lord," Mother muttered as she got up and walked over to put Roger down in the playpen, on his tummy the way he liked. She stood up and turned around, hands on hips. "Does he have any other friends around here? Anyone he can talk to? Or did you and Carl just pitch him out in town and leave?"

Chief was beginning to look like a whipped puppy, shoulders slumped, head burrowed in. "Well, he goes to the Catholic church. He knows Father Mohan, and me and Carl meet him down at Sho'nuf Barbecue once in a while, for breakfast." He lit his Lucky, took a drag, and leaned forward, his elbows resting on his knees, watching the cigarette cupped in his hand.

"Opened up a shoe shop when he first got here and was damn good at it, too, but he kinda let that drift. Last year, sold it to a fellow from up in the north end of the county. Young fellow had a family he needed to support. Now old Z, he drinks too much and we have to let him sleep it off at the jail once in a while. I think it's more so he'll have company than anything else." Chief glanced up at her, eyes like a baby calf's. "He rents a room over at the boardinghouse on Wood Avenue."

"He's such a sweet man. I can't believe you haven't been more supportive, Red."

Chief's shoulders sagged again and his head hung lower, maybe a little too low. He said he sure did agree. Probably old Z needed a woman's touch.

Mother was jerking off her apron before she realized that maybe all this might have been premeditated. She grabbed her cigarettes off the side table, knowing Z liked a smoke, and then got a good look at the chief—the picture of gloom. She put the pack of Camels in her pocket more slowly now, "Am I falling into your snare quickly enough?"

And the chief, all innocence: "I ain't told you nothing but the facts . . . just like they stand."

"Oh sure, just as you knew I'd hear them."

"I can't handle no man that goes and gets soft on me. That's women's—"

"Don't you dare say it."

"Okay," he said, so sweetly, "but you need to go on over there and do something with him 'cause he's all het up, and I can't stand to see no man het up. Besides . . . you're my neighborhood assistant." He glanced sideways at her. "Remember?" The chief was so pleased at having conned her that he had to turn back and look down at the floor to hide the grin.

I had stashed the crayons and my Captain Marvel comic, getting ready, too, because of course she would need my help. “No, Aggie,” she said. “You have to stay here with the baby, in case he wakes up. Jane won’t be back from Marilyn’s house until . . .” Suddenly she changed her mind. “No”—smiling—“this won’t take long. You come with me. Chief can babysit.”

“What?” He was already stubbing out his cigarette, up off the glider, his hands fumbling with his policeman’s belt, fingering the top of his nightstick. “Us bachelors, we don’t know nothing about kids. . . . No, no, you don’t wanta leave no helpless baby with me.”

“Yes, I do.”

“What if it wakes up?”

“We’ll be right across the street.”

“Yeah, but . . .” Chief edged over to the playpen, glancing down at Roger like he was peering over the rim of the Grand Canyon.

“You want someone to speak to Mr. Zanino, don’t you?”

“Well, yeah, but . . .”

She was already to the door. “Be back in a while. Don’t worry, I’ll send Aggie to check on you.”

We were crossing the street, Mother with this satisfied smirk, when he yelled to us, “Be sure and clean out that dresser, too.” That, of course, instantly woke Roger. We could hear him whimpering and then starting to yell when the chief tried to pick him up. We hurried on in the house, but after a few minutes Mother took pity on him—Roger—and sent me back across the street. When I got there, the chief was trying to bounce him into happiness, practically shaking his poor little baby teeth loose.

Chapter 57

She stayed a long time. Intermittently, we would see Vincent coming out with a load of trash, stacking it on the curb, waving to us, and then going back inside.

Late in the afternoon she came back, just in time to feed Rog, rushing through all of us on the porch, grabbing up her apron in passing, and telling me to bring the baby to the kitchen. Chief picked up Roger to take him. By now he had gotten the hang of holding him, and Roger seemed to like sucking on his badge. When we got back to the kitchen, she was grabbing a jar of baby food out of the cabinet and wiping off the high chair tray. She put Roger in and popped the top off the Gerber's creamed chicken, handed it to me, and rushed to the fridge to get out some hamburger.

"Jane," she called. "Jane, front and center." She called again and knew Jane was back from visiting because we could hear the record player going.

Jane stuck her head through the kitchen door. "Something wrong?"

"No, I want you to get on the bike and go down to Hill's and get a loaf of that new French bread they have in the bread section."

"Wow, what's the occasion? We never have that."

"Guests for supper."

"We all stood there waiting for her to tell us. She was busy getting the stove turned on and looking for an onion in the potato bin. Finally she stood up holding the onion and saw Jane hadn't moved and we were all watching.

"Z, Mr. Z. We're having him for dinner."

"You're having a prisoner for supper?"

Mother gave her a look.

"Yes, ma'am, I'm going, but I'll need some money."

Mother searched her pockets and, finding nothing, looked to the chief. "Would you like to stay for supper?"

"Well, I—"

"Good, you may contribute the bread." Mother peeled off the outside layers of the onion and began dicing.

It took him a second to realize. Chief reached in his pocket, got out a quarter, and flipped it to Jane.

"Be back," she said.

"Having a supper and all, that's nice. I didn't mean you should go to no trouble."

"I know you didn't. I want to. He's such a nice man, and he's had so much misery."

"Yeah, he has . . . but did you . . . did you happen to get that dresser cleaned out?"

"Yes, Red." She glared at him. "Yes, as an afterthought, I cleaned it out. I put the stuff that wasn't worth saving in the trash, and I put the other things in a bag for you to take to the Salvation Army, and then I realized none of it was worth saving so I disposed of it all—most all of it. I'll tell you what I kept later."

The onion was beginning to sizzle. After a few more minutes of stirring, she dumped the mound of ground beef in the bottom of the Dutch oven. Hamburger steam and the smell of onion rose up to fill the kitchen.

"This is going to be Mr. Z's farewell supper. Well, not his farewell supper, but close to it. As soon as we can get everything worked out, he's going home."

Chief sat down heavily in one of the kitchen chairs, dropping his arms on the table. "I didn't mean for you to run him off."

She didn't turn around from the counter, where she had begun to chop green peppers. "We had a long talk. Seeing the scarves today was cathartic for him. It brought back the memory of one of his wife's scarves—one she had been wearing the last time he saw her." She scooped up the peppers and dumped them in with the onions and turned to face the chief.

"He is so grateful to you and Carl and everyone here in town who helped him, but he really wants to go home. And I don't think he realized it until now. He wants to go home. He doesn't belong here. He still has a couple of cousins there and he thinks an old uncle and, he hopes, some of the old neighbors. He feels guilty about leaving them, like he has run out on them. I told him that we understood completely—that you understand completely. This dinner, it's to let him know we support his decision." She paused and looked up at the chief. "We do, don't we?"

"Well, yeah . . . I guess so."

"He's afraid he will seem ungrateful." She grabbed salt and pepper out of the cabinet above the counter and began to shake it into the hamburger mix. "I told him that was non-sense. We want his happiness. More than anything, we"—she pointed the salt at Chief—"*we* want his happiness."

"Well, hell—'course we do. But he's here in America . . .ain't that enough?"

Mother let the salt and pepper shakers bang down on the counter. "Red, honestly!"

"Well, now looka here . . ." Chief stood up from his seat and began enunciating on his fingers, trying to be practical, as he saw it. First finger: "Now our town here, got its name from a town in Italy." Second finger: "We're right on the river, and Florence, Italy, it's right on a river over there." Third finger: "Well, hell, their river probably ain't got the same name as our river, but it's the same general idea . . . ain't it?"

"Sure . . . right."

Chapter 58

Jane and I got into the spirit of the occasion. It was the first time we had had formal dinner guests. We set the table on the screen porch after we took off all the old books and baby toys and pulled it from the other end where it sat alongside the playpen. We lined it up with the glider. Jane and I and Hercule would sit on the glider side. Mother and the chief would be on either end and Vincent and Mr. Z opposite us. Mother told us we could use her glass candleholders, the ones she had brought from Nashville—wedding presents. Jane was in her element, gathering magnolia leaves from the side yard to arrange in a circular pattern around the candles. Ivy leaves from the vine in the backyard were placed under the glasses—coasters. As a final touch, Jane rushed to our bedroom and turned on the record player. Tony Bennett came wafting out of the window onto the porch, again.

"Well . . . well, lovely." Mother brought out the bread in a basket, hot and wrapped in a red-and-white-checkered napkin. She readjusted a few magnolia leaves to make room. The only change she made was to put Mr. Z, as guest of honor, at the head of the table and place Chief beside Vincent.

"Don't you have a place for your father?"

"He won't be home in time, because he never is. And besides, we don't have any room." Jane and I were loath to amend our stunning arrangement.

"He probably won't, but set a place next to me." She insisted on it. We did, but he didn't get an ivy leaf coaster and it did, we felt, upset the symmetry of things.

Now Mr. Z, as he came up the front walk, was a changed man. Chief must have taken him by his boardinghouse, because when he stepped through the screen door, he had on dark pants and a white long-sleeved shirt without a collar, and a vest—and he smelled good—and he was grinning, his white teeth showing under the mustache.

Jane had put on lipstick. I had no idea how she came by it. Not to be outdone, I had rushed to our bedroom and combed my hair.

"Buona sera, signora bella." He had brought her a bouquet of flowers—black-eyed Susans and daisies—from Mrs. Brownlee's backyard. He bowed and gave them to her. His graying hair was slicked down and curled up slightly in the back. There was a speck of dried blood on his neck from a fresh shave. Chief and Vincent were standing behind him, proud parents.

When they finally got in the door and past Mother—who was still going on and on about Z's flowers—Chief pulled out another bottle of German wine and, for us, three Coca-Colas. Mother sent me to the kitchen for four orange juice glasses. We could drink our Cokes right out of the bottle. She explained that it was the proper way to drink Coca-Cola.

Mother and Jane brought out oversize bowls of spaghetti and salad. Mr. Z rushed around to help Mother with her chair. She asked Chief to do the honors with his Zippo, as the sun was beginning to fade out of the tops of the trees in Mrs. Brownlee's backyard.

From the moment the candles sputtered into a soft glow, even I could see that we had been transformed. I had never before eaten by candlelight and was amazed at how we all looked so much better, so much softer. It brought to mind a world my mother might have inhabited. We might have been in a giant bubble floating on up to Nashville or out over the ocean to Italy, on our way to the marvelous unknown—the candles, the music, our little table crowded with this strange mix of age and assorted backgrounds—knowing as little as I did at the time of the seductive powers of candlelight and music and German wine.

We—Jane and Hercule and me—were not that much involved in the dinner conversation. I could only sit and imagine some erudite comment I might make if called upon. I wasn't.

Mother and Chief and Mr. Z. talked about what Mr. Z would do when he got back home—start another shoe repair business, most likely. Perhaps expand into importing American shoes to sell—the chief's suggestion. Z had saved a little money. He sat there looking into the candlelight, wondering what his cousin Giorgio was doing or if his aunt Anna had moved to Modena where her children all lived now. He hadn't contacted them in so long, hadn't known where to write.

"My country, she is so beautiful, like Alabama." He paused before he came clean. "To be truthful, *sono egualmente niente*—they are nothing alike." Then he raised his orange juice glass to Mama: "*Excepta* for *la bella donna*." She blushed on cue.

"You know it'll be changed; it won't be the same over there now." Chief was trying to be practical.

"*Naturalmente, naturalmente,* but I will be there. . . . *Il mio cuore è pieno.*" Mr. Z was already transitioning back to the motherland.

Chapter 59

"Before we have dessert," Mother said, "I want to read you something I found at Mrs. Brownlee's today, while I was cleaning out the bedroom chest of drawers." Chief shifted in his chair. "I'll give it to you as soon as I read it, Red. Don't worry."

We cleared the table and brought out sugar cookies and as we began to eat, Mother began to read. "It's a letter that Sammy, her oldest son, sent home to his mother while he was a prisoner of war."

"I don't think—," the chief began.

Mother interrupted. "Red, it will give the children some idea of what it was like over there, really like over there." And she began before he could stop her.

March 1944

Dear Ma,

Hope this letter finds you in the best of health. We are getting along swell here so don't worry about me. I am getting plenty of nourishing food and hope this will all be over soon. I am tired of playing bridge and sitting around all day. Nothing much else is going on. Your last letter only took 6 weeks to get here. I do really appreciate letters from home. Red Cross packages come in all the time so I have plenty of candy, etc. Don't worry!! The Red Cross has also sent in baseball equipment and we have started a baseball league. Daniel organized it and we have a swell time. He makes sure we all get the proper amount of exercise. So you see, I am well taken care of.

Hope that leak in the roof you talked about gets fixed soon. Carl suggested that you should ask Dummy if he can fix it, which I think is a good idea.

At this point, Mother stopped and explained to Vincent that there was mention of him in the letter. Vincent seemed pleased, nodding and pointing to the roof, as he remembered mending it.

If not, Jonnie and I will be home soon and repair it for you.

Well, I must stop now and get ready to go to a play that is being put on by some of the other fellows.

Always your loving son,

Sammy

As Mother finished the letter, Chief was fumbling with his fork, turning it end over end on the tablecloth. Z was watching his wine, tilting the little that was left back and forth in the glass.

"Well," she said, folding it and putting it back in its envelope, "I just wanted to . . . I wanted the children to hear what it was like over there . . . during that time.I found this tucked in underneath her blouses. She must have particularly wanted to keep this one."

"You had a baseball team?" Hercule had brightened at the mention of it. "Chief, was you on da team?"

Chief looked up, realizing he was being asked something. "Yeah, I was, buddy. I sure was. And . . . let me see . . . I was the third baseman."

Jane said, "I bet our father was the pitcher, wasn't he, Chief."

Chief smiled. "Yeah, I believe you're right, he was the pitcher." He nodded slowly. "He was always the pitcher . . . saving our butts." He looked up, embarrassed. "Saving the game . . . when it was close."

"And you had plays," Jane said, "I never knew that. It was nice of the Germans to let you put on plays in the prison camp. It's just like we do sometimes, using our parachute as a curtain."

"Were you in the plays Mr. Zanino?" I asked.

Mr. Z laughed. "Ah, yes." He turned to the chief. "Remember, I was Aunt Prissy in zee play?" Chief smiled, nodding. "Soooo funny, I was so funny, making everyone laugh, using the blanket for a skirt, and then I trip over myself coming on the stage—terrible." Mr. Zanino moved the wine around in his glass again, looking up at the ceiling, grinning. "I look so foolish, but it was good to give everyone the big laugh because . . . remember?" He turned back to the chief.

"Quel giorno il ragazzo in caserma di Sammy era stato assassinato."

Chief interrupted, "Yeah, yeah, Z."

Z heeded the chief and was silent, drinking down the rest of his wine.

I had recognized only two words—*assassinato*, and "Sammy"—but since I had already read that part of the journal, I guessed Mr. Z must be talking about the shooting in Sammy's barracks. Still, I did not see my father as that man—as Daniel—kneeling on a rough-hewn barracks floor, holding a dying man in his arms. That was no one I knew. Maybe someone I might be afraid to know.

I picked up the last piece of my French bread brimming with melted butter and polished it off, unable to make any connection between these men sitting here with us at our abundant table and the cold, starving misery of a POW camp—as all the while it must have been, to them, a memory burning to the touch.

Mr. Zanino smiled benignly at my appetite and asked Mother if there was perhaps a drop left in the bottle. She said since he was the guest of honor, he should rightfully have the rest of it. We all watched as she poured and he drank.

And with that, the party for Mr. Zanino was over. The candles were flickering in the last bit of wax left in their holders. The tablecloth had spaghetti stains on it. Tony

Bennett was stuck in a groove. Jane got up to fix it. Mama slowly folded the letter and handed it to the chief. "Here, that wasn't too painful, was it?"

It hadn't been painful. It also hadn't been anywhere near the truth—if the journal was the truth.

April 25, 1945

Could hardly make it to morning appel. One of the guards came to look me over. Thought for sure I was a goner. Daniel says he is going to find something for us to eat come hell or high water. If we don't get something soon, probably won't make any difference to me— watery soup and a piece of black bread from the Krauts once every couple of days, if they bring that. Billy, one of our fellows from Arkansas, was taken off yesterday.

They said for his own protection. I didn't know what they were talking about until Daniel told me the fellow is a Jew. Daniel went to Van Guten to protest—but nothing. Can't believe they took him and not me. I think Daniel is giving guards extra cigarettes to keep them from bothering me. My leg is so swollen, the whole thing is stiff—mean-looking crimson streaks running all the way to my hip. P.M.

Tonight Red took the knife to my leg again. Nobody had to hold me down this time. I couldn't feel a thing. Daniel, pacing back and forth in front of my bunk, says he will get me something to eat somewhere—somehow.

I hope so!!

April 26, 1945

Along about midnight Daniel woke us up, out of breath, shaking all over – never before seen him shaking like that. Had two loaves of kriegesbrot, a roll of sausage and some wilted cabbage leaves–could smell it before I saw it. He told us –shut up and eat it because there wasn't enough to go around except for our room. Black German bread–and the best thing I ever ate in my life. Probably weeks old, but we didn't care. The sausage was mostly sawdust, but a feast to us. It–the sausage–didn't stay down long, scalded my stomach something awful–but it was good while we were eating it–mouth-watering good. We don't know where he came by it– figured he must have swallowed his pride and pleaded with Herr Commandant–we didn't ask. We ate it and didn't ask. I'm thinking we don't want to know where he got it. Today, more planes–think maybe we can hear tanks in the distance –or just more wishful thinking?

P.M.

Tonight we see explosions–bursts of light out on the horizon.

Chapter 60

In the light of the next day, all the commotion over Mr. Z leaving had died away. Mother said she would be responsible for getting the papers he would need to travel back to Italy, but it would, she believed, take several months. Everyone went back to work.

Chief came in for his usual afternoon visit. Mother brought out the usual tea and again, asked a question about the war, this time trying to enter it through the mayor. "So, what was our mayor like, as a soldier, I mean?" She dropped an extra piece of mint into his glass.

"Probably as good or bad as the rest of us." Chief took the glass and changed the subject. "Tell me something . . . when was the last time Daniel saw Mrs. Brownlee?" He took one of her sugar cookies off the plate.

"What do you mean, *saw her*?"

"Visited with her."

"Well, he came to visit here when he first got back from overseas, while we were still living up in Nashville. He came down one weekend, you know, to pay his respects and bring her a few items he had brought back that had belonged to Jonnie. After all, two sons lost, and one of them had been in his squad—and he had known both of them since he was a boy. He told me he felt he had to."

"So you're telling me they didn't visit on a regular basis?"

Mama shrugged. "No. Not that I know of. She did tell me one time, when we first moved here, that Daniel had been a comfort to her boys, that she would always be indebted to him for that. But so many people have said that about Daniel." She paused, taking a deep drag on her cigarette, blowing out the smoke in his direction. "You know that better than I do. You were there, in prison camp with them. You tell me."

"What about before the war?"

"He told me he did spend a lot of time at the Brownlee house when he was a boy," she said. "Back then they were close, I suppose. Like Carl told us, Daniel was the leader on their team. He played the goalie or some such."

"He was the quarterback."

"Whatever, I was never much interested in sports."

"I can see that." Chief asked for more tea, and after she had filled his glass, "You know, maybe if you'd come out of them books long enough, you might find it ain't so bad round here."

Mother busied herself with stabbing out her cigarette. "You should be the one talking about varied interests. All any of you ever talk about is football and hunting, in that order."

"Well now, if you'd ever take the kids to a football game on Friday nights during the season, they might like it and you might, too."

"I do not like football. It's too violent. I don't want—I hope the boys don't want to play when they get older."

"Hell, you don't know, 'cause you've never seen it here. Round here it's more like a community gathering. Carl, he don't never watch the games. He stands round talking to people and eating dogs, and last year, we even had a losing season. Nobody cared . . . well, almost nobody cared."

She studied her fingernails.

"I'll get y'all some tickets when the season starts."

"Thank you, no."

"For the kids."

"No, I said. No, thank you."

Chief sat there, determined. "How about—"

She grabbed the empty tea pitcher and stood up. "Have you ever been called a *Holy Roller*? Jane has and she didn't like it—and I can't say that I blame her. God, at the time I didn't even know what it meant. I would have liked very much to strangle the little smart aleck who hurt Jane's feelings, but rather than spend the rest of my days in your jail, I preferred to avoid that kind of altercation altogether." She walked away, back to the kitchen.

"Hell," he muttered to himself, and then he called after her, "I knew I shouldn't of got in no discussion with you. I always come out on the short end of that stick. Am I gonna have to bring you another bottle of wine for that one? Are you that put out with me?"

She came back in carrying a pitcher half-full of fresh-brewed tea. "What did you really want, Chief? You didn't come over here to talk football."

"All right, I'll get off my soapbox, but I'm bound to say this before I do. It ain't the end of the world, getting your feelings hurt. The end of the world is when you leave it, gone forever, and you can't take nothing back and you can't make no amends—that's the end of the world."

She stood there tapping her fingers on the side of the tea pitcher.

"Okay," he said. "Well now here's the thing. The probate judge gave me permission to break into Mrs. Brownlee's safe-deposit box yesterday. I was looking for some next of kin and maybe some money to handle the burial expenses, you know? The burial wasn't much, but the town shouldn't have to pay if she could afford it." He stopped and finished his tea.

Mother waited.

"I found her will in the safe-deposit box."

"That's probably where I would put mine."

"And she left the house, the only thing she really owned, to Daniel."

She stared at him for a moment, squinting. "Why in the world would she do a thing like that?"

"I don't know. Do you think Daniel knew about it?"

"I imagine if Daniel had known about it, he would have had it sold by now and used the money to save any errant souls he might dig up."

Strangely enough, Chief was insulted. He got up out of his chair and headed for the door. "I can tell you this—when you're the one having your butt saved, you're damn happy he's there saving it."

"I didn't mean . . . I'm just tired of—"

"Tell Daniel I want to talk to him—alone."

Chapter 61

Around six that evening, Chief parked his car at the curb and waited. She had told him Daniel was usually later than expected. Chief sat there for two hours, smoking and waiting. He was out of his car as soon as he saw our father driving down the street. They met in the front yard. I couldn't hear it. I could only watch them shake hands and begin talking. After a minute or so, they walked toward the house. "I don't want it," he was saying. "God knows I don't want it, Red. I'd feel like a Judas." He swung the porch door open hard. It slammed back against the screen, letting in flies. "Why did she do that?" He stopped abruptly and turned to look at the chief. "They could be alive if it weren't for me."

The chief's head slumped forward. "We been over this, what, probably a thousand times? I feel like I'm on the boat again, for Christ's sake, coming home with you and Carl, sitting up all those nights in them damn bull sessions we had. It was war. *It was war*. Things like that happen in war. Me and Carl see that. Why can't you?"

"Things like that? *Things like that?*" Our father walked over to the rocker and sank into it as if his legs might buckle. Chief watched him, then moved to the glider, pushed aside some of Hercule's Lincoln Logs and took a seat. He reached wearily into his shirt pocket, pulled out a pack, and offered one. I had never seen a cigarette touch my father's lips. He had always told us it was not good for a Christian man to smoke, but this night he was putting it to his lips and letting Chief light it for him without knowing he was doing it.

They both sat back, staring into the dark yard, exhaling long streams of smoke that drifted out through the screen. There seemed to be a familiarity, an ease, I had never seen in him before.

"When we got back, I brought her the journal."

Chief took off his hat and ran fingers through his flat-top, shaking his head. "Hell, I know it— and you shouldn't of done that." He sighed. "Been looking for the damn thing ever since—"

"It was all that was left of Jonnie," he interrupted, "of both of them. For Christ's sake, Red, what did you want me to do, throw it in the trash? Jonnie always told me if anything ever happened to him, I should bring it back to her." He looked down, watching his hand roll the cigarette between his fingers. "I don't think she ever even opened it. She thanked me, but she didn't open it when I was with her—probably thought it would bring back too many memories. I didn't blame her."

"I been trying to keep a lookout for it, but I ain't seen hide nor hair." Chief rocked back.

They stared out across the front lawns of the houses on Tripoli Circle. "You needn't have worried," Daniel said.

The leaves on the oak in Mrs. Brownlee's yard rustled in the breeze that always stirred briefly just after sundown in the summertime. Chief looked at his cigarette, pinched between his forefinger and thumb, watching the fire get closer and closer. "I ain't the man you are, Daniel, never was. I'da took it and threw it overboard. I don't like nothing sitting around reminds me of that time. But Carl, you'd think he was gonna wet his pants 'bout what we might find in that house, callin' me every night. 'Least I ain't that big of a sissy."

The chief moved the cigarette in his fingers and studied it, now just an inch of paper and ember. "Funny how people imagine who you are, even if you aren't that person at all." He reached over to an ashtray and stubbed it out. "Reason I left Memphis—had to do with me having to kill a man when I first come on the police force. I wasn't no more than nineteen. After that, everybody was always talking about what a stud I was, and that didn't have a damn thing to do with it. I was scared shitless when I had to pull that trigger—scared I was gonna get killed and just as scared I was gonna kill somebody." Chief pulled out his lighter, flicked the flint several times till it lit up, then closed the top on the flame. "Taking away a life to save your own, there's always a question there."

Daniel jerked around, glaring at the chief. "That's not what I meant to do. I never did that."

"Oh no . . . ," Chief began quickly to backpedal. "I wasn't meaning you—it was me I was meaning, up in Memphis." He popped his Zippo open and closed again, lighting the fire and just as quickly smothering it. "It all has to do with the circumstance, don't it? Hell, look at me, there I was, not six months after I left Memphis, dropping bombs, killing hundreds at a time, hundreds . . . at a time."

He didn't look at Daniel. "Why, if you was to think about that too much . . ." And he began flipping the Zippo again. "That's why I don't . . . think about it too much."

My father got up and stood over Chief. "Remember," he said, "I told you then, if you wanted a great place to live, come on back here. Remember that?"

"I'm here, ain't I?" Chief got up slowly, looking out at the lights that were coming on in the houses all up and down Tripoli Circle, faint glows through curtained windows. "I never thought I would get the chance, but I knew if I ever did, I'd end up here. You fellows always made it sound so fine. One of these days I might try to buy me a house right here on Tripoli Circle—get tired of renting."

My father walked to the screened porch door, turned the knob, and held it open, clearly asking the chief to leave.

"Ah, bullshit, Daniel, you got family. You're a lucky man. We all are." He studied Daniel for a moment. "Don't you ever feel lucky . . . lucky to be here?" When Daniel didn't respond, Chief stepped through the threshold to the outside, breathing in the night air. "Somebody's having pot roast for supper. Remember how Jonnie used to tell us he could smell it in the air when he was on his bike and coming home after football practice?" He picked up the evening paper that had been thrown on the steps and handed it to Daniel. "Nice night." And it was a nice night, a little bit of a breeze still coming out of the west. The smell of the river was in it, and the pot roast.

"Well, I got to do some patrolling. Just wanted to come by and tell you 'bout the will and tell you Judge Longshore says to get your butt down to his chambers first chance you get."

"I'm not taking it, Red."

"Right." Chief raised his hand as he walked off. "Tell the judge that."

Chapter 62

As I turned away from the window, the hem of her skirt hit me in the face. She had been standing behind me the whole time.

She glared at me, not saying a word, until she was sure he had left the porch.

"What," she yelled her whisper, "have I told you about eavesdropping?"

"Nothing."

"What in the world do you mean, *nothing*?"

"Nothing." I remember shrugging, as if I had never heard the word before. It was my knee-jerk defense and it probably wouldn't work, but it was worth a try as there was no other out. "No, ma'am, I don't remember you ever telling me nothing about eavesdropping."

"*Anything* about eavesdropping, and I didn't need to tell you because you should know it is rude and impolite, to say the least."

I was about to say that in this particular case, it would be like the pot calling the kettle black, but then I knew it would only add to her ire. In addition, she would be incensed because I was using clichés, and I would quickly have to think of three words that meant "the pot calling the kettle black." While I was trying to think of them, I was saved by the bell—a reprieve, a pardon, an amnesty—when our father called to her from the kitchen, asking if he might have some late supper—thank you God. On occasions such as this, I was sure there must be one.

Chapter 63

The evening wore on to way past dark. I stayed huddled in my room, afraid of another encounter with her, promising God that if He would only keep her from ever finding out I had stolen the journal and, worse, read parts of it, I would become a missionary and live on a mountaintop in Peru for the rest of my life, spreading the word to the Peruvians and llamas or whatever else one found on a mountaintop in Peru. As it turned out, God must have had all the missionaries He needed.

Jane came in from returning the record player to Marilyn McClure. We got ready for bed. Mother called to us from the kitchen to turn out the lights and to make sure Hercule was tucked in. She never darkened our door, which only added to my misery.

After a time, the house settled into a stillness that usually meant she had gone to bed, too. He was probably out in his garage office, working. All the houses on Tripoli Circle that I could see from my window were asleep now.

I thought I knew what she would do next, but try as I might to stay awake, I couldn't. I would periodically drift off and then wake with a start, afraid I might miss it.

Finally, late in the evening, I saw a shadow duck under the rope that cordoned off Mrs. Brownlee's yard and watched as she tried the front door, which was locked. Her shadow disappeared around the back of the house, probably going in through the kitchen. With a glass pane broken out, there was no way to secure that door. Minutes later, the beam of a flashlight appeared in the boys' upstairs bedroom window. It faded as she must have walked to the corner to look in Jonnie's desk, where she had seen me find it. Then the light began to move around the room, sometimes going out. I guessed she was standing there in the dark, thinking about where the journal might be if it wasn't in the desk. Who would want to read it and have to sneak it out to get a look?

After a while, the light went out. A minute after that, I could see her shadow emerge from the back of the house, slip under the chief's rope, and come home. And I waited.

She tiptoed right up to my bed and whispered, not wanting to wake the others, "I imagine it must be under your mattress." I lay there motionless, pretending sleep, but she would have none of it. "It's where you hide everything that's important. Get up. I'm waiting."

I remember that I got off the bed slowly, embarrassed by my pathetic child's hiding place. She had known precisely where to look. Her fingers felt between the mattress and bedsprings. "Do you think I never change your sheets?" It was sarcastic and meant to be hurtful.

In the darkness I couldn't see the journal as she pulled it out, but I saw the white envelope I had put it in flutter to the floor, and suddenly I was on the verge of tears. “Have you read this or did you just steal it, like some common thief?”

“I—”

“Don’t you dare give me any excuses, not after what you’ve done, not after I told you expressly not to take it. Just own up to it and tell me, have you read it?”

“I’m sorry . . . sorry. I shoulda—”

“Answer me: Did you read it?”

“Yes, ma’am”—in a whisper—“all except for the last pages . . . that somebody musta stole out of the back,” I said, trying to take some of the onus off my head.

“How could you do that? How could you take it when I told you not to and then read it and not tell me what you knew?”

“I didn’t know anything, honest, I—”

“Don’t you know what trouble I’m in with him?”

I stood there in the darkness, stupidly shaking my head.

It only gave fuel to her mounting panic. “What do you think all that business with the vacation money was about, and that meltdown he had at the river picnic? Do you think he took the money just to foil your juvenile plans? Do you think it’s commonplace for a grown man to subject himself to snakebites? Have you been living in a wonderland? Your father is in terrible trouble. Don’t you see that?” Her voice was getting too loud, but it was the only alternative she had to actually hitting me. “What is the matter with you that you don’t see that?”

The importance of the little journal, the importance of it to her, began to settle in, along with the fact that I had lied to her and had, in the beginning, thought of it as nothing more than a trivial transgression. There in the dark, for lack of anything else left to me, I began to try to mount some pitiful little defense. "It's . . . just an old journal . . . like a diary. It's not even good like a mystery. You won't like it 'cause . . ."

She held up her hand for me to stop. Jane was beginning to stir in her bed, and probably more important, she could no longer stand to be there with me. My only blessing was that there in the dark, I couldn't see her face. "Go back to sleep. I'll deal with you in the morning." And she walked out, taking it with her.

As we inch up in the world, we are all bound in some way, at some time, to betray our mothers—our first line of defense in this life. It's part of pulling away, but the first time is wrenching. It is as much a physical ordeal as mental. At least it was for me. I remember that a great wave of despair began to sweep over me. I felt faint and nauseated at the same time as I began to realize what I had done, or in this case had not done.

I lay back down in the bed, curled in a ball, holding my stomach. Presently I heard her come out on the porch and take a seat in the rocker. She switched on the table lamp and opened to the first page of the journal, but before she started reading, she looked over to my window, and although she couldn't see me through the curtains, she pointed a finger. "Go to sleep."

After a long while I drifted off, relieving, for the moment, my misery.

Chapter 64

Mother must have finished reading it while I dozed. I woke to the creaking of the screen porch door. She was standing there, holding it open for Daniel as he came around from the garage.

She said she couldn't come out there to him and leave the children alone. He must come inside and talk with her. He came in. She pointed him to a chair. He sat. His arm was still bandaged where the rattler had gotten to him. There were others, a moccasin bite on his leg, another on top of his foot. He had been barefooted that night. Jane had told me about it. He had stood there after the first one struck, seeming to wait for the others to do the same, his face lifted up to the heavens, the snake on his foot hanging there, not letting go. He looked now as if days of sleep would never be enough to bring him back.

He was in the middle of planning his Sunday sermon, he said. The prodigal son was his subject. She said it was more important for them to talk than for him to do his sermon. That was fine, he said. He would listen to what she had to say while he looked up some passage in his Bible he had brought along.

She sighed, seeing his inattention, but she plunged ahead, probably feeling, in her long ignorance of it, she needed to make up for lost time. "I read the journal—all that was there." She held it up. "I went over to Mrs. Brownlee's earlier tonight and got it." She paused, watching him, and when he didn't respond, didn't look at the thing in her hand: "I had seen it earlier, when we were cleaning out the house, in among some other things in Jonnie's desk." He nodded, as if he had known it was inevitable. "I had wanted to read it but hadn't had the chance until tonight," she lied.

He sat rigid, as if waiting for physical blows. "Did the children . . . ?"

"Only me," she lied again.

He opened his Bible, slowly running his fingers along the columns. "I'm thankful for that," he said, almost to himself. "Children shouldn't have to know—" His voice cracked. He began lifting the pages, turning them one at a time and placing them down again gently. "A lot of the fellows"—trying to see the words—"a lot of them kept journals." A drop of moisture fell on the page. He lifted his hand, rubbing his forehead, shielding himself from her. "I remember . . . some fellows . . . they kept them on pieces of paper. Some wrote on the inside of used cigarette packs." He stopped turning, wiped his eyes, took a pencil out of his shirt pocket, and began a tentative underline. "Miss Delaney, down at the library, sent that little journal Jonnie carried in his shirt pocket. Must have had it when he jumped, the day our ship went down." There was a long silence as he finished marking and then sat there, staring at the page.

"Funny the things people take with them . . . or don't." He took a long, deep breath and let it out slowly. "I forgot to wear my captain's bars that day . . . and my dog tags. Germans could have shot me for being a spy." He stayed there, still looking at the page, biting his lip, trying so hard. "I always thought the Lord must have saved me for some other . . ." He reached into his back pocket, pulling out a wrinkled handkerchief, wiping at his eyes. I squeezed mine shut.

"I could tell from his journal"—she was trying her best to comfort him—"that you were Jonnie's hero. They all looked up to you."

He held the handkerchief tight in the same hand that supported his forehead, his elbow tucked in against the other arm that gripped his waist, pulling into himself. "Not in the end . . . I wasn't. It was like Aunt Lib said, I didn't have it in me . . . when push came to shove."

"Your aunt Lib was a sickly old fool. Everybody knew that. The chief told me that. Listen, sweetheart"—she moved in closer—"you did the best you could . . . whatever you did." She patted his knee, began rubbing it. He sat back and sighed, looking at her in a benevolent, condescending way, a little smile, as if she were no more akin to his world than a Martian. She saw that look, the one he had lapsed into so often. She took her hand away and leaned back lamely, tired of trying to cajole him, to placate him, to love him—ready to move on now, no matter where it might take them.

Chapter 65

"What did the missing pages at the end of the journal—what did they say, Daniel?" The overhead fan slowly cranked around pushing down a small breeze. It was as old as the first Christmas and the motor was about to go, so it made a soft grinding noise every time it turned a full circle. I remember counting ten rotations before he said, "I was doing good works, Sara. I was."

She leaned forward again. "You *are* doing good works, Daniel. You are now."

He held the Bible up to her—in retrospect, swearing his innocence? I don't know. I'll never know for sure.

"I went over there," he said, "to see if I could help. That's why I went over there that night. After you told me about her being out sweeping the sidewalk half-dressed. I knew she must have gone completely round the bend. She would have to go to a nursing home. They would clean out the house."

I saw Mother stiffen. This was not what she had asked about, not what she thought she had asked. "Daniel . . . what are you talking about . . . Mrs. Brownlee?"

"I needed to think of the reputation of the church, Sara. Of Carl and Red and . . ." He trailed off. "Of me, of me. I was thinking of me, damn it." He hit himself in the chest hard, with the Bible. "Goddamn it, I was thinking of me and not anybody else."

"Oh, my God . . . Daniel?" She stared at him. Her hand shook as she lit up and took a deep drag, holding the smoke in her lungs. After a long moment, she managed to breathe the smoke out. "Whatever you did over there, I—"

"I walked in that night, she thought I was Jonnie. She was that far gone. I asked if I could have the journal back." He looked away from her, down at the floor, ashamed that he had asked anything for himself.

"Whatever you did . . ."

He was long past hearing her. "She took me up to the boys' room, took the journal out of the manila envelope it was in when I gave it to her. She had never even opened it. It was still sealed. She started to hand it to me, but just as quickly jerked it back, chastising me for not cleaning up my room."

He looked at Mother, those big beautiful blue eyes begging her to understand. "I tried to humor her. I told her I would clean the room if she would go make me a glass of tea. When she was gone, I tore out the last few pages, so the journal would be there if she ever looked for it. I couldn't hurt her feelings by taking the whole thing."

Mother didn't move, sitting there holding her cigarette suspended in the air like some mannequin in a storefront window, afraid to breathe, petrified by what she might hear next. "You always were considerate . . . *are* considerate."

"While I was closing up the desk, I heard a little cry. Nothing big, just a little cry. When I got to the bottom of the stairs, she had fallen. Probably had done it many times, what with all the junk on those stairs, all over that house."

His face was open and caring, like he had always meant to be, wanted to be. "I helped her up—brought her a glass of water. She said she felt fine when I left . . . God as my witness, she was fine. Maybe she stumbled again . . . afterward. . . . I don't know."

Mother closed her eyes and she breathed again. "It wasn't your fault, Daniel, if she fell after you left. It wasn't."

He was shaking his head. "*No*, I stole out of there like some thief in the night—like his brothers when they left Joseph to die in the desert . . . like before, just like before, goddamn it, just like before." He slammed his fists into the glider cushion. "When I had a chance to stand up like a man . . ." His was seeing something else now, swimming back up from the long ago. "The commandant . . . he lined them all up—I coulda saved them. I coulda saved Sammy, if I had just stood up."

Mother had a quizzical look on her face, not able to make sense out of his disjointed ramblings. "Daniel, sweetheart, whatever you're talking about, you can't be perfect for everybody. You're a fellow who came home from a war, like a million others. You did the best you could."

He looked up, sneering at her. "No, I didn't." His voice was getting louder now, feeling the freedom of confession. "It was the last day of camp. We knew we were going to be liberated any minute. Hell, we *were* liberated . . . not fifteen minutes after it happened. Not a minute after Van Guten had . . . run away. Our tanks came and busted down the gate."

Just as quickly, his demeanor changed back to pleading. "But I didn't know it the night before. All I knew was, I had to get them food, they were counting on me. They were starving. It coulda been another three weeks, another three months. I didn't know. I couldn't look into the future. You see that, don't you?"

"Yes, I—"

"All the other guards were leaving, not wanting to be captured . . . all except for Van *Gut* and his goons.

"*Damn it*, what is the matter with me . . . that I always fail?"

"Daniel, I don't know what you did or what you're talking about, but you don't *always* fail." She reached out, trying to touch his arm. "Look at your life, at what you've accomplished. Everybody says you're a hero . . . Chief . . . and Carl . . . and everybody."

He pulled back, jerked away. "It's all done now, anyway." He stood up quickly, purposefully. "God gave me a cross."

That was more than she could tolerate. "You gave *yourself* a cross, Daniel. If you would just—" In that moment of trying, once again, to protect him, to cajole him one more time, she became a stranger.

"What do you know about it? I'm the one who was over there—*not you.*"

"What about forgiveness, Daniel? You're always talking about it for other people. What about for you?"

He put his head down and began to pray, touching the Bible to his forehead, beseeching his unforgiving God, blocking out anything else she might say. Finally she stopped trying and leaned back in the glider, the light of the reading lamp catching her tears.

His prayer got louder, more fervent—reminiscent of his Sunday sermons at Redeemer. It woke Jane. She came to the window to lie on the bed with me, looking out. "What's going on? Is she sick—is he praying her well?"

He finished. I think it must have been his final attempt to keep us safe here on earth. He laid the Bible on the table beside Mother and pointed to it. "All the answers are there, Sara, all of them are there, if you would only seek the Lord."

"All right, Daniel." It was all she could muster.

Chapter 66

He walked to the screen door, pulled it open, and stood there looking out. I have often wondered what he saw on that last night, looking up and down the length of Tripoli Circle, all the houses gone dark—a microcosm of the world he had fought so hard to save. Maybe their stalag—all of his charges huddled over a cold stove, half-starving, looking to him, waiting for him to bring food, to save them. I like to think it wasn't that. I like to think he might have been transported back to a cold, clear wintry night in England, still warm and well fed. He is opening the door to a pub where they have been celebrating a mission in which they all came back without a scratch. They are stepping out into snowflakes that melt on his leather officer's jacket, closing the door on the last strains of "Lili Marleen," all together there, laughing, looking up at the stars, arms casually around shoulders, walking off into the white swirl. It's what I liked to think.

"Daniel," she said lamely, "*everybody* looked up to you."

He closed the screen quietly and walked off.

She got up, went to the door, and halfheartedly called after him, but gave up when she saw that he wasn't going to answer—wasn't even going to turn around. The top of his head passed under the streetlamp on Tripoli. He walked once around the circle and then off into the dark.

I told myself he was going out for a stroll, as he had on so many nights—to help him sleep, he had said.

She came back to sit in her rocker and take up a mystery, but it sat in her lap unopened as she rocked back and forth, her eyes closed to the tears. Jonnie's journal lay there quietly, almost unnoticed, on the side table under the lamplight. After a while, the creaking of her chair finally sent Jane and me to sleep on my bed.

Chapter 67

That night, our mother was free-falling with no place to grab a handhold and no knowledge of how far to the bottom and no horizon to find her bearings. It is like that, for a time, when someone you love is taken away. Jane and I could only sit and watch, because the reality of death never truly happens for a child—not until it is reflected in the adults left living.

It was around three in the morning when I was jerked awake by the siren wailing off in the distance and coming closer. A dimly reflected wash of orange firelight soaked the walls of our screened porch.

"Get up"—I poked Jane—"Mrs. Brownlee's house is on fire."

We pushed aside our lace curtains, crawled through the window, and were coming out the screened door when she, hardly recognizable, came running around the side yard from back of the house. "Have you seen him?" And then, already impatient with us: *"Have you?"*

"Ma'am?" We were barely awake, watching the fire, and had no idea what she meant, not then.

"Sit down, right here, and don't you dare move."

We nodded that we would not move one inch and watched as she frantically scanned the yard, then looked up and down the length of Tripoli Circle, then pushed past us and took the front steps two at a time into the house. "Maybe he came in when I wasn't looking—maybe he's in bed." The screened door slammed after her.

Perhaps it was somehow our fault that she was so upset. Jane looked at me accusingly. "Did you finish drying the dishes tonight—all of them? It was *not* my night."

"Of course I dried all the dishes, stupid. That's not it . . . whatever it is."

The other houses on Tripoli Circle were beginning to wake up, lights flickering on at the Olivers' and the Pruitts'. The lumbering fire truck pulled to the curb as the siren's whine died away, its massive engine still humming with auxiliary gear. Firemen began rushing about, pulling out hoses, wrenching open our one fire hydrant on Tripoli Circle. In the distance, we could hear the backup coming.

I began to have some vague notion. Even if he was in the burning house, he would get out. He always got out. In every close call, he was always saved—on the football field, in the POW camp, in the church up on Sand Mountain. It would be a miracle if he *didn't* get out.

Off in the distance the chief's car was coming, dome light circling. I breathed easier. He would know what to do.

Mr. Oliver stood in his yard in his postman's trousers, one suspender stretched over a shoulder. Lights had blinked on at the Wilsons' house. Hercule woke up and came out to take his place with us, rubbing his eyes.

Mother, having made her search, hurried back out of the house, coming to stand in front of us. We pointed to the burning house. Surely she must be interested. Suddenly the window glass in Jonnie's room blew out, sending shards sprinkling down to the slate porch below. Flames curled out around the shutters.

"I called the fire department," she said, "when I heard the shot—" She corrected herself. "Heard it start . . . saw the flames." It would be years before I would let myself make the connection she had already made—between the hunting rifles in the boys' room and the sound she had heard that night.

I tugged on her skirt and tried to give some little comfort, because it had been for me. "Chief came while you were gone."

She bolted out across the lawn, stumbling on the curb, losing one of her shoes. We watched her calling to the chief and running toward the burning house. She was almost to the azaleas Jonnie had fallen into, almost to the first step of the front porch, before Chief caught her by the arm and pulled her back hard.

She stood there yelling at him, some incoherent something we couldn't understand above the fray.

"What is she doing?" Jane was in tears now. "What has come over her? I know she can't find him, but he's never here anyway, probably down at the church . . . or something."

"Jane, I think . . . maybe . . ."

"What? What do you think?"

"I . . . I don't know."

The chief, still holding on to Mother's arm, had walked over to his car and was using the radio.

"Where is he? He needs to be here to help her," Jane said, looking at me suspiciously now. I shrugged and kept my eyes fixed on the fire. She turned to look back at the flames and didn't ask again. In a few minutes, the ambulance he must have called coasted to a stop behind the chief's car. Mama yanked free of the chief, turned and walked slowly back toward us, picking up her shoe in the process, not realizing she had.

"Oh, God," Jane murmured, finally realizing what might be possible. She clasped her hands together hard and began whispering into them.

Mother moved past us, pulled open the screen door, went inside to the porch, and slumped down in her rocker.

Our attention was drawn back to the flames. Enormous fountains of water were spewing up out of the hoses, arcing into the night and back down again on the Brownlee roof. "Mama, they've got all the hoses going now."

I got no answer. I looked back. She had picked up his Bible and was leafing through it.

"Mama, dare spraying water on da Pruitts' roof and da Olivers', too."

She didn't answer Hercule. She had pulled the missing pages of the journal out of the back of his Bible and was reading them by the porch lamplight.

April 27, 1945

A.M.

All sitting on the ground for appel. Leg is on fire—and fever.

Writing a few lines to take my mind off it— waiting for Herr Commandant to show.

11:30 Came strutting out mad as a hornet, shouting, wanting to know who stole the food last night. Whoever stole it killed one of his guards—slit his throat.

Van Gut—walks between the rows pointing out ten men— Sammy, the fourth one.

Lines them up.

Says he will give us one hour.

If the coward doesn't stand up, he will shoot all ten.

Everyone silent.

Red whispers, Goddamn it Daniel, don't stand up, he'll kill us all.

Old Sammy winks at me.

Van Gut wouldn't dare

Our tanks here any minute.

Got one whole hour.

P.M.
Didn't give us any hour
My Sam–all ten–gone.
Ma, I lov
1st Lt Jon

Chapter 68

The flames were out by the time one of the firemen leaned a ladder against the side of the house. He used his ax to clear the remnants of the window frame leading into Jonnie's room. I remember hearing the window glass spilling down to the ground, a soft, tinkling sound. Then he climbed through.

Mother had come to sit with us on the front steps, taking Hercule in her arms, holding him tight in her lap. She seemed resigned now, even calm. I had snuggled up close to her on one side and Jane on the other. We were what was left.

The fireman inside the house came to the front door and beckoned to the chief. Both Chief Kelly and the fire chief walked in and didn't come back out.

I got up and went inside. It was my right to read the last pages, too. They were there, what was left of them, bits and pieces in the ashtray where she had burned them. I wouldn't know until years later what they had said.

As I came back out the screen door, Chief was coming out of Mrs. Brownlee's. He walked over and said something to the mayor, who had just arrived in his pants and pajama top. Several of the other men in the neighborhood had gathered around by then. They all looked over to us and then turned back to more conversation. Presently, Chief held his hand up to call for the two drivers who were leaning against their ambulance, smoking. They let cigarettes drop to the ground, stepped on them, and then turned to pull out their stretcher, which had come once again to Tripoli Circle.

Chief walked toward us. I shut my eyes and put my hands up to my face and my face in my lap. In my child's mind, I had the idea that if I didn't breathe, time might stand still and whatever might be coming next, couldn't.

"Had to wait till the fire was out to go in through the window. Upstairs door had something blocking it from the inside." He took off his chief's hat and cleared his throat, standing in front of us, trying to block our view, looking to Mother. "Now I know how you are, Sara, but they ain't nothing you can do 'bout this here, so just as well stay put." The ambulance attendants were coming slowly out the door, carrying their burden. Mother started to rise, but he held her shoulder. "For the children? Ain't nothing they need to see." And for once, she took his advice.

Chapter 69

"Your daddy . . . he was a true American hero," Chief began. "Better'n all the rest of us put toget—"

"I told your father," she interrupted him, "I had told him . . . there was a light on in Mrs. Brownlee's house, upstairs. He went over to see if there was someone in there who shouldn't be." She looked up at the chief, holding his gaze, adamant that their stories coalesce. "Suddenly there was a deafening explosion and flames filled the boys' room. . . ."

The chief coughed loudly and took up the story. "Probably a short in the wiring," forgetting in his lie that the electricity was still cut off. "Happens in these old houses . . . old wiring. Never can tell what mighta been up there in all that trash; coulda been some old ammunition . . . hunting ammo . . . some varmint chewing through the wiring . . . something like that. I told the neighbors just now, probably hunting ammo . . . done spoiled." He cleared his throat again and stood at attention to put his hat back on, looking over to Mrs. Brownlee's as the ambulance, lights on, backed out of its parking place. I thought he might salute.

Jane had not moved, her eyes fixed on the smoldering house as she listened. "Our father, was in there . . . you're sure?"

"He was, sweetheart . . . he was tryin' . . ." Jane grabbed Mother's arm.

"He was trying to help, Jane. He was always trying to help."

"Nobody coulda done nothing," Chief was saying. "Fire was too hot, up there in that room. That's why I stopped your mama. She coulda got inside the house, but the main fire was up there in Jonnie's room . . . and . . . that's where he was at."

"You could have saved him, you *could have*." Jane bolted and ran inside.

Chief took off his hat, beginning again his mantra now, encased in it the sum total of the love he felt for our father—for all those who had shared with him the freezing nights and starving days. "Your daddy, he was a American hero . . . is all I can say." He put his hat back on.

Smoke drifted up through the roofing shingles of Mrs. Brownlee's house—all its memories, like slithering ghosts, wandering out into the night air.

Suddenly I was cold and pulled myself into a crumpled little ball, my only warmth her arm around my shoulder, and I said what I could think of to comfort her. "I think he wanted to go back and be with them. I think he hadn't been happy since he left them."

Chief turned away, walking slowly back across the street. Hercule buried his head in Mama's blouse. We sat there and watched for the longest time—until the firemen began to wind up their hoses and undo them from the fire hydrant; until the Pruitt sisters went back inside and the lights in their kitchen came on and we knew they were deciding what to cook and bring over; until the sky began to show itself back of the trees behind Mrs. Brownlee's house and Hercule was sound asleep in Mama's arms.

"If I had given it to you . . . ," I began, the importance of the journal, the shame of having kept it to myself, flooding in on me. Perhaps I was responsible for this—for all of this. "You mighta been able to . . ." But she knew what I was about to say and she saved me. And I am sure to this day that she meant to save me from a child's indiscretion that could have weighed down like a mighty anchor on the adult I was to become. Mothers, perfect mothers, are like that.

"I'm glad you didn't give me the journal before," she said. She may not have meant it; in that moment she probably didn't mean it. She could have easily passed on to the next generation the suffering in hers, but she somehow swallowed her own anguish and said it, and for me in that defenseless moment it was the blessed truth. "It wouldn't have helped," she said. "I wouldn't have known what to do about it anyway. It would only have added to my angst." She kissed the top of Hercule's head and pulled me closer. I felt the knot in my stomach begin to ease.

"It was," she said, trying to couch it in terms that I could understand—that she could live with, "like the football game."

By then I was half listening, watching the wispy threads of smoke rise in the first light of day, up where he had flown his plane on all those early mornings, with all those boys. "Ma'am . . . what?"

"How fate, capricious as it is, intervenes," she said, and when I didn't answer: "The football game, the mayor's story about the football game."

"Oh yeah." I nodded, remembering the mayor standing there in the kitchen telling us—another fable now—how the ball came floating down through the night air into his outstretched arms and he became a hero forever, not even imagining what might have happened had he dropped it.

Chapter 70

The summer was almost over by the time we got down to the beach. We did not, however, use the proceeds from the sale of what was left of Mrs. Brownlee's house to finance our trip. No, Mother had insisted that should go to Church of the Redeemer.

The way we got the money was this: Days after the fire and days after the funeral—after Mayor Carl had tried and failed to get through the eulogy, breaking down in great sobs, saying later he was not sure what had come over him; after the Pruitt sisters and everybody else on Tripoli Circle had brought over food and told us how sorry they were, what a tragic accident it was, and what a hero our father had been in the war and on the football field and on that one last night of the fire, thinking someone might have been in the house and going in to save them; after Mother had decided that the best use of his old garage office would be for Vincent to move in and make it his home; after Vincent had begun repainting it and adding a bathroom; after all of us had gone down to the train station to see Mr. Zanino off to Italy, and Jane and I had drawn Italian flags on construction paper and waved them as the train pulled out; and after Chief, dressed in a tie and starched shirt, had brought over tickets for the fall football season, in a sack that included a bottle of German wine.

I had been on the screen porch when he came bearing gifts. I had immediately accepted on our behalf. Mother had looked up from her reading, shaking her head and searching the ceiling, but she had smiled.

After all of that, Mother had asked him what he was going to do with the soft drink bottles in Mrs. Brownlee's house. The chief had said that it appeared to him it was our house now—what was left of it—and that if we wanted to get the deposits back on all those bottles, and there were hundreds, it was fine with him.

So she had said to us, "Your first entrepreneurial venture," and when we squinted our eyes, unsure of what that meant, she added, "As in capitalism at work, money grabbing . . . your first real job."

Jane and I and Hercule spent days loading bottles into the Radio Flyer. Each time we had a wagonload, we would take it down to Hill's grocery and get our deposit and then run all the way back to the house with the money. It was like finding a gold mine and digging until all the veins were played out—in the basement, in the kitchen, in her old garage. The Pruitt sisters, watching from behind their curtains, came out to tell us they had some bottles stacked in their garage that were getting in the way of parking their cars and we would be doing them a great favor, since we were dirty anyway, to come over and take the dusty old things off their hands—no matter that I had seen them pouring perfectly good Coca-Cola down the drain of their kitchen sink as I passed by with a load.

At the end of the day we all looked like chimneysweeps, covered with soot from the fire—perhaps some sort of anointing from the fellows—but at three whole cents a bottle, we were not in the least concerned with appearances, not even Jane. It was making us rich beyond our wildest dreams and keeping us from our dreams.

When the last bottle had been exchanged for the last three cents, we gathered for a meeting to decide what should be done. Hercule and I were delighted with the idea of going to the beach, pleased to be getting out of town, away from all the doleful looks we were getting everywhere we went. Jane, remembering his kindness, was not so sure it was a good idea. Maybe we needed to save it; maybe we needed to give it away. He might be looking down on us, saddened that we were so self-absorbed. Hercule and I were about to object, vehemently, when Mother intervened. No, she said, the person she had known, back before, he would have wanted us to go—would have insisted on it. It was really the money we had saved and hidden in the sugar canister, brought back to us again. On further thought, she said, we must go.

And then, I don't recall the other particulars, as if by magic we were at the beach, sitting underneath a huge umbrella and watching the late afternoon sun settle down into wispy pink-and-orange clouds far out on the horizon. Jane was holding the baby and letting him kick his feet in the water. Hercule was diving in the waves, and soon enough Mother called us all to come inside to our beach cabin built right out on the sand—ours for one whole week. We played the radio and danced while we helped Mama peel shrimp and cook up a big mound of rice smothered with a mouthwatering sauce made from a recipe she said she had discovered while she was a stewardess and living in Jamaica once long ago—or was it Paris, France? We were never quite sure.

Epilogue

It's all still there, Tripoli Circle—Sears, Roebuck houses being that sturdy. Even today I can visit and stand in the shadow of Mrs. Brownlee's house, rebuilt now, with new azaleas trimming her front porch—all of its weathered old self gone. The old oak tree is there, its branches hollowed out or fallen, and the sidewalk, patched concrete. And our house, so small now that I marvel at how we ever lived there, six of us crowded into two small bedrooms and one bath, at a time when I felt there was all the room in the world.

The afternoon sun ricochets off his old garage window, as if he had just switched on the lamp and were standing by. He is, still standing by.

Author's Note

In addition to my mother, my thanks to two individuals who did so much to inform this story. My uncle, Jonathan McDavid Cunningham, who kept a steady stream of letters coming home during World War II—in much of this manuscript they are used verbatim. And Rutledge Laurens Jr., who was shot down and spent eighteen months in a POW camp in Germany. One made it back. The other—like thousands — plot F, row 3, grave 80, the American Cemetery, Cambridge, England. Both were and are proud members of the Mighty Eighth.

Acknowledgements

Everlasting thanks to Harvey-Jane Kowal for her expertise and encouragement and for passing me on to my brilliant copy editor, Sona Vogel. And as always, thanks to my wonderful sisters, Sal and Jo. I am grateful to the fine folks at the Mighty Eighth Museum in Pooler, Georgia, especially their very helpful library personnel. Thanks to the World War Two Museum in New Orleans, a wonderful, ever expanding, resource. And to the Liberty Foundation for the great ride aboard their beautifully restored B-17, *Liberty Belle*.

10351828R00213

Made in the USA
Charleston, SC
28 November 2011